Always You

Scarlett Avery

Edited by John Hudspith

Proofread by Chrissy Becker and Jamie Betts

Cover designed by Murphy Rae

Always You © **Scarlett Avery**

It Was Always You series

ISBN 978-1-77498-154-2

Dedication

To those of us who aren't expecting Prince Charming to save us. You'd much prefer a tattooed badass who's more than happy to corrupt you...

Chapter 1

Jules

In the shit show that is my life, this break is a godsend.

I scoop up the rest of my salsa. "I could live off these huevos rancheros burritos and the pulled pork ones. Nothing surpasses breakfast from Mamá Carlota." I pop the last bite into my mouth.

"I agree," my best friend says.

"Now I'm stuffed." I lean back in the garden chair, close my eyes, lift my face and do a sun salutation as I rub my tummy. "Thanks again for looking out for me."

"It's not over yet," Sydney says. "I got us your favorite from Mamá Carlota as a post breakfast sugar rush."

I meet her gaze. "You got *tres leches* cake?"

"I did. I also got flan." Her blue eyes twinkle. "*And* I stopped by Sticky Fingers to buy you a jar of *dulce de leche*—they were just displaying them when I got there."

Damn.

Left to my own devices, I could eat *dulce de leche* with a spoon straight from the jar—

Wait a minute.

I narrow my eyes at Sydney. "You're buttering me up."

"Why would you say that?"

I swing my attention to the house to make sure my evil step-mother isn't at an earshot. "You're an even worse actress than my stupid stepsisters."

"I take offense to that. I consider myself far more capable of delivering believable lines than Olive and Petula—even if I'm only a lowly blue-collar worker who will never grace the red carpet."

We laugh.

Hillary poo-poos manual labor. It's beneath her. She has dreams of multi-million-dollar contracts and shelves lined with Oscars. She's banking on her talentless daughters to make her a bona fide stage mom.

"Regardless, the answer is no to whatever you're about to ask, Syd," I say.

"Don't be like that."

I cock an eyebrow. "What do you have up your sleeve?"

She scoots her chair closer to mine and brushes stands of her red hair behind her ears. "You're not going to work today."

"This is LA and all, but since it's only nine a.m., it's not hot enough for you to suffer from heatstroke."

"Seriously, Jules, you need to take the day off."

"I can't."

"Yes, you can."

"No, I can't. It's like I'm living with a ticking time bomb strapped to my chest. I *have* to work."

Sydney places a hand over mine, her blue eyes filled with emotion. "I know the responsibility of your dad's business falls squarely on your shoulders, and I also know Hillary is of no help other than to burn through money and put you further into debt."

I wince.

My stomach is in knots over my stepmom's over-the-top expenses.

"Since your dad passed away eight months ago and ever since, you've been working yourself to the bone." Syd pouts. "Look at you." She waves a finger at me. "You don't sleep, forget to eat, and no longer bother with makeup. You bite your nails from all the stress you're under. And, I know for a fact you haven't had a haircut in forever." She pulls at my ridiculously long, blonde braid. "I'm all for a curtain of hair, but not this," she waves a frantic finger this time. "You're only twenty-three, Jules, your father wouldn't want this life for you. I'm sure his heart is breaking up in Heaven."

Sydney is right. I have given up on pretty much everything except for my father's dream.

My own heart constricts, the familiar ache lodging deep inside my soul. Losing one parent is tragic. Two? Well, there are no words to express the depth of that kind of sorrow.

"While the three wicked witches are off to their chichi star-studded ball," Sydney says, "you and I will be swimming smack dab in an ocean of sexy domineering studs."

I scrunch my nose. "Was that German?"

"No, that was English for I, Sydney Malone, am the luckiest bitch in LA because I was selected to receive this month's vendor's complimentary tickets for Mr. Gallagher's theme party that's taking place tonight."

"Seriously?"

She nods.

Now she has my full attention.

"I wouldn't lie about something that important." she says, lifting her chin. "I received the text super early this morning and I could hardly contain my excitement. I jumped out of bed, drove to Mamá Carlota, and then drove here because I had to tell you in person."

"It's like winning the lottery."

"Pretty much," she says. "We've been working for Mr. Gallagher for two years, and this is the first time I get selected. This is a big deal. No way am I missing out. I can't afford the hefty member's fee and this is my chance to find out what happens behind closed doors when LA's crème de la crème gets down and dirty."

The sad, sad state of my finances wouldn't even cover the taxes, let alone the hefty member's fee. "I see."

"And you're my plus one."

"What about Austin?"

"He's going away with his best friend for a weekend of manly outdoors activities. It's you and me, babe."

I pounder on her words.

Sydney and her brother Austin have a successful landscaping business. Larkin Gallagher is one of their best clients. Syd and Austin not only take care of the property surrounding Mr. Gallagher's luxurious Quintus Hotel, they also take care of the property surrounding his other businesses. They even take care of his massive Malibu property and all the other opulent houses he owns and rents. One of the many perks of being one of Larkin Gallagher's vendors is the monthly lottery-ticket style draw to enter a world of naughty pleasures. Dark Compulsion is an exclusive adult club annexed to the Quintus Hotel. Syd does all the floral arrangements for both the hotel and the kinky club. She swears sex lingers in the air hours after the action dies down. It sounds illicit... and intriguing.

I arch a brow. "What's the theme tonight?"

She bumps her shoulder to mine. "So, you are interested."

"Maybe."

She shoots me a mocking side gaze. "Right."

"Just tell me."

"*Ruined.*"

"What?"

"The theme of tonight's party is *Ruined.* I'm guessing you can replace the ruined with defiled. From the text message it promises dirty as fuck fun."

I nod, taking in the full weight of her words. "I don't think I can keep up with a theme like that. That's a hell of a lot of pressure, and I might turn out to be a huge disappointment for an unsuspecting guy." Fear and worry tightening my stomach.

"It's been a while for you, Jules—"

"More like a *very* long while."

"Not that I want to rub your face in it, but you could pass as a born-again virgin."

"Glad to see you're on my side." I purse my lips. "Now I'm even more worried."

"Don't be," she says. "I found out via one of the theme party organizers I've befriended, the men at Dark Compulsion are domineering alphas—"

"What does that even mean?"

"It means, your job is to surrender and let go."

"Oh."

"Do this for yourself, Jules," Syd says. "For one night, forget about everything that's weighing heavy on you and spend the evening with a man who will do all sorts of lewd things to your body and blow your mind."

"Oh." Holy Jesus, that sounds so wrong, yet so right.

I chew the inside of my mouth, pondering on her revelation.

Maybe my shattered self could use a respite for one night.

"Even if I agree to come with you—not that I've decided yet —I have nothing to wear."

Syd grins. "Oh, girlfriend, I have you covered—including

dress, shoes, hair, and makeup. I've already pulled in favors from my clients. You're going to be the belle of the naughty ball."

Chapter 2

Levi

Three security guards built like Mack Trucks, posted side-by-side in a military stance in front of Dark Compulsion, man the doorway to heaven—the exclusive adult club we frequently visit for a night of hedonistic pleasure.

"I'm glad I'm here tonight," my buddy Jace says as we queue up behind a line of people. "I've been too consumed with work and my son lately to come here, so I intend on making up for it. My dick is fucking ready."

"So is mine," my buddy Rod says.

"Theme parties promise *a lot* of fun," my buddy Beckett says.

I'm still getting used to his new edgy haircut and his blond tips.

Jace nods. "Wicked. Dirty. Filthy fun."

"Fresh pussy to conquer," Rod says. "You can't go wrong with that."

"You mean, fresh pussy to get *Ruined*," Beckett says.

The guys laugh.

"I'm so jetlagged, I'm here for one reason—the spectacular food," I say.

Jace's head swings to me, his eyes widen in shock.

Rod's head jerks back, his narrowed eyes peering at me. "Did you leave your dick in Europe, Levi?"

I chuckle. "It was a joke."

"Yeah, well, don't quit your day job, Aldridge," Beckett says. He's still staring at me like I have two heads.

As former rock stars, my buddies take pussy seriously. I love pussy. A lot. But pussy is a religion for these three. And the more, the better.

After flashing our club rings and scanning our club ID cards, one of the beefy bouncers lets us in to the trio of beautiful hostesses waiting for us behind the welcome desk. They hand us each a white envelope embossed with the letters D and C in silver with instructions not to open them until we're told. I tuck mine in the pocket of my suit jacket. My buddies mimic me. Surprise, surprise, we're all adorned in black bespoke suits sans the ties.

The main party room is packed with eager bodies clad in designer clothing. If you're looking to rub elbows with some of the richest, most powerful and wealthiest men and women in LA, this is it.

"Since we're only allowed two drinks tonight, I suggest we get started."

My gaze slides to Beckett, and I nod.

The four of us head to the long bar that dominates the back of the room. The bartender recognizes us and reaches for a top-shelf whiskey.

With tumblers of whiskey in hand, it's time to check out our options. As we stride through the crowd, women crane their necks to catch a better view. At this point in the evening, it's about enjoying the view.

With theme parties, we arrive with our own playmate or we hook up with one after a little flirtation. Either way, the choice is ours. Tonight is different. We're randomly paired. This guarantees an instant connection, or you might end up with someone who doesn't get your dick hard. Beauty isn't always enough to get your cock to cooperate.

For the next half hour, we roam around, checking out beauty after beauty. We strike up a conversation here and there, but keep it brief. Like always, the women are hot, but so far, I'm not enthralled.

We gather near the bar for our second drink.

Larkin Gallagher approaches us. "You gentlemen must be adulting hard because it's been a while since you've come out to play." As usual, bodyguards flank him—two badass beasts who could crush skulls with one hand. I guess when you're at Larkin's level, having permanent shadows is a requirement. He owns Dark Compulsion, the Quintus Hotel, and a long list of businesses. The man has an enviable net worth that makes many dot com multibillionaires look like they have play money.

"Zeus." I lift my tumbler in salute.

Larkin tips his head in response.

Privacy is paramount at Dark Compulsion. That's one of Larkin's immutable, abiding principles. As such, each club member is assigned a randomly selected name. Larkin's club name is quite fitting.

"Gentlemen," Larkin says.

"I have an excuse for being MIA," Jace says. "My thriving business and my son's needs have kept me too busy lately to show up. I can't speak for these fools." He points at us.

"Asshole," Beckett says.

I shake my head.

"Idiot," Rod says.

We all laugh.

Larkin doesn't.

I don't think I've ever seen the man smile since I've been a member.

He's way too intense if you ask me.

"I gather the promise of unsuspecting souls brought you out," Larkin says.

"*Ruined?*" Rod cocks a brow. "You bet I'm showing up, even though I landed at LAX from Dublin three hours ago and I'm jetlagged as fuck."

"For once I agree with him," I say. "I got back early this afternoon from an intense weeklong business trip to London. I'm looking forward to unwinding... inside an inviting pussy."

Larkin's attention shifts to me. "You're in luck, Ignatius," he says using my club name. "The selection abounds tonight. Given the theme, it's safe to say our guests are dying to be dominated by the right alphas. I have no doubt you gentlemen are up for the challenge."

"Damn right." Rod puffs his chest out like a peacock.

"I'm locked and loaded," Jace says.

"The selection is so tempting, I might even have to play tonight," Larkin says.

"Wow," I say. "The women must be something else for you to deviate from the norm." He's all about business and nothing but the business to hook up with a woman during theme parties.

"You're correct, Ignatius. Based on the profiles, we have an interesting bunch."

"How so?"

"The women tonight are like little lambs headed to the slaughter—innocent, but not too innocent."

"Right up my alley," I say.

"I would gladly sacrifice myself and offer to *Ruin* two or three little lambs, but you have strict rules," Beckett says.

"Indeed." Larkin nods. "Tonight, it's straight or gay, but no poly fun allowed."

"Pity," Beckett says.

The guy is unlikely to ever turn down a threesome, foursome, or even a fivesome. Personally, I'm too greedy to share.

"Holy. Fuck." Jace's eyes are wide.

"What?" Beckett searches the crowd.

"Coming our way." Jace cocks his head.

It's my turn to search the crowd.

I do a double take.

Two women approach us—a beautiful redhead and a drop-dead gorgeous woman with long, blonde hair falling over one shoulder.

"Whoa." Rod says. "She has legs for days."

And they'd look damn good wrapped around my neck.

My eyes are glued to the knockout blonde, admiring to her cobalt-blue dress and the risqué split cutting up her right leg, stopping short of the Promised Land.

Fuck. Me.

I *need* to know if she's wearing a lace, mesh, satin or sheer thong underneath, or if she's daring enough to have gone commando.

Larkin checks the iPad he's holding. "Mauvelous," he says, locking eyes with the redhead dressed in black.

Contrary to members, guests get a Crayola color as a temporary club name. They also get purple cuffs to easily identify them.

"I'm glad you came out to play."

"Zeus," Mauvelous says. "Thank you for the invitation." She grins wide.

"It's my pleasure," Larkin says.

"I'm so ready for tonight." The redhead with the blue eyes rubs her hands together.

"You're going to have a night of depraved fun." Larkin's gaze moves to the blonde whose eyes are as big as dinner plates after that bold statement. "I see you didn't come alone."

"No, I didn't," Mauvelous says, bubbling with excitement. "This is my best friend, Wild Strawberry."

"Thank you so much for the invitation, Zeus," the blonde says.

Her voice is soft and so fucking melodic.

Kudos to Larkin for keeping the music low enough to encourage conversation.

"Wild Strawberry," Larkin says. "That's quite the name. A lucky guy will discover if you're *wild* and *sweet*."

Her cheeks burst into flames.

And... I'm hard.

After a round of introductions, we're all eyeing each other. The redhead monopolizes Jace's attention, while Rod and Beckett practically enter in a duel to secure the blonde's attention.

Over my dead body.

I'm not a religious guy, but right now, I'm praying to God, Wild Strawberry is my match. If not, it might be a battle between whoever she's paired with and me to determine who has the biggest balls. The evening has just begun, but for the life of me, I can't fathom spending the night with another woman and I can't explain why. There's something about this blonde goddess that's drawing me to her like a strong magnetic pull.

I peek in her direction and catch her checking me out.

Busted.

Under the chandeliers, I can't tell if her eyes are hazel-green or green. Regardless, they're like two precious gemstones staring back at me.

I wink.

She bites her lower lip, as a hint of color creeps up her cheeks.

Don't do that, precious. It's driving me fucking wild.

My eyes eat up every inch of her.

She's not model tall, but she's not short either.

Her body is banging.

Fuck, she's delicious.

Images of freeing her body from that dress cloud my mind. The cobalt-blue shade is elegant as fuck, and she wears it to perfection. I suspect it hides a sensual view.

Larkin zooms his attention to the redhead. "Did you just arrive?"

"Yes," she says. "I gave my bestie the grand tour of the hotel before coming here."

Larkin checks his watch. "You only have ten minutes left to mingle, ogle and eye-fuck," he says.

We chuckle.

"It will make it much easier for you later when it comes to finding your perfect match for the evening... in case Lady Luck isn't on your side the first time around."

The redhead and the blonde frown their confusion.

"Trust me on this," Larkin says. "You want to get a scope of who else came out to play tonight before the MC steps on stage."

Larkin has a wicked paring game plan for tonight. This should be interesting.

"I regret we didn't get here sooner," the redhead says. "We're at a disadvantage now."

"A lot can happen in ten minutes," Larkin says. "Sometimes, one look is all it takes."

Amen to that.

"Then, we'll work the room." The redhead grabs her friend's arm, pulling her away.

When the blonde turns around, the world stops spinning.

Goddammit.

The beaded fabric of her dress covers the front of her body, but the back... more than makes up for the small level of modesty she was displaying when she was walking towards us. Only a thin strip of cobalt-blue glass beads holds the sleeves of her dress together across the top of her back, leaving the rest of her skin exposed in a dramatic V, plunging all the way down to the crack of her fine ass. Jesus, you could bounce a quarter off that ass.

I cock my head to the side to appreciate the unbelievable view.

I want to claim and own every inch of her, right mother-fucking now.

Fuck, I'm hard all over again.

Larkin catches me eye-fucking her.

He lifts an appreciative eyebrow and nods.

I shake my head in response because it's not as if I can capture Wild Strawberry's beauty into words.

My eyes follow the blonde closely as she floats around the room, and it doesn't escape my notice how she keeps stealing glances my way.

"Ladies and gentlemen." A woman's voice resonates through the speakers. I'm so taken by Wild Strawberry's intoxicating beauty, I didn't even notice her get on stage. "Please." The voluptuous brunette adorned in a yellow flowy dress shouts into the microphone, quieting the crowd. "If I can have your attention."

"Things are about to get interesting." Larkin nods. "Good luck tonight, gentlemen."

My buddies nod.

I don't.

I didn't come here looking for a fight, but that's what's likely to happen.

I refuse to watch another man claim Wild Strawberry's pretty little ass.

Let the games begin.

Chapter 3

Jules

Sweet *mother mercy.*

The men here tonight are unbelievably handsome. I mean, so smoking hot, someone needs to crank the A/C way down.

Are stunning good looks a requirement to becoming a member? If so, I approve.

Phew.

Nothing could've prepared me for the drop-dead gorgeousness I now know as Ignatius. While my best friend was hyperventilating over the star power surrounding Zeus, I was too busy losing myself in the most mesmerizing aqua-blue ocean.

Who has eyes that color?

Jace Halsey, Beckett Christensen, and Rod Wolfe are nothing to sneeze at. After all, we're talking about former rock stars. I was in awe, but I was under Ignatius's spell. I couldn't stop staring at him, my heart pummeling my chest.

The man is dangerously hot.

Like, I'm-willing-to-sell-my-soul-to-the-devil-if-it-means-I'll-get-paired-with-you hot.

Here's-my-thong-sorry-it's-so-dripping-wet hot.

I-might-need-to-lie-down-with-you-on-top-of-me-for-the-next-two-hours hot.

Please-*ruin*-me hot.

One glance from this stranger heated my blood and stirred desire low in my belly. The way he ate me up with his eyes set my skin ablaze. I had to blink several times to steady myself when he blinded me with his dazzling smile.

I was going on about not wanting to be paired up with someone I wasn't attracted to, but I didn't expect to be facing an even bigger conundrum. What happens when you're so attracted to a man, you just want to climb him like a tree?

"My club name is Selestia and I'm your MC for tonight," the curvy woman on stage says. "Welcome to a night that promises to wreak havoc on a lot of underwear."

I'm already there.

"Judging from the insane level of sexiness present tonight, bypassing underwear altogether should've been a requirement."

Another round of laughter rumbles across the room.

I glance in Sydney's direction.

She grins from ear to ear.

"Let me explain the rules of the game," the MC says. "I'm sure everyone here is eager to meet their match. I saw a couple of you already eye-fucking each other. Naughty, naughty."

The crowd laughs.

An irresistible force compels me to look over my shoulder.

Ignatius is staring straight at me.

So are his three buddies.

Oh boy.

"The first rule is to make sure you respect the club's rules." I return my attention to the MC. "If you don't, you'll get unceremoniously thrown out on your ass. No exceptions."

Good thing Sydney insisted I read every line of the NDA and club rules before signing my life away.

"Now, let's get down to the good stuff," the MC says. "When you walked in, you should've received a white envelope. Please have it handy."

I rummage through my clutch until my fingers clasp around the envelope.

"Remember, hookups with more than one guest or member aren't allowed tonight—so no threesomes, foursomes, fivesomes, reverse harems, or harems."

Holy Jesus.

"Don't be greedy, unless you're determined to piss off Zeus." She pauses. "You must be curious to find out how you were paired up. First and foremost, you were matched base on your sexual preferences. Second, the goddess of serendipity is to thank—or blame—for the rest. Now, it's up to the goddess of seduction and the god of sex to work their magic. You have ten seconds to accept or reject your match. If you like what you see, remain eyes locked. If not, stand side by side. Once the music starts, you'll have sixty seconds to pair up with another match."

Please be good to me, God.

"One last thing, the safe word for the evening is *red*. It's a bit predictable, but it's easy to remember." The MC points to the ceiling. "Drumroll, please."

Right on cue, the sound of drums echoes around us.

A few seconds later, she does a throat slash gesture with her hand and the soundtrack stops. "All right boys and girls, tear open those envelopes. Find your match. And, go get *Ruined.*"

A few happy cheers erupt as people discover their match.

My heart palpitates as my impatient fingers rip open the white envelope. I pull out a lime-green laminated card with a bar code on one side and a number on the other. I flash it to

Sydney. She flashes me an orange card before lifting it over her head.

All color drains from her face.

I follow her line of sight.

Dear God.

Her match is a tower.

Tattoos run up his neck and shaven skull, and down his hands. If his considerable height, thick neck, massive hands, and feet are any clue, his cock must rival that of a horse. The top four buttons of his purple shirt are open, exposing an impressive eight-pack. The man's biceps are like tree trunks. So are his powerful thighs.

I'm guessing, he works out. A lot.

Syd looks at me. Her eyes are so wide, they take over her face. She blinks a few times before moving her bewildered gaze to her match.

There's no two ways about it, the man looks threatening.

The beast flashes Sydney a telling grin that sends chills down *my* spine.

Forget about ruining her pussy, he's going to destroy her.

Here goes nothing.

Armed with fake courage, I hold my card up and turn in a circle, looking for my match, all the while saying a little prayer.

Hail Mary full of Grace—

My heart lurches when my eyes land on a lime-green card that's an exact replica of mine.

Recognition—and satisfaction—shines bright in Ignatius's blue eyes before he flashes me a row of perfect white teeth.

His blinding smile is killer, and I'm the lucky girl on the receiving end of it.

He stalks towards me.

I do a happy dance inside, but maintain a cool exterior.

A sexy salsa beat seeps through the speakers, starting to count down.

Rumbling murmurs and footsteps indicate unhappy campers are buzzing about in their search for the perfect match.

My eyes don't waver from his—my perfect match.

He stares at me, his devastating blue eyes unblinking.

I swear an electrical current is charging the space between us.

How I manage not to melt in a pool of lust under the intensity of his gaze, I'll never know.

"Time's up, boys and girls," the MC says. "You either found a more suited match or you'll sit it out for the evening."

I glance over my shoulder in an attempt to locate Sydney. I can't find her anywhere. She must've moved deeper into the crowd.

Shit.

"Your best friend is in good hands." It's as if Ignatius could read my mind.

My worried eyes meet his.

"Trust me. I know her match."

I'm not sure if he's talking about the beast or another guy.

Syd praised the pristine reputation of the club.

Relax.

"Okay. Thanks."

"Let's go stand over there or else we might get stampeded as people make their way to their rooms," he says, jerking his head.

"Okay." My repertoire of vocabulary has dwindled since I stepped into this club.

He interlaces his fingers with mine and pulls me out of the way.

"You didn't want to trade me in?" A half-smile curls his beautiful lips.

Hell to the no.

I shake my head. "And you?"

He lets his gaze linger over me with blatant hunger. "Fuck no."

I'm excited—and terrified—by his unwavering tone.

I'm sure this guy's experience trumps mine by a long shot.

I hope I don't disappointment him.

"So, we're a match, Wild Strawberry," he says.

This close, I have no other choice but to take him all in.

He's tall, so much so, I have to tilt my head back to meet his insane gaze—even with my five-inch heels. I'm compelled to run my fingers through his silky smooth, thick, wavy brown hair. Some men are hot because they ooze confidence and they know how to work their best assets. Some men are hot because God was good to them from birth. This tall piece of man candy falls into both categories. His eyes rival precious jewels and enhance his straight nose. His strong jaw is dusted with a 5 o'clock shadow that makes him so much more irresistible. And then, there's his sexy mouth...

Damn.

I'd be willing to bet a vital organ his black suit cut to perfection hides a formidable body. Even by LA standards, the sheer perfection of this man is a dead giveaway he's not human. He can't be.

Bolstered by this fortuitous turn of events, so immensely grateful Lady Luck was looking out for me and I won't have to be someone's baby girl or spend the rest of the evening around the buffet table, I say, "Fuck, you're hot."

Very eloquent, Jules.

My handsome match laughs.

Even his laugh is sexy.

Is there anything that isn't perfect about this man?

To save face, I force myself out of my he's-too-hot-to-think stupor. "I mean, it appears we're a match."

He leans into me, eclipsing everyone around us, his lips flirting with my earlobe. I'm certain the scent of his intoxicating cologne comes in an absurdly expensive glass bottle that's uniquely eau-de-freaking-hotness.

"I much preferred, *Fuck, you're hot* because that's how I feel about you."

My cheeks flush.

"I was willing to fight off any man here if the deck wasn't stacked in my favor."

"Oh."

"Looks like I won't have to throw any punches or break someone's jaw."

"Looks like it," I say with a lopsided grin.

He pulls away from me, and I miss the warmth emanating from his body.

He reaches out and brushes a finger down the front of my dress—between my breasts. Since the design doesn't allow for a bra, there's no hiding how my nipples tighten with need.

He narrows his eyes, his gaze fixed on my chest, and he bites his lower lip, stifling a moan. "You look like a goddamn wet dream in that dress."

Me? A sexy man's wet dream?

No one has ever said anything remotely close to that to me before.

Maybe I unknowingly entered the gates of Heaven.

"Thank you," I say in a shaky voice. My heart is beating so fast, I fear it might pop.

"Is this your first time at the club?"

I nod. "Yes, it is."

"So, you're a club virgin?"

"I am."

"I get to pop your club cherry."

"Should I be worried?" My bravado is wearing thin.

"Absolutely."

For a second, I'm not sure if he's serious or joking.

"I'll take great pleasure in *ruining* you," he says with an intensity in his strong face that makes me shiver from head to toe. "Are you looking forward to it?" His low, seductive tone travels all the way to my clit.

I'm so out of my league, but fuck if that's going to stop me.

"Yes," I say in a meek voice.

"Good." He flashes a wicked grin that's all sin and sex.

"Since most of you have been paired up, it's time to turn the heat way up," the MC says. "Your room numbers are on the card. Guests, you'll find a screen near the elevators. Scan your card and you'll be presented with a map pinpointing your room's location. Please remember, by scanning your card, you give your match access to your hard limits. Now, go and get dirty."

Giddy laughter echoes from behind Ignatius.

He's too tall for me to see what's going on, but I suspect happily paired couples are shuffling out of the room.

The tall, blue-eyed hottie glances down at me. "I'll soon find out. What are your hard limits?"

"Is that a deal breaker?" Nerves twists my stomach.

"No." He shakes his head. "I'd rather hear it from you."

"Um..."

"Nothing will shock me."

"I know the Eros Den is closed tonight, but that's the last place you'd ever find me." Syd has told me about the kinky dungeon where some pretty crazy shit happens. "I'm not into anything hardcore or scary."

"Neither am I."

Phew.

"What about dominance?"

"I've never experienced anything like that before," I say.

"But you're open to it?"

With you I am. "I think so."

"What else?"

"It's not an issue tonight, but a ménage doesn't appeal to me."

"I don't like to share," he says.

"Oh, and no to anal sex."

A second ticks by.

Then another.

"We'll leave it off the table for tonight." He says that like there'll be other hookups where anal sex might be a possibility.

Sydney warned me. Tonight is about living out a fantasy most women have within safe boundaries—a one-time steamy hookup with a complete stranger.

No real names.

No contact numbers.

No encores.

You walk away.

"Do you have hard limits?" Best to know now.

"I have zero interest in a woman who's looking for a master. I'm not looking for a slave. Having 24/7 control over a needy soul isn't on my to-do list. I have a demanding and fulfilling career. And, no matter how much you beg, you're not getting my cock unless it's wrapped up."

His crude words cause my head to jerk back in surprise.

"You're okay with that?"

"Absolutely." My voice comes out faint.

Ignatius crowds my personal space with all of his imposing presence. "Good. That leaves plenty room for us to have filthy, dirty fun."

Relief washes over me.

I would've been crushed if he decided he wanted someone more adventurous.

"Let me spell it out for you, Wild Strawberry." There's a warning undertone in his words. "Just in case it wasn't already crystal clear, this isn't a fairytale ball—"

"I know." Okay, I get it. I'm a little wet behind the ears, but I'm miffed he feels the need to point that out.

"I won't be offering you sweet nothings and conversation." He ignores my acknowledgment. "Once you get up to our room, I want you stripped of that cock-hardening dress that looks like it was sewn onto your sinful body."

My heart is one breath away from lurching from my rib cage.

"I want you waiting naked—with a blindfold covering your eyes—ready for me to devour every inch of you."

My eager pussy palpitates.

"If anything is too much, use the safe word and everything stops. If you don't, be warned, I won't hold back, and I expect you to give me everything tonight. By the time I'm done with you, I'll have marked you in a way that will *ruin* you for any other man."

I fight to keep my breathing even. Heck, I fight to keep breathing.

"I intend on using you in every possible way so I can bring you immense pleasure. Be warned, you'll feel my cock inside you for days to come."

I struggle not to let the impact of his words show, but God, I swear I'm going to come from what just came out of his beautiful mouth.

"Every step you'll take, you'll be reminded of our illicit night."

His lustful gaze sears me in place.

I'm speechless.

He reaches out and brushes the back of his fingers across my hardened nipple. "Your body belongs to me tonight."

My flaming lady-parts combust. I'm so turned on, I'm dripping. It's with herculean effort, I don't fan between my legs.

He leans close, his hot breath feathering across my lips. "Take it or leave it?"

His words should horrify me—send me running for the hills—because let's face it, what he promises is a pretty tall order and I'm so out of my element it's not even funny. Yet, every cell in my body hums in anticipation, and my neglected pussy clenches with desire. Everything about this sexy stranger turns me on so damn much. Such a strong reaction to a man is a first for me.

God have mercy on me, but if this is the only time in my life I'm lucky enough to be invited to a naughty party like this, no way am I chickening out.

I came here to forget.

My mind won't be preoccupied with all the problems weighing heavy on my shoulders when this delicious man is pounding the ever-loving fuck out of my pussy.

"Take it," I say.

"Good answer, Wild Strawberry."

His fingers trace a line down the bare skin of my back until they slide down my butt crack.

I gasp and clench my cheeks together.

He cups my ass with both hands and squeezes.

I moan, as a sensual tremor courses throughout my body, ending at my clit.

"Your ass is a fucking work of art," he says.

"A do lot of squats."

Seriously, Jules? That's your answer?

"I appreciate that. A lot." He chuckles. "I can't wait to nestle my cock between your bouncy cheeks."

My body stiffens.

"Relax. I didn't say I was going to fuck your ass. We've established it's one of your hard limits." My shoulders slump in relief. "I intend on nudging my cock between your pillows."

That sounds so dirty.

"I'll allow it," I lift a defying chin.

I have no idea where that came from.

He pulls his head back so our eyes meet. "Is that so?"

"Yes." I'm bursting with newfound confidence.

He takes a step forward, forcing me back against the wall, pinning me there.

I'm wedged between a hard place and, well... a hard place.

"Let's get one thing straight. *I* control this ride."

"O—okay."

He leans down, heat radiating from his lips, and my breath catches in my throat. One hand rests on my waist, the other interlacing our fingers together. His aqua-blue eyes flick from my mouth to my eyes. He hold my gaze for a long beat before lowering his parted lips until they're hovering above mine.

I convey with my eyes a million thoughts without speaking a word, but he seems intent on teasing me. On torturing me.

A short eternity passes between us.

"Please kiss me." *If you don't, I know beyond any shadow of doubt, I might die.* The desperate tone in my voice is foreign to me. I've never wanted a man to claim my lips this much in my life.

He grants my wish.

Our mouths meet with a flurry of emotions, kissing like we're both literally drowning. Shockwaves of heat zip through me, threatening to make me dizzy. I clasp his cheek with my palm to deepen the kiss, cursing my other hand isn't free to cup his gorgeous face. I drink him in, the taste of strong liquor on his tongue. It's so all-encompassing, I forget to breathe.

Fuck breathing, this is all I need.

I'm drowning in his kiss with no desire to be rescued.

"More," I say between kisses, threading my fingers through the strands of his hair.

He cups my face. "Greedy little thing," he says before slamming his mouth over mine. His possession is unreal.

I moan when his tongue slips inside my mouth.

Jesus, this guy knows what he's doing.

His kiss is like flooring his foot on my desire's accelerator. Goosebumps pebble up and down my body, and I shiver. I snake my other arm around his neck, bringing us closer together, my body molding to his and I melt into his warmth.

I lose all concept of time until he pulls away from me.

I let out a grunt of frustration.

"You wore the perfect dress for tonight." A slow smile widens on his face as his hand travels down my body. "The sinful slit gives me easy access to your pussy."

He robs me of a response when his fingers snake under my dress, finding my thong before sliding between my pussy lips.

I gasp.

He groans in a low, deep voice, making me shudder. "You're so fucking wet. Is that for me?"

"Y—yes."

"I'm a lucky bastard." His fingers continue exploring me.

"Others will see us"

"That's the point."

Jesus.

My eyes move left, then right, but his body blocks my view.

From the desperate moans echoing around us, I can only assume we're not the only ones doing naughty things.

This is crazy.

I've never been this promiscuous. Ever.

Sydney warned me the whole hedonistic vibe floating in the air once I stepped into the club might awaken dormant urges.

I'd snorted a laugh, convinced I'd never fall into that trap.

Look at me now...

Then again, the man towering over me is sexy as fuck.

Languorous fingers continue exploring my wetness, teasing my clit, causing my thighs to tremble and my finger-nails to bite into his forearms to prevent my legs from giving out.

A throaty, sex-filled sound I don't recognize leaves my lips.

His masterful fingers take me higher and higher.

Heat and pleasure roll in waves through my body.

I've never been at the edge of a cliff, ready to dive headfirst like this before.

I reach out for his cock because it's only polite to return the favor, but he stops me.

"No, this is about you. There's plenty of time for you to take care of my cock."

Copy that.

His fingers keep rubbing circles around my clit until I'm almost seeing stars before he sinks them deep inside me, making me moan as my eyes slam shut.

"Eyes on me."

The excruciating ache between my legs is unbearable, but I find it in me to obey his order.

"Better." His fingers are still toying with my pussy.

"God." I'm breathless. "You're going to make me come right here in front of all these people?"

His aqua eyes blink and his lips twitch in a wicked smile. "I am."

Alarm bells should ring in my head, because good girls like

me don't do things like this. But right now, I'm far too consumed by the pleasure his fingers are dragging out of me.

He alternates between teasing my clit and filling my pulsing pussy.

The orgasm threatens closer and closer.

I'm powerless to stop the groan that escapes my throat.

How did he manage to bring me right to the brink so quickly?

This man, this total stranger, is in control of my body, playing me like a maestro, strumming the strings of his instrument.

As if he knows I'm close, he picks up the pace.

"I'm nearly there..."

"Don't hold back."

His response startles me because I didn't realize I'd spoken the words aloud.

My hips tremble as he skates over my clit again, and again, and again.

My need to stay decent is swept away in a tidal wave of desire. I should feel ashamed at what I'm allowing this stranger to do to me, but I don't. The wrongness—no, the boldness—feels so incredibly good on me, a foreign, new sensation.

Jesus.

My skin tingles.

My vision blurs.

My breath hitches.

My mouth drops open, but no sound comes out.

"Come for me," he says and presses my clit like it's a launch button.

I let go.

The force of my orgasm literally chokes me.

Heat burns in my core as I shatter in an exquisite, passionate climax that leaves me breathless. I swear my pussy spasms for a solid minute before the shaking in my thighs subsides.

As I struggle to snap out of the haze of arousal he's put me in, he pulls his fingers from my pussy and brings them to his lips. With his eyes boring into mine, he cleans up my juices with his tongue.

"Holy... uh..."

I blink.

I blink again.

Did he actually do that in the open like this?

"Um." I'm at a loss for words.

"Your club name suits you to a T," he says. "That was wild *and* you're a sweet little thing."

Un-fucking-believable.

I don't have a reply for that.

This is more than I ever could've expected from tonight.

"You get a head start," he says.

I frown my confusion.

"Get your fine ass up to our room. You already know what I expect of you."

I nod. "I do."

As I stride in the direction of a group of people rushing to the elevators, it doesn't go unnoticed the number of couples making out in plain view. Considering how many women—and men—are on their knees with their mouths stuffed with cocks, Ignatius's corruption is tame in comparison.

I do a double take.

A head of red hair eagerly bobs up and down a long and meaty cock. The black dress is a dead giveaway.

Sydney found her match.

The attractive man wearing a crisp white shirt that's unbuttoned, exposing a chest covered with colorful tattoos, is unquestionably badass, but he's not as scary looking as her original match. There's no way she could've handled that beast.

Syd's alpha locks eyes with me, and he licks his lips as he tightens his grip around my best friend's hair.

Wow.

My cheeks flush.

I've never seen my best friend in the throes of passion. Not only did I turn into an exhibitionist, it also seems I'm a voyeur. I guess it's par for the course since everything is getting thrown out the window tonight.

Freaked out by my lustful reaction, I head towards the elevators. As I'm about to cross the threshold, I look over my shoulder.

Ignatius is staring at me with a raised eyebrow.

His gaze drifts from the guy Syd is sucking off to mine.

I'm startled by the possessiveness I read in his eyes. It turns me on even more than I already am... and that says a lot considering how my body is humming.

"Go. Now," he says.

A rush of heat blooms between my legs, causing my poor clit to tingle all over again.

I nod and scurry out of the room, too eager to get *Ruined*.

Chapter 4

Levi

W*ild Strawberry is my perfect match.*
What are the odds?

Dark Compulsion tends to attract some of the most beautiful women in LA. Members and guests are highly desirable, so attraction is rarely an issue. Everything is compounded when it comes to Wild Strawberry. The second I laid eyes on the blonde with the mesmerizing hazel-green eyes, I wanted her with every fiber of my straining cock.

I can't explain it.

Given our luck tonight, it's like we were fated.

Although, I didn't expect things to go from hello to me licking her juices off my fingers after making her come. It's a kinky party and all, but I tend to show more restraint than my buddies.

Fuck, that was damn hot.

I adjust my cock. I'm so turned on the fucker is hard as steel.

Eager to kick things up a notch—or twenty—I strut across the floor, scanning the room to locate my buddies. Beckett and

Jace are nowhere to be seen, but a woman on her knees with jet black hair is worshiping Rod's cock.

He grins at me.

I grin back and exit the main party room.

I don't bother scanning my card. I know where I'm going. I bypass the elevators and the queue of people waiting, preferring to take the stairs two by two up to the third floor. I stroll down the hallway until I reach our room. I scan the card and push open the door. The heels of my shoes tap against the hardwood floor as I make my way from the foyer to the bedroom.

A satisfied grin stretches my lips at the inviting sight I'm unlikely to forget anytime soon.

Damn.

My cock twitches in my pants.

My eyes shift from Wild Strawberry's discarded cobalt-blue dress and black lacy lingerie on the chaise to her body. Her form-fitted dress hinted at all the wonderful things going on beneath it, but seeing it in the flesh leaves me salivating.

She's a knockout—in and out of clothes.

I take my time to appreciate all of her.

She obeyed me like a docile little lamb.

She's waiting, naked, blindfolded, her long hair falling behind her back, her hands clasped together on her lap.

Fucking perfect.

I remove my suit jacket and place it next to her dress before toeing off my shoes and removing my socks. As I stride to her, I free my shirt from the confinement of my pants.

"It's you," she says in a breathy voice as I sit next to her. "I recognize your cologne."

I lean into her. "You were paying attention."

This close and without any other distractions, the lovely scent of her delicate perfume tickles my nostrils.

"How could I not? Everything about you is hard to forget."

"Oh, I'm hard alright."

She lets out a quick breath at that.

"I like you, Wild Strawberry."

"Ditto." She shifts on the bed. "You have some weird effect over me."

"It's the same for me," I say. "I've been to many of these theme parties and I can't remember wanting a woman this much."

"Really?"

"Really."

"Gosh. I was so worried," she says.

"Worried about what?"

"I wouldn't be able to satisfy a guy like you..."

"You have everything to satisfy me... in spades."

"Oh," she says in a low voice.

I reach out and twist a strand of her hair around a finger before setting it free. "You have beautiful hair." My gaze lands between her legs. "Too bad your Brazilian prevents me from figuring out if you're a natural blonde."

She laughs. "I'm a dark blonde, but I got highlights, so it's more honey blonde."

"I see."

My eyes drop to her heaving chest, zooming in on her breasts.

Like the rest of her, her tits are fucking perfect. Unable to resist, I reach out and grope them, feeling their weight. They're a nice size and they're natural. Her beautiful pink nipples are begging for my touch. I lean forward and pepper little kisses along her neck and collarbone as I brush the back of my fingers against the hard peaks. I taunt them and roll them in a teasing way that leaves her squirming under my touch.

"You're so responsive."

She swallows a moan.

I hold her tits in my hands, admiring them, before lowering my head and latching my lips over one hard nipple. I suck it before moving my attention to her other nipple. When I bite gently against it, a choked cry slips from her lips.

I do it again, and again, until her rosy nipples turn a seductive dark shade of red. I pull away from her to admire my handiwork.

Fucking beautiful.

"The blindfold should heighten your senses." I let go of her tits.

"It does," she says, her voice trembling.

"You like that?"

"I do."

My fingers drag across the skin of her taut stomach.

She groans.

I trace a line between her bellybutton and the entrance of her pussy, stopping shy from exploring between her lips. "Do you know what I want to do to you?"

"No," she says, her breaths heavy.

"I want you fully exposed and vulnerable—"

"I think I already am."

"This is merely the warmup. What I have in store for you will blow your mind."

"Now you're worrying me."

"Trust me, you'll be thanking me," I say. "I want you splayed out across the bed like an offering. I want to give you so much pleasure, you forget your own name."

"Oh."

"Can you handle that?"

"Yes." Her voice comes out high-pitched.

"You're sure about that?"

"Yes, I can handle that." Confidence radiates in her statement.

"There's one catch, though."

"Um. Okay..." She frowns. "What is it?"

"I want to restrain your wrists."

"Wh—wh—what?"

"Not with handcuffs, ropes, tape, zip ties or chains—"

"Chains? Is that a thing?"

"It's more hardcore, and not suitable for a novice, but yes, chain wrist cuffs are a thing."

She sucks in a sharp breath. "Oh gosh."

Her head drops, almost in defeat.

I place two fingers underneath her chin, lifting her head up, regardless of the fact she can't see me. "I'm not talking about anything that extreme. I'm talking about silk ties—"

"I'm okay with that."

"You're very trusting."

She considers me for a beat. "You haven't given me any reason not to trust you, Ignatius."

My cock throbs.

"I like that answer."

She offers a shy smile.

I cup her face between my palms and slam my mouth against hers, claiming it. Her pouty lips part and our tongues meet. Sweet notes of champagne hit my tongue full force.

I groan.

There's nothing chaste about this kiss. It's a dominant, possessive kiss—like I fucking own her.

She places her hands on my forearms as if begging me not to stop.

No chance of that happening, little one.

For a few long beats, we're all tongue as I devour her mouth.

I could kiss her like this for an eternity, but I'm too eager to taste her other set of lips.

I stand up and scoop her into my arms.

She yells. "Where are we going?"

"To paradise."

"I see."

I place her slender body in the middle of the king size bed.

I open the nightstand and find what I need. I pull out the silk ties and place the box of condoms on top for easy access.

"Reach over your head and hold on to the headboard rails."

These modern industrial metal beds are esthetically pleasing and serve double duty.

She obeys.

I make quick work of the silk ties around her wrists. "Pull against them."

She does as she's told.

"Too tight?"

"No, I'm okay."

"You're sure?"

She nods. "I am."

"Since it's our first time together, I won't bind your legs."

"Okay."

"What's the safe word?"

"Um..."

"What's the color of *strawberries?*"

She giggles. "Red."

"That's right, Wild Strawberry." I chuckle. "So, what's your safe word?"

"Red."

"We won't do anything extreme, but I tend to get a little kinky. If anything is way out of your comfort zone, use the safe word."

"I will."

"Now you're ready to play," I say. "Part your legs."

She does.

I climb on the bed.

I grab her legs and spread them further apart, settling my weight between them.

My eyes are glued to her pretty pink pussy. "Look at that beautiful sight."

Her body shivers.

I lie down on the bed, and lower my head until I can inhale her heady scent.

Fucking heaven.

I slip the tip of my tongue between her pussy lips.

She gasps a sharp breath of surprise.

I slip my tongue further in.

She pants in a strangled voice as she pulls on the bonds.

"What do you think you're doing?"

"It's too much," she says.

"Do you need to use your safe word?"

"I never said that." Her tone is indignant.

"Just checking."

"I'm not used to being with a man who's this talented with his fingers and his tongue."

"Sounds like you're upgrading tonight."

She laughs. "Big time."

"Now that you've distracted me, I'm going to have to make up for those precious minutes lost."

"It doesn't sound like it's going to bode too well for me."

"On the contrary."

I resume my mission.

Pinning her legs open, my mouth begins to work her sensitive flesh with the same intensity that I'd kissed her mouth.

She yelps as my tongue pushes inside her.

I double my efforts, pumping my tongue in and out of her slick pussy.

"Your tongue... I love what it's doing to me."

I replace my tongue with two fingers as I close my lips around her clit.

She thrashes and whimpers as I play her like a damn violin.

"Dear God, my whole body is going to shatter into a million pieces."

I pull my mouth away from her intoxicating pussy, but leave my fingers lodged deep in her warmth.

I might not be able to see her eyes, but her heavy panting tells the whole story.

"I didn't use the safe word," she says. "Why did you stop?"

I tsk.

She pulls her lower lip between her teeth.

A second goes by.

Then another.

"I want your mouth on my pussy," she says.

"You're already addicted to my tongue?"

"Yes... and to you."

I didn't see that coming.

"I'm giving you a respite."

That's a partial lie.

If I don't pace myself, I'm going to ravage this woman to the point of no return.

"I don't need a break. I need your mouth."

"Demanding little one. What do you want from me?"

"Please, make me forget."

"Forget what?"

"Err... I'm not thinking straight. It's all your fault." She worries her lower lip. "Sex is never this mind-blowing... I'm blurting out nonsense."

She's not getting off that easily.

"Forget what?"

She turns her head as a response.

"Tell me what you want to forget, and I'll make it happen."

I withdraw my fingers, then plunging them back in along with a third one.

She gasps, her body arching off the bed. "Not tonight. For one night, I want to feel. Please."

This is supposed to be an illicit night. This isn't the time or place to psychoanalyze her life. As it stands, I may never see her again.

I drop the subject.

"All right. You want to feel? Hold on for the ride."

She moans as I pump my fingers in and out of her, plunging into her with an increased intensity that makes me desperate to sink my hard cock into her. I close my lips over her clit, causing her back to arch off the bed all over again.

Two slow, wicked thrusts, and she reaches the precipice. Her screams of ecstasy bounce off the walls as she rides my face —and my hand—like a woman possessed, wringing every last drop of pleasure from my fingers while her tight pussy clenches and pulses with her climax.

I pull my fingers out and get off the bed.

A frustrated whine tears from her lips.

"I can't fuck you fully dressed."

"Oh, of course." She lets out a shy laugh.

I strip naked, roll on a condom in record time and climb back on the bed.

I lift her legs so they rest on the crook of my arms, lining my cock at her entrance.

I hope I survive this.

"You're so goddamn beautiful," I say, inching in.

She clamps down on me, making it difficult to slide in further.

On second thought, I'm not going to survive this.

That is one tight pussy.

I withdraw and then push in again, further this time.

A pleading moan leaves her lips.

"Can I feed you more of my cock?"

"Yes." She's breathless.

I push deeper, forcing my way.

Even though she's slippery wet, it's still a struggle.

She groans. "You're huge."

"I'm a big guy."

"No, you're huge. And so, so hard."

"I told you how much I wanted you."

"I still can't believe you feel this way about me. I mean, we just met."

"Believe it," I say. "When it's right, it's right."

"I like hearing that." She smiles.

I take advantage of the moment to bury myself as far as I can until I'm completely inside her.

She gasps.

I grind my hips. "Do you like having my big cock in your pussy?"

"Yes, I do."

"So do I."

Adulting has robbed me of my free time, and it's been a long while since I've allowed myself a night of carnal debauchery.

My instant attraction for her, coupled with a long period of abstinence, unleashes my feral nature. I let go of her legs, angle my body so my pelvis rubs against her clit and fuck her like an animal.

It's a good thing she's bound to the bed. I wouldn't have made it with her hands on me, scratching at my back and ass, or wrapped behind my neck.

"Show me how much you appreciate the way I worship your pussy. Come for me."

"I—I can't believe I'm going to come again— I'm close."

Thank the fuck God.

"You're ready to come hard for me?"

"Oh, yes," she says. "Oh, oh, oh... I wish I knew your real name."

Fucking club rules.

For some insane reason, I've never wanted to hear *Levi* fall from a woman's lips as I make her come as I do right now.

"Ignatius. Oh, Ignatius!"

Fuck, that sounds so wrong.

I don't have time to dwell on it.

Her climax comes crashing in like a wave, hitting the shore with full force. It's so intense, her body convulses, fighting against the ties, forcing me to hold her down.

She cries out a sob of pleasure as she freefalls, her pussy clenching in staccato pulses around my cock.

"That's it. Take it all."

I relish how she milks me with her body.

"I could watch you come all night long," I say.

She's too busy shuddering with the aftershocks of her orgasm to respond.

Fuck, she's beautiful.

My balls contract, reminding me of my looming climax.

I move deep inside her, pumping my cock in and out of her with determination. I swear I've never been this hard in my life.

She's still clamping the muscles of her pussy around my cock, which only seals my fate.

The orgasm I've been holding at bay rears its head and I'm a breath away from exploding. Resolved in my promise to brand her body in a way she'll never forget, I pull out of her, yank off the condom and toss it aside. I pull off her blindfold and untie her hands. I might not know her real name, but I need this connection.

"Holy shit," she says, blinking a few times, her eyes

adjusting to the dim light, before zooming in on my hand stroking my cock at an infernal pace.

"I want your eyes on me when I come."

She licks her lips in response.

I jerk my cock with a few rough strokes, grunting like a caveman. "I need you to see what you do to me."

A few more hard strokes and I'm done.

I jet my warm cum all over her stomach as my climactic grunts take over the room.

When she reaches out and runs her fingers across her stomach covered with my release, smearing it across her tits, I nearly come again.

Fuck.

My heart drums against my chest so hard, I fear I'm about to have a heart attack.

I have to coax myself to regulate my heartbeat.

Judging by her heavy breathing, I'm guessing I'm not alone.

It seems to take an eternity before my feet touch the ground, and for my breathing to slow to almost normal.

"That was hot," she says.

"Not bad for a first round."

Her jaw drops open.

"You made me come twice."

"Three times, but who's counting."

"That's well past my quota for one night—"

"You asked me to make you forget," I say. "I take an oath very seriously. Lucky for me—and you—the night is still young. Let's aim for another few rounds."

Her gorgeous hazel-green eyes take over her face. "You can't be serious."

"Be careful what you wish for."

Chapter 5

Jules

Darkness surrounds me when I open my eyes.

For a second, I'm lost, until a warm, hard body stirs next to me, and I'm transported to last night—and earlier this morning—as saucy images loop in my head.

It wasn't a dream.

Thank God.

What time is it?

I force my eyes to focus on the clock sitting on the nightstand.

Four o'clock?

Shit.

Sydney must be worried.

I pull the sheet off my body and attempt to climb off the high California King bed. When I move my legs, I groan internally. Our sex marathon depleted everything in me. My legs feel like Jell-O and my pussy is still pulsating from the vigorous workout. From the first thrust, I was stretched to the max. Ignatius's remarkable size was a lot to handle, but the pleasure of the fullness overruled the discomfort, so I didn't complain. Now, I'm paying the price for fucking a man with a big cock.

I bite my lip to stifle a grunt as I push myself off the bed and I wobble a bit when I stand up.

I look over my shoulder at the gorgeous man sleeping peacefully. He looks more like a boy than an alpha right now.

My eyes trail over his delectable torso, stopping at his spectacular tattooed chest. I was dying to ask him about them, but last night wasn't a date.

Sigh.

I should get a move on, but I can't pull my eyes away from him. My fingers itch to run along the fine layer of scruff adorning his jawline. To mess up his thick wavy hair, which is styled a little longer on top. The craving to slide back into bed, so we can go for another couple of rounds, blooms between my legs. I wish I could taste his full lips one more time before escaping, but I don't want to wake him and I sure as hell don't want to come across like the silly girl who falls for a one-night stand.

Even in the lowlight, it's impossible to remain unaffected by his good looks. I can't ever recall having such a strong physical reaction to a man upon sight. I've heard of insta-lust, it's just never happened to me. My perfect match is the quintessential irresistible Hollywood playboy every girl wants, and last night, he was all mine. I asked him to make me forget, and he rose to the challenge.

Thank you for the most amazing night of my life.

I blow him a kiss.

I wish I could stay here in this luxury suite with this beautiful stranger and never step into my tragic, chaotic and lonely life again, but I can't.

One night.

I knew the deal before stepping into the club.

I sigh.

Get out of here, Jules.

I tiptoe towards the chaise and slide into my clothes and heels, a pang of overwhelming sadness engulfing me.

This makes no sense.

I shake off this weird trance I'm under.

In the dark, I smooth down my dress and comb my fingers through my freshly fucked hair. I'm sure I look like a hot mess, but checking my reflection in the mirror is too risky.

You need to get out of here, Jules.

My hand is curled around the bedroom door handle when I spy a pen and small notepad on the dressing table. Without bothering to second-guess myself, I tear off a page and pen a brief note.

> *Ignatius,*
>
> *Thank you for helping me to forget and thank you for making me feel again. I'm sure this note screams newbie and it's probably gauche, but since we're unlikely to ever see each other again, I'm okay with that. I won't forget you anytime soon.*
>
> *—Stay well, Wild Strawberry, aka, J.S.*

I'm not breaking the rules per se. I didn't write my full name, just my initials. I drop the note on the pillow next to him and tiptoe out of the bedroom. I stand in the hallway for way too long before coaxing my feet to move. Once I reach the lobby, I check my phone. Sydney texted me three hours ago to let me know she was heading out.

Wow.

Hillary also texted me to let me know she was spending the

night at her boyfriend's Malibu house with her daughters. It's unlikely I'll see her until much later today since they're going sailing and then off to another party. She also texted me a long list of chores she expects me to do around the house since it's Sunday.

Great.

While the three witches enjoy a leisurely Sunday, I'll be pulling God knows how many hours at the office in my attempt to save Daddy's company before going back to the house to play maid.

Fuck my life.

Chapter 6

Levi

A lazy smile stretches my lips as I turn over, searching for the woman I intend to enjoy a few times before breakfast. I pat the bed, expecting to find her sinful hot body, but it's just the mattress.

What the fuck?

I sit up straight in bed.

She's gone?

Like the sexy blonde, the beautiful blue dress is nowhere to be seen, only her subtle perfume lingers.

I search for the time and nearly fall out of bed in shock.

Eleven a.m.?

Being jetlagged, coupled with a wild night of sex, threw my body's internal clock out of whack. I rake my fingers through my hair and let out a long sigh as I close my eyes. When I open them again, I catch sight of a note lost in the sea of tangled white sheets. I snatch it off the bed. It only takes me a quick glance to read it. I can't help but chuckle.

"Yeah, that screams newbie, but it's pretty adorable."

Adorable?

That's a word I reserve only for my little nephew.

Aldridge, you sound more like a teenage girl than a twenty-seven-year-old executive.

I chuckle at my silliness.

Even though Wild Strawberry escaped, I'm still under her spell.

Jesus.

Images of our filthy time together flash in front of my eyes, and my balls draw up at the memory. Hours on end of over-the-top sex and I still want her. I didn't expect her to be unabashed. I fucking loved her wild side. And I fucking hate there won't be an encore.

I read the note one more time.

J. S.

Who are you, sweetness?

Chapter 7

Levi

Mondays are hell. That's a given.

Tuesdays should be bearable.

Dealing with two brutal days in a row is daunting.

I spent most of yesterday catching up and updating my brother on my meetings while I was in London. Meetings that promise a flurry of talented British artists looking to make their mark on this side of the pond. As much as my body hates to have to adjust to the jetlag, the potential of new and lucrative business more than makes up for the temporary discomfort.

"Who the fuck does he think he is?" My brother isn't mincing his words. "We're behind some of the biggest concerts in the last decade. Joel fucking Banner just landed from gay old London," he says in a crappy British accent, "and he thinks he can tell us how to run our business. Again, who the fuck does he think he is?"

"Stop pacing, Linc. You're making me dizzy."

"It's either I pace or I wring Joel fucking Banner's neck."

Dealing with a bunch of finicky clients is a lousy way to kick off your day.

I'm equally vexed, but one of us has to maintain a cool head.

We just ended an excruciating meeting with Joel Banner and his three bandmates at our Culver City office-slash-studio. They're the four British rock stars behind the chart-topping group Brawn Impulse. Joel Banner is their lead singer and Linc's main point of contention right now.

"Their manager needs to rein them in." My brother points an agitated finger at me. "They're acting like spoiled kids in desperate need of a good spanking. My son is more mature for God sakes."

"Their manager is a snob, and it's clear Joel calls the shots."

"Joel fucking Banner." Linc shakes his head.

The four band members and their snooty manager scampered out of here in a cyclone of indignation at our reluctance to roll over like dogs to accommodate their unreasonable last-minute requests.

"Sit the fuck down, Linc."

He glares at me, but grants my wish.

He drops his ass in the seat across from me like a four-year-old sent to timeout. He even crosses his arms over his large chest and scowls at me.

"You look like you're about to burst," I say.

"I'm well past that." He lets out a long-suffering sigh. "Working with musicians can be like working with prima donnas—and I'm aware I signed up for this kind of bratty attitude when I chose this profession—but Joel fucking Banner takes the fucking cake." Linc jams his fingers through his hair.

Linc is six years older than me. Together we're co-CEOs of Lumen Opus Productions. The music industry is all we know. Like our dad, uncles, and grandfather, we're part of the team of experts and tradesmen who work in the background to make musicians look good when they're on stage, rocking out their fans at concerts. Linc's former boss was a bigshot in the industry, but he was difficult to work with, hence he went through employees like you go through tissue when fighting a cold. It was a constant revolving door. Linc was one of the rare ones who could handle this guy's volatile temper. Since he didn't have kids, he accepted Linc's offer of a buyout to continue his legacy. My brother was only twenty-five at the time, but eager to prove himself. I joined him the minute I graduated from the American Film Institute Conservatory. Linc designs the actual the stage, while I'm the light show guy. Together, we make magic.

"Joel has the gall to bring a list of demands as long as the goddamn Golden Gate Bridge a month before their Vegas concert because he wants to upstage another British band that had a sold-out concert in Madison Square Garden last night?" Linc balls his hand into a fist. "This isn't fucking kindergarten. If it weren't for our friendship with Holt, I would've thrown Joel's British ass out for having so little respect for what we do."

"He's clueless of the nightmare involved behind making such dramatic changes at this stage of the game."

"Damn fucking right he is."

If Joel wasn't linked to a good friend, Linc would've chewed up out and spat him out.

Holt Christensen commissioned us for this gig. Beckett's older brother is the head of a record label that's making waves in the industry. He's living in London now, but he has offices in LA and New York. Joel's band is signed under Holt's label. The guys are talented, but they're a royal pain in the ass—especially the band leader.

Holt wasn't always a record label exec.

Once upon a time, Rod Wolfe, Beckett Christensen, Jace Halsey, and Holt Christensen were known as the formidable musicians behind Random Misconception, aka one of the biggest rock bands of our time. Linc and I designed the stage and light show for their farewell tour. I was young when I secured that contract. I was hungry, too. It's the concert that put our company on the map.

Today, the four rock gods run successful companies. They're acing their second careers. Along with being badass execs, Rod, Beckett, Jace, and Holt are paper billionaires.

Years ago, our buddy Gage Hollingsworth needed seed money to propel an ingenious idea to the next level. We jumped in. Jace's older brother Jagger and his cousin Lochlan Berkshire are also investors. It was a risk, but the gamble paid off. It's mind-boggling to think StreamTunes has become a multibillion-dollar company as the leader in audio streaming services. The valuation of Gage's company is approaching the twenty-billion-dollar mark. Once he buys us out, we'll become bona fide billionaires.

Except for Beckett.

He's a multibillionaire in his own right. The company he owns with his business partner is kicking butt as a market leader. The rest of us will be rich. Pretty boy Beckett will be filthy rich.

"*I want to become a bloody legend, not just another musician, mate.*" Linc mimics Joel in an atrocious British accent. "We design fucking stages. We don't perform miracles—"

"I'll concede he's got a bit of a diva complex—"

"The pompous ass thinks he can walk in here and dictate how we do our job? *Chill out, mate. Money isn't an issue for us lads.*" Linc mocks Joel again. "This has nothing to do with money, you British prick. Like he knows the first thing about building a stage with a wow factor."

Joel managed to push his buttons during a meeting that extended by over an hour—precious time we'll never get back.

Linc snatches a rogue pen off the conference room table and taps it to the beat of his annoyance.

I open my mouth to say something to calm him down, but the alarm on my phone rings. "I have to go."

"The four o'clock meeting with the lawyers?"

"Yes."

"I forgot."

"I allotted time after our meeting with Joel and company for us to brainstorm, but now I'm pressed for time."

"Thanks for taking one for the team," my brother says, his tone softening.

"No problem. You can't possibly miss your son's first playoff soccer game of the season." Micah is playing off another top-ranking school. It's a big deal.

My brother chuckles. "He's predicting a 3-0 win. The boy has balls."

"And ambition."

Micah wants to grow up to become the team captain who brings the FIFA World Cup to America. Linc is a firm believer in dreaming big.

Micah is Linc's world.

He loves that boy so much, he'd sacrifice anything for that tiny human. In fact, he has.

The only reason my brother didn't jump in as a Stream-Tunes investor was because he was in the middle of an acrimonious divorce and a bitter custody battle. He was bleeding red *and* seeing red. He didn't want to give his wife the opportunity to siphon more out of him than she already had during their sham of a marriage.

"Enjoy the father-son time, while I pore over tedious legalese."

"Divide and conquer," my brother says.

"It's the only way."

Chapter 8

Jules

I *had such high hopes.*

My eyes are glued to the ceiling as the elevator descends to the lobby.

Sydney, bless her, mentioned my father's creation to one of her rich clients. I need an investor, a partner, or someone to take over the company. I'm walking a fine line, and time is running out. I was supposed to meet her contact, but when I got to his office, his assistant informed me he had to get on a plane to Chicago for a family emergency. I hope whatever his family member is dealing with isn't life threatening.

When I reach the lobby, I step out of the elevator, pull out my phone and text Sydney. She insisted on an update after my meeting.

Her response is quick.

She's as disappointed as I am, and like me, she hopes her client is still interested in meeting with me when he gets back to LA.

Fingers crossed.

With that thought making the butterflies in my belly soar at the reminder of my precarious situation, I heave a sigh and I'm about to head outside to hail a taxi to drive me back to the office, when my phone rings.

So, you're still alive.

In any other circumstance, I would let Hillary's call go to voicemail, but because I haven't seen her—or her daughters—since Saturday morning, I'm dying to know why she's MIA.

"Hillary," I say, accepting the call.

"*Jules.*" When she drawls my name, it means bad news.

"What do you want, Hillary?" I cut to the chase.

"It sounds like you didn't miss me or the girls. I'm a little hurt."

I roll my eyes at the phone. "You're all adults. You want to spend time at your boyfriend's place, that's your prerogative."

"Well, yes, I had a lovely time with Florian. His rented Malibu house is *so* much more comfortable than your father's crammed house."

Bitch.

"Our relationship is unfolding beautifully."

I have no desire to hear about how quickly she moved on after Dad's death.

"The duke is such a great father figure for my daughters."

Fucking Duke Florian Thauvin de la Poutaille.

Hillary can't shut up about the French duke she bumped into at the bank four months ago because he claims he has ties to the next King of France's family. Any imbecile can do a quick Google search to find out the last King of France was executed by guillotine over two centuries ago. Hillary prefers wearing blinders.

"I'm sure you didn't call me to tell me about your extended weekend at Florian's."

"You're right."

She allows for a long pause.

A strange fleeting emotion passes through me, but I ignore it.

"Spit it out, Hillary." *I don't have time for this shit.*

I move away from the elevators so I'm not in the way.

"I want out," Hillary says.

I frown at the phone. "What do you mean?"

"Hollywood is so last century when it comes to acting."

According to whom?

I yo-yo between curiosity and irritation. "What does Hollywood have to do with your previous statement?"

"You know what they say about New York? If you can make it there..."

"Enough with the clichés." I swear, the woman's communication skills are deplorable.

"My little green olive and my little patch of patchouli have a much better chance of shining on Broadway than in Hollywood."

I hate those ridiculous nicknames.

"Even as stunning blondes and after the breast augmentations, they can't get cast."

Eye roll. "Olive and Petula are moving to pursue their acting career?"

She snorts. "I wouldn't let them go on their own. They still need their mother."

"Hillary, Olive is twenty-one and Petula is twenty-four. They're grown women—"

"They still need my guidance."

Okay, whatever. "So, what does that mean?" I still don't understand the gist of this conversation.

"The duke, the girls, and I are moving to New York."

"What?"

"Florian is coming with us—"

"You've only been seeing him for four months. Are you

really going to uproot your life and move across the country with a man you barely know?"

"The duke promises a much better life for me than remaining a single mom."

"You're going to marry him?"

"I believe it's in the stars for me. But this isn't about me. It's about my girls. The duke has incredible contacts in New York and he believes he can open doors on Broadway for my little green olive and my little patch of patchouli."

I'm baffled.

"Your plans don't involve me, then."

"You're not my child, Jules. You didn't come out of my womb."

I shudder at the disturbing thought.

"And you don't have my last name. Not to mention, you've never made an effort with Florian. He has the distinct impression you dislike him."

That's because I do.

Royal title or not, the guy is sleazy.

Annoyance flares. "Why aren't we having this conversation face to face at the house?"

"I doubt I'll be coming back to that tiny box when I can live in the lap of luxury at my boyfriend's rented Malibu place. Florian hired professional movers. They'll take care of packing all our belongings. Once they're done, they'll leave the master keys with you. You won't have to worry your pretty little head. It'll all be handled."

Wow. I'm at a loss for words.

"So, you see dear Jules, this is the end of the road for us. We'll be leaving LA within a month—"

"A month? You've been planning this for a while, but it's only now you tell me?"

"Everything came together for us over the weekend. Florian

found us a beautiful apartment near Central Park. I wanted to wait until that was secured before telling you. We couldn't rush things. A man of his stature requires a certain level of accommodation. It's not like we can live in Harlem or any other suspicious neighborhood. We're both royalty."

Had she not just pulled the rug from under my feet, I'd be laughing my damn head off right now.

"Unbelievable," I say.

"Stop pretending you're going to miss us, Jules." I can imagine the smug look on her face. "You can't tolerate us—"

"That's beside the point, Hillary." I'm sure my voice carries, but right now, it's the least of my concerns. "You could've had the courtesy of warning me in advance—"

"Now that we have our ducks in a row, I'm warning you—"

"On the eve of your departure? That's hardly a warning. It's a conclusion."

"Back to my opening statement."

What a freaking cow.

"I want out of the house and your father's rinky-dink company—"

"You never seem to have any problem submitting your bogus expenses to said rinky-dink company—"

"Anyway, the sinking ship is all yours. I want nothing to do with it. Never did. I certainly don't want to be associated with it any longer. It reflects negatively on me. I want you to buy out my shares."

"Wh—what?"

"I need the cash—"

"But—"

"My only reason for living is to help Olive and Petula get their careers off the ground when we land in New York. I need money for that to happen. Hence, why I also want my share of the house in cash."

Her words have the same devastating effect as a cataclysmic earthquake.

I grip a wall to avoid collapsing to my knees. "You can't be serious."

"Oh, I am, dear Jules. My lawyer will be in touch with yours."

"But, I don't have a lawyer."

"There's no shortage of lawyers in LA."

"You know full well I don't have that kind of money. It's not like I can sell my soul in lieu of payment."

"It's not my fault your father was a piss poor businessman."

My blood boils.

"For some quick cash, sell the house. LA is such a hot real estate market. Even if it is a dodgy neighborhood—"

"Silver Lake is a good neighborhood."

"There you go. The house will sell in the blink of an eye."

Crap. I walked right into that one. "And where will I live?"

"You're not my child, therefore you're not my responsibility. Your mother died well before I came into the picture. True, your father's accident came as a shock to all of us, but that doesn't make you my daughter."

My teeth grind and my hand tightens in a fist, as my anger threatens to boil over.

If I could reach through the phone and press against that woman's throat until she suffocates, I would.

"I'm dead serious, Jules. Your father left me fifty percent of the house and forty-nine percent of a company that has never generated a cent of profit—"

"You burned through his insurance."

I refused to believe Daddy would do me wrong by designating Hillary as his beneficiary. It's only when I overheard Hillary gloat to Olive and Petula about how she was able to convince my father to change his will, everything made sense.

She called it a stroke of genius. Her timing was my curse. Everything was finalized a week before Dad's death.

"Your father left *me* the money to take care of my girls... and you."

"I never saw a dime of that money," I say. "You spent it all on stupid acting classes, acting coaches, personal trainers, dietitians, boob jobs, extensions, monthly visits to a pricey Beverly Hills salon, and regular trips to the tanning salon for Olive and Petula. The rest, you spent on all the furniture you insisted on upgrading after my father's death and on all that fake art—"

"They're reproduction paintings—"

"A copy of a Monet or van Gogh painted by some random artist in China is fake."

"It's still *real* art."

I grip my phone with both hands, bringing it close to my mouth as I seethe. "News flash, Hillary. You pretend your fake art is real, and a chimpanzee has more acting skills than your daughters."

"You know nothing about showbusiness or art. Florian says the paintings add a touch of sophistication to your father's crappy house, and he also says my girls have Oscar-worthy careers."

Florian says this.

Florian says that.

I get it. The French duke knows everything.

"To answer your accusatory question about the insurance money, you still have a roof over your pretty head. That's where the money went. So shut the fuck up with your complaining. I've had enough of this conversation."

"You called me."

"Enough back and forth. I want my money before I leave LA. You have thirty days to buy me out."

My heart is beating at warp speed and my head hurts so badly it's like a construction crew is jackhammering in there.

"Oh, one last thing, Jules."

"What?"

"In case you plan on going psycho on our personal items still in your father's Cracker Jack box house... you know like, burning or dumping everything at the Salvation Army. Don't even think about it. I'll sue your ass faster than you can say oops."

My fear mixes with annoyance. "You'd sue me?"

Her threat is like I've been punched in the guts, and I almost topple over in my heels, putting out a hand to steady myself against the wall once more.

She lets out a demonic laugh. "You bet your bottom dollar."

She never made any effort to be nice to me, but I never imagined she'd take pleasure in seeing me destitute.

"One last thing before I go."

"What now?"

"I did your last three remaining employees a favor."

Attrition has been a problem since Daddy died. The employees weren't jumping up and down when Hillary and I stepped in. Since she didn't show her bitchy face often, I guess attrition was caused by my inexperience to run a company.

I furrow my brows. "In what sense?"

"Once you buy me out, your father's company will crumble like a deck of cards. I called them to warn them of things to come and suggested they find new jobs because your days are numbered."

Her revelation knocks me askew. "You did what?"

"I'm sure they dropped their letters of resignation on your desk as they rushed out the door. You can thank me later. I saved you from having that difficult conversation."

"You raving bitch." My body vibrates with rage.

"Enjoy the rest of your day," she says before ending the call.

A text message pops on my screen.

Then another.

And another.

Judging from who they're from and variations of the same *I'm really sorry to do this, Jules, but...* opening line, I don't have to read the messages in full to know what this pertains to. In a way, I should be relieved since making payroll was always so stressful, involving so much juggling, it would deplete me of all my energy.

I'm not sure how long I stand in the lobby of this fancy building, clutching my phone. It must be a while, because my legs start to hurt. There's no equity left in the house. Daddy used it all to keep the company afloat. And profits from the business are as foreign as snow in Miami. In other words, I'm knee-deep in shit.

The weight that is my life settles on my shoulders, as heavy as an elephant.

My mind races for a solution, but none comes.

All the air seems to evaporate around me.

What am I going to do?

Where am I going to find the money to buy Hillary out?

Where am I going to live?

How am I going to survive this?

My stomach twists and catapults bile into my throat as I struggle not to throw up.

I'm doomed.

As tears prickle behind my eyes, I bite hard against my lower lip, determined not to show any cracks in my armor. My first instinct is to call Syd because I could use a shoulder to cry on, but I need to get out of here before the panic that's beginning to ebb turns into sheer terror. On the verge of an avalanche of tears, I turn around, dead set on rushing out of here before anyone sees me lose it, but I don't go far. I slam right into a wall of muscle.

"Careful there." Strong hands grip my shoulders.

"I— I'm sorry," I say, my eyes trained to the floor.

I'm not going to cry.

I repeat the mantra over and over again, but it's in vain. My body starts to tremble.

I'm fucking crying.

"Are you okay?" the man says.

Huh?

I recognize that voice. It's the same deep, sexy voice that murmured filthy things in my ear in a luxurious suite at Dark Compulsion while the unwavering alpha fucking me made me come over and over again.

I glance up and my heart stops.

Unforgettable aqua blue eyes stare down at me.

I blink.

I blink again.

I blink one more time for good measure.

The gorgeous man staring down at me has been the star of my dirty dreams for the past two nights.

Am I dreaming?

I'm having a shitty day so far, God wouldn't be so cruel as to conjure up a mirage.

"Ignatius?"

He blinks. His expression is a total mystery. "Wild Strawberry?" The club names sound a bit ridiculous in real life. He scans the surrounding space, then focuses on me. "Did someone hurt you?"

God, he's a witness to my sad, sad state.

"This is so embarrassing." I avert my gaze, wiping away the tears streaking down my face with trembling hands.

His strong fingers tip my chin, raising my face up. He stares at me with careful sympathy, like he can read my soul. "Why are you crying?"

"It's nothing," I say.

He cocks an eyebrow. "You're a terrible liar. What's going on?"

My lips part, like I could spill all my hurt into the palms of his hands, and he'd make it all better.

Ridiculous.

Mom is dead.

Dad is dead.

My grandparents on Dad's side died a few years ago.

Mom's parents passed away when I was a kid.

I'm running a company I have no business running.

My bank account is anemic. And my credit cards... maxed out. I'm up to my eyeballs in debt and drowning fast.

My loneliness weighs on me every waking hour of the day.

I ache for the family I lost.

I ache for the sense of safety that was my companion until the day I buried my dad.

I only have my pain left. Nothing else.

There isn't anything this gorgeous man with the beautiful mouth and the kind eyes can do to help.

I push the mountain of emotions down, tucking them deep inside, allowing them to eat at what's left of my soul. What's left of me.

"I'm not budging until you talk to me." He crosses his arms over his way chest.

His determination breaks my resolve.

"It's been one of those bad days," I say in a low voice.

"We've all had them."

"I've been on a winning streak of so many back to back godawful days, I can't remember anything else." My shoulders slump. "It's starting to wear me down."

Concern shines bright in his eyes and the stunning aqua shade shifts into a stormy blue as his jaw sets.

Why am I spilling my guts to a man who is, for all intents and purposes, still a stranger?

He looks over my head, searching for something, but I'm not sure what.

"Come on, let's get out of the way," he says and drags me to the front of the lobby, not even waiting for my response.

I stare up at him.

"What's your name?"

"I thought we weren't supposed to exchange real names?"

"That only applies at the club. We obeyed the rules, but when we're in the real world, we abide by different rules, J.S.," he says with a light chuckle.

My cheeks blush.

"You got my note?"

"I did. And for the record, you were wrong."

I furrow my brows. "In what sense?"

"We meet again."

"We do," I say with a small smile.

His expression changes, turning more serious. "Can I be honest?"

I nod, because I'm still awestruck.

"I haven't been able to stop thinking about you since we hooked up." My pulse jumps at his admission. "I really wanted to know who you were. In fact, it was a burning need."

Butterflies erupt inside me.

Oh.

My.

God.

"It's the same for me. When I wasn't consumed with all this drama—aka my life—you were on my mind."

I spent the better part of Sunday at the office. Sydney came over on Sunday evening to keep me company and help me with my long list of stupid house chores. All the while, we exchanged naughty stories. Her alpha was undeniably an experienced lover, but he didn't rock her world the way the man standing in front of me did mine.

"Are you going to keep me in suspense much longer, J.S.?"

"My name is Jules Salinger."

"Pleased to meet you, Jules Salinger." He flashes me a smile that makes me forget all my woes. "My name is Levi Aldridge."

"It's a pleasure to meet you, Levi."

"So, you're having a challenging day?"

"To say the least."

"I know that you don't know much about me, but I'm a great listener."

"It's okay." I shake my head. "I don't want to trouble you. I'll figure it out." As it stands, only a crystal ball—or a million dollars—can help me figure out my next step.

"It's no trouble, Jules."

I love hearing my name on his lips.

I consider him for a long beat.

"Listen, whatever you're dealing with is weighing on you. Sometimes you just need to get it off your chest."

I let out a heavy sigh. "Okay."

"Good." He smiles. "I just ended a meeting with my lawyers, and I was heading to the convenience store for a chocolate bar because I'm starved. If we're going to talk, we might as well do it in front of a hearty meal and great wine. It's only half past five, but why don't we have an early dinner? I know a phenomenal Italian restaurant not too far."

"I—uh... Are you sure? I don't want you to change your evening plans on my account."

"I know what I want and that's spending the evening with *you*." His voice drops a notch or two, sounding wholly seductive, although I'm unsure if that's on purpose or not. Regardless, my pussy approves.

"Oh," I say, brushing a strand of hair behind my ear.

"Do you work in this building?"

"No." I give him a quick rundown, but don't mention Hillary. "I took a taxi here. I didn't want to deal with parking, or worse, a ticket." *And my shitty car is unreliable.*

"My Audi SUV is parked in the garage. Let's take my wheels and I'll drive you back to your office after dinner."

"Okay." I don't have it in me to argue. In this shit storm that is my life, Levi Aldridge is a beacon of light. I'd have to be stupid not to take him up on his offer.

Chapter 9

Levi

Mexican culture defines El Pueblo, but before that, this was the old Los Angeles enclave—and heart—of Little Italy. After a bit of a downslide, the neighborhood is now bustling and Italian culture shines again. It's home to some kickass restaurants. Zia Josefina is one of my favorites.

"Hey, Levi," a brunette says when I step inside, hand-in-hand with Jules.

"Hey, Carmela."

"*Come stai, bello?*" the forty something-year-old woman says in Italian.

Translation: *How are you, handsome?*

"*Va bene, bella,*" I say. "It's good to see you again."

Translation: *I'm good, beautiful*

She huffs and shoots me a dubious side gaze in response—the kind your mom gives you when she doesn't believe a word of your lie.

She comes and stands in front of me with a hand on her jutted hip. "Now, you're too good for us?"

I let go of Jules's hand and drop it on Carmela's shoulder.

"No, *carina*, I've been busy lately, and I've also been spending a lot more time in Europe on business. That's why you haven't seen me in a while."

"You work too much," she says.

"Says the woman who practically lives in her restaurant."

"I have to keep myself busy or else I'll go crazy. Not to mention, it's the only way for me to get away from four teenage boys."

"It's the same for me, minus the teenagers."

She laughs.

Her eyes shift to the blonde standing next to me. "You bring a beautiful girl to my restaurant?"

"Carmela, this is Jules."

"Your girlfriend?"

Carmela loves to meddle in my personal life. She's tried to hook me up with her cousins, nieces, friends, and even some of her female patrons.

"*A friend*," I say.

"Well, that's a first."

She's right. Other than Dad, Linc, and Micah, I never bring anyone here.

"It's a pleasure to meet you, Carmela," Jules says with a little wave.

"Likewise," Carmela says. She gives us both a lingering onceover. "Hmm..."

I squint my eyes at her. "Hmm, what?"

"You two make a stunning couple."

Great.

"And we'll be sure to send you an invitation to the wedding. Now, can you please take us to our table? I'm starving and I can't wait for Jules to discover how delicious your food is."

"Nice diversion tactic, Levi," Carmela says.

"I do my best."

She laughs.

"Follow me." She waves. "I reserved your favorite table when I saw your name pop up on our reservation app."

I wrap an arm around Jules and follow Carmela. She's still laughing.

~

"This restaurant ruined it for me," Jules says, finishing her last bite. "Those are the best meatballs I've ever tasted in my life, and I doubt I'll ever taste anything close to this until I make it to Italy."

"It's a family recipe," I say "Spaghetti and meatballs isn't a traditional Italian dish—neither is the eye-popping size of those babies—but Carmela doesn't care because it's one of her best-selling dishes." The juicy and succulent meatballs at Zia Josefina are the size of baseballs.

"I can see why."

Since it's her first time here, I ordered for both of us. After a tasty Caesar salad, we dived headfirst into a generous platter of spaghetti and meatballs for two.

"More wine, Jules?"

"No, thank you. A third glass would be pushing it."

"Fair enough. Dessert?"

"Absolutely, but can we wait a bit?"

"Just say the word."

I gesture for our waiter to top up our glasses of sparkling water.

"How old are you?"

I cock an eyebrow.

Her question comes of the blue.

"You were wearing a sharp black suit at the club and today

you're sporting a well cut dark-gray one. It's uncommon among guys my age."

"You're also wearing a suit."

She's gorgeous, yet unassuming in her lavender suit, but it's a far cry from the sexy dress she wore Saturday night.

"I was meeting with a potential investor. I wanted to make the right first impression. You seem to live in a suit."

When you hang out with fashion icons who happen to be former rock stars, it influences your style.

"How old are *you*?" I turn the tables on her.

"Hey, I asked you first."

"Perhaps, but you left yourself wide open with that statement. Come on, spit it out."

"I'm twenty-three," she says. "And you?"

"Twenty-seven—"

"You're so much younger than the guy my best friend hooked up with at the club." She blurts that out before her face turns beet red. "Oh gosh, that was loud." Concerned eyes scour the restaurant before meeting mine. "I shouldn't be airing our *naughty* laundry in public like this."

"No one knows what club you're talking about."

"Thank God," she says with a giggle.

"And yes, I'm twenty-two years his junior, but the guy is in phenomenal shape."

"He has a hell of a body."

I cock my head to the side. "Is that so?"

Her eyes widen. "He has nothing on you."

I chuckle.

"Sydney is a sucker for a little silver on a man. She says older guys make for far better lovers because they know what they're doing."

"Do you share her opinion?" I

She bites her lower lip, a move that makes my cock swell. "I wouldn't know." She shrugs. "I prefer guys my age... or a few years older."

"Looks like I fall within that window."

"Looks like it."

"Did I meet your expectations as a lover?"

Memories of Saturday night—*her taste, her moans, her soft silky skin under my touch, her tight pussy milking my cock, the sinful way she submitted so beautifully to me, her cries of ecstasy*—own my mind, and I can't divorce myself from them or the drop-dead gorgeous blonde sitting across from me.

A devilish expression veils her hazel-green eyes.

I'm not the only one who's transported back to our sexy time.

"You smashed any expectations, Levi Aldridge."

There's no helping the grin that tugs across my face.

"I've never done anything like that before," she says.

"You're no longer a club virgin."

"That's not what I was talking about," she says. "I mean, I've never had a one-night stand before."

"Never?"

"Never." She works her bottom lip. "It's the same for all the things you did to me in public right after we found out we were a match..."

"I pushed you out of your comfort zone?"

"You did."

"Is that a good thing?"

She nods. "I tagged along with Sydney because I'd made the decision to do the opposite of anything the normal, sensible Jules would do. That was the lure of the theme party. One night. Instant connection. No names. Just sex. Cautious little old me wouldn't dream of doing anything that wild. Dark Compulsion was a safe environment to unleash a side of me I didn't know existed." She pauses. "When responsible, color-within-the-lines Jules started to freak out, you always managed to say something or do something to calm me down. You helped me break the leash on sensible Jules. You helped me forget."

Her words humble me.

"I'm repeating myself, but I'm so thankful you were my match, Levi."

One look at her, and I could tell she was a fish out of water, but that's what attracted me to her so damn much. There's no greater pleasure than to initiate a willing soul.

"Same here, sweetness."

"You still feel that way after the fact?"

"After sampling everything you have to offer? Hell, yeah."

Her cheeks turn a beautiful shade of pink–Wild Strawberry indeed.

Goddamn, she's adorable.

There I go using that word again.

I can't help it.

She's a rare balance of innocence and sexy siren.

"So, Jules Salinger, I know your name and your age, but I don't know what upset you so much earlier." I rest my back against the seat. "Talk to me."

She flashes a hesitant look, her bright smile now gone.

"A problem shared is a problem halved," I say.

She plays around with her cuticles for a few beats before fixing me with her hazel-green eyes.

Awkwardness crackles between us.

Just when I'm certain I stepped into a pile of shit and ready myself to backtrack, with a heavy sigh, she launches into story mode.

"I'm an orphan—"

"Did you just lose your parents? Is that why you were crying?"

She shakes her head. "My mom died four years ago."

"I'm sorry to hear that. Was she sick?"

"It was an accident."

"Shit. A car accident?"

"No. She supervised building managers for a rental company. She was doing an inspection round for an upcoming renovation of an older building when an air conditioning unit dropped like a meteor from the twelfth floor onto her head."

I'm speechless.

"She died on impact. Daddy and I were devastated. She was full of life. She kissed me goodbye on that morning and by the time I came back from school, she was dead."

I reach out for her hand and squeeze it. "I'm sure you miss her every single day."

A surprised face snaps up to mine. "You say that like you know what it's like to lose your mother."

I offer a sad smile. "I don't mean to usurp your story, but yes, I know what it's like. I also lost my mom."

She places her other hand on top of mine. "Oh, God, Levi. You know how much it hurts."

I nod. "It fucking hurts."

"I didn't think I would ever recover from such a tragic loss. For the longest time, Daddy walked around like a ghost. It was so hard on him, he started sleeping in the guest room. He couldn't handle the emptiness of his bed. Like me, he cried a lot." She pauses and takes a breath. "He was an engineer by trade, but I think he started tinkering around as a way to keep his mind busy."

"Cars?"

"No. Dad was an avid cyclist. He started bringing home broken bikes and repairing them. Then he graduated to motor-cycles. When he couldn't sleep at night, I knew I'd find him in the garage. After an injury, he got a gym membership so he could rehabilitate. That's how he was forced to embrace indoor cycling. He had a beef with the stationary bikes on the market. He got it in his head he could come up with a smart indoor bike that fuelled your workout and pushed you beyond your limits. Before long, it became an obsession. Time went by, and his tinkering turned into something real. Fueled with excitement—and the promise of a better life—he went all in. Unfortunately, there were a lot of bugs with the technology, and manufacturing the equipment in America was—is—ridiculously expensive."

"Why not go to China? It would've been considerably cheaper."

"Dad never cared for made in China products. He wanted the bikes to be made in America. He was such a patriot. In the past few months, I discovered a number of reputable sources in Vietnam that are far cheaper, but I'm strapped for cash. Hopping on a plane to meet with those manufacturers to check out their facilities isn't part of the budget. Not to mention, I don't speak a word of Vietnamese and from my understanding, not everyone is fluent in English."

"There are consultants right here in Los Angeles who can act as the middleman and negotiate on your behalf. They have a good grasp of the language, or they're natives."

"I didn't even know that." She hangs her head low.

"Being in business doesn't mean you know everything."

Her eyes snap up to mine. "Well, in my case, I feel like I know nothing."

"You're being too hard on yourself."

"I fucked everything up."

"What do you mean?"

"I inherited the responsibilities of the company when Daddy died. I have a degree in kinesiology from Los Angeles City College and a business administration certificate. I don't have a bachelor's degree or an MBA. Until my father's passing,

I was a personal trainer at a chain of boutique gyms. I only worked part-time in the family business because there wasn't enough money to cover yet another paycheck. In other words, I'm not equipped for the job."

"So, you're overwhelmed and things are tight?"

She nods. "It was a juggling act to pay my last three employees. Needless to say, there's no money left for me once I'm done with payroll."

"No savings?"

"Daddy sunk every last dime into manufacturing the bicycles and prototypes of other smart exercise gym equipment. He was so certain of his vision, he applied to be a contestant on that TV reality show where a bunch of billionaires decide to partner up with you or not."

"Wow. He was serious."

"He was unwavering in his belief. He was hoping to win the jackpot by becoming that lucky guy one of the billionaires partnered up with, or at least, he was praying the massive exposure from his fifteen minutes of fame would translate into free publicity and a ton of preorders."

"I assume it never happened?"

Her gaze falls to the table. "A car running a red light slammed right into him while he was on his bicycle during his evening ride. He died three days before an assistant producer from the show called the office. I couldn't even take his place—"

"Why not?"

"I didn't know the ins and outs of the business. I blew a chance of a lifetime because of my inexperience—" She chokes up.

I get up, circle the table, sit next to her, and wrap her in my arms. I brush her hair off her face before wiping her tears away with my thumb.

"You don't have to continue if this is too hard."

"I'll be okay."

"Only if you're sure."

"I am. Other than my best friend Sydney, no one knows what I've been dealing with for the past eight months. It's a heavy burden to carry. We may still be practically strangers, but sharing this with you has somehow lightened my load."

"Good. Tell me more."

"Hillary Twatt is making my life a living hell."

My brows dip.

"My evil stepmother," she says.

My frown deepens. "Your stepmother's last name is Twatt?"

She nods.

"For real?"

She nods again. "She refused to become Mrs. Salinger. Something about being able to trace her roots to British royalty. I'm thankful she kept her name, but curiosity ate at me, so I did a Google search. The royal connection never came up—and I looked hard. However, a not so flattering British meaning for her last name did. Quite fitting, if you ask me. She also wanted to keep her last name for her daughters' sake."

"So, you don't get along with your stepmother and step-sisters."

She shakes her head.

Jules explains why she was in Beverly Hills and how her hopes were crushed when Sydney's contact was a no-show due to unforeseeable circumstances. She talks about her deceased parents. Then, she tells me all about her evil, scheming social climber stepmother. She explains how her dad and Hillary met —a Fourth of July barbecue at a colleague's house. She also gives me the rundown on her useless fame-hungry stepsisters and Hillary's dick duke boyfriend.

Her story is more over the top than a reality show. "Is Petula and Olive's father out of the picture?"

"They have different fathers," she says. "And yes, they're out of the picture."

"Deadbeat dads?"

"Both are illegitimate, aka bastard babies." She lets out a wry laugh. "Until she suckered my father into marrying her, Hillary was a career mistress. She's not even ashamed to admit it."

"Few women would be shouting that out on megaphones."

"Other than her daughters and being a stage mom, Hillary doesn't have many accomplishments. I guess that's why she makes being a homewrecker part of her curriculum vitae."

"Good one." I laugh.

"The men are also to blame for their philandering, but Hillary made it her mission to target men wearing a ring on their left hand. It was like an aphrodisiac to her. From what I've overheard here and there, her lovers were generous until they got tired of her. At which point, they'd conveniently find a way to ghost her. That's what happened with Petula's dad."

"Regardless if the guy ghosted her or not, Hillary could've gone after him for child support."

"Hillary has a thing for foreign men—hence, the French duke and her daughters' fathers—which begs the question why on earth she ended up with my father. Daddy was as red, white, and blue as can be. American through and through." She shakes her head. "In any case, one night, while Daddy and Hillary were out, Petula and Olive were sitting in the garden, drinking, and complaining about their sad, sad lives—"

"What were those ungrateful bitches complaining about?"

"They were lamenting about how their mother ended up with a pauper instead of latching onto a rich man who could help them achieve their Hollywood dreams. From their silly giggles, it was obvious they were drunk. I was a personal trainer at the time and one of my clients canceled his appointment—the last of the day for me. After the three Witches of Eastwick entered our lives, I made it a point to tiptoe around the house. The Twatt sisters didn't know I was home early. Eavesdropping on their conversation, I found out Petula's father is Irish. When Hillary started putting pressure on him to man up and take care of her and their daughter, despite the fact he was married, he disappeared to Ireland. Hillary tried to find him, but it was in vain. The name Patrick Murphy is common over there, making it impossible for her to track down her baby daddy."

"What a cluster fuck of a situation."

She lifts a finger in the air. "But there's more. Olive's father was a forty-something Canadian director who worked in the film industry, traveling back and forth from LA to Toronto. Even though the cheater was married, he made Hillary big promises. She believed him. He even bought a house under his name so she would have a roof over her head for her and her daughters. She didn't expect he'd die in a traffic accident while he was in London for a film premiere a few months before giving birth. Hillary tried to sue his estate because she had smartened up enough and had collected DNA, aka strands of the guy's hair, as proof of paternity. Alas, laws are different across the border, it's prohibitive to sue rich people, and apparently, the cheater's wife is a ballsy American boss lady who you don't want to mess with. Translation, Hillary got squat, and she lost the place she was living in since it fell under her deceased lover's estate."

"What a crazy, tragic story."

"As crazy and tragic as Hillary Twatt herself."

I nod.

She tells me about her stepmother's cunt move with her last three employees.

There's so much weight in what she just shared, it nearly crushes the table.

"I'm going to be homeless by the time I figure out how to buy out Hillary."

Everything about her indicates she's a strong woman, but that's a shit load of stuff to handle on your own when you're that young and over your head.

So much makes sense now. "That's what you were trying to forget on Saturday night?"

"Yes." She sighs. "I wanted to quiet my mind. It was for a brief moment, but it was worth it. I don't regret a thing. Since our time together, things went from bad to catastrophic. And here I am, swimming upstream of the Niagara Falls without a hope of survival." Her shoulders slump in defeat.

My hand settles over hers. "Don't say that."

"It's not looking too good for me, Levi," she says. "I'm so utterly consumed with the fear of losing Daddy's company."

"Have you tried hiring someone to oversee the areas where you lack knowledge, or even hiring a CEO?"

She nods. "I have. I don't have the budget to hire someone with the skills that would help the business take off. The two guys I hired as marketing directors didn't last long. One quit after a week. I fired the other one after catching Petula on her knees, wearing only a G-string, sucking him off in one of the storage rooms at the office."

"Yikes."

"Yeah. He had zero input on the company during the two weeks he was here, but he managed to find time to fuck my good-for-nothing stepsister every chance he had."

The Twatt women are something else.

"How many stationary bikes did your father manufacture?"

"We have a hundred CycleThonix bikes—and three extra

as prototypes—but we can't sell them until we get the app to work. That's my Achilles' heel right now."

"That's a lot of bikes."

"Daddy got a significant price break for producing that many, and he wanted to have enough merchandise for when sales kick in."

"He didn't believe in half measures."

"No, he didn't. Daddy was all in or all out."

"The name is catchy," I say.

She smiles. "I came up with it. Daddy did a lot of triathlons, so Thonix is a play on marathon and tonic. The brand is Fit Thonix."

"Clever." I return her smile. "How about the other equipment? How many did he get produced?"

"We have a stepper (StepThonix), stairmaster (Stair-Thonix), eliptical (ElipThonix) and a treadmill (TreadThonix). Daddy produced only three prototypes of each for testing purposes."

"Catchy names. Very memorable."

"That was my contribution to the business."

"Branding is everything. It seems you underestimate yourself."

She responds with a shy smile.

"Where is everything stored?"

"In the warehouse of an office I can go longer afford to rent."

"Can I see them?"

She grabs her phone, but I stop her.

"No, I want to *see* the prototypes and the stationary bikes. I don't want to see a photo."

She flinches.

"If I'm going to help you, I need to know what we're working with here."

"You—you're going to help me?"

"I know a thing or two about running a successful business, I have solid contacts, and friends with deep pockets. And I have a little money myself." The shell-shocked expression on her beautiful face remains. "When it comes to apps, it's all about finding a kickass coder, one who's thorough enough to triple test his—or her—work. The good ones come at a hefty price."

For a long moment she stares at me, wide-eyed.

I can't tell how she feels about what I said.

She takes me into her embrace. "Thank you."

Two words, but it's like the weight of the world just lifted off her shoulders.

She nuzzles her nose, hiding her face against my chest, holding me tight.

Her body convulses, and she starts crying.

She's inconsolable.

Fuck.

Every protective fiber in me flares. More than anything, I want to make all her worries and fears disappear.

I shift, wrapping my arms around her, pulling her close to me.

I drop a soft kiss on the top of her head. "You're no longer alone, sweetness."

Chapter 10

Jules

Thank you, God, for answering my prayers.

"On second thought, I changed my mind," Levi says.

Disappointment washes over me.

I pull away from him. "What do you mean?"

"You've dealt with enough for one day. Let's talk about something other than business."

My heart thundering. "You're not going to help me?"

He shakes his head. "That's not what I said. I want to know everything there is to know about your dad's business, but not right now."

"Um... okay." I'm not sure where he's going with this.

"We can talk about business tomorrow morning. Feeling your body against mine makes me crave more. I want a repeat of Saturday night, Jules. You robbed me of that when you left in the middle of the night."

I'm at a loss for words. I'm not used to eliciting this kind of hunger in a man.

"I remember the sensation of your lips against mine," he says. "Every time I've jerked off in the past few days, you were my go-to spank bank dream girl, leaving me with a fist full of cum." Tingles sizzle through my body. "And you know what?"

"What?"

His hot gaze drifts up and down my body. I'm talking 5-alarm fire hot. It's the same searing look he flashed my way when we found out we were a match at the theme party... the one that makes my knees go soft.

"I have a pretty vivid imagination. I remember every touch, every thrust, and every moan. But being with you trumps the fantasies by a long shot."

Oh wow.

"Really?"

"I wasn't talking bullshit. I've never felt this kind of connection with anyone before."

"It's the same for me." I hesitate, plucking up the courage to confess. "If we're being honest, I've thought of you—of us— every time I touched myself since I left the club. I thought a lot about... your mouth."

A cocky smile twists his lips. "In what sense?"

"Your dirty, filthy mouth drives me crazy, Levi."

"Because of the things I said?" He leans into me. "Or because of the things I did with my mouth?"

"Both."

As if to taunt me, he licks his lips, drawing a soft sigh from me.

I've said too much. "I can't believe I admitted to that," I say.

"It doesn't get any better than this, Jules. You want me as much as I want you." His potent words flame my desire. "Did you like being blindfolded?"

Heat creeps up my cheeks.

"I take it that's a yes," he says.

"I didn't expect to like it as much as I did. It was a powerful thing, removing one of my senses. All the remaining ones seemed to heighten. I was totally focused on your touch, your kiss... or your tongue, down there—"

He tsks. "Down there?"

"Between my pussy lips," I say, my voice low.

He chuckles. "The newly uninhibited girl is still shy."

"Maybe just a little." I giggle like said girl.

"Tell me you want what we shared again."

I suck in a deep breath, let it out, and nod.

He shakes his head. "Not good enough. I want words."

"I want a repeat of what we shared, Levi."

"Good, because so do I." I can't help my wide smile. "It's early, so it must still be quiet at the club." He snatches his phone off the table. "Let's see if I can book a playroom at Dark Compulsion or get a suite at the Quintus Hotel."

I peek over his shoulder as he opens an app and books a room.

"Done! I get to fuck you to my heart's content tonight."

"Very romantic, Casanova."

"You weren't complaining Saturday night."

It's not like I can argue with him.

The man sated needs I didn't even know I had.

I crave the feel of his cock deep inside my needy pussy.

Silence engulfs us for a few beats. "What do you want me to do to you tonight?" His voice dropped a notch, sounding way too seductive.

I may not have much experience with domineering men, but something tells me I won't have much of a choice in the matter. Suits me just fine.

"I'll leave the decision in your capable hands," I say.

"You're such a quick learner." Desire pools in his eyes. "And you're such a good girl."

He's so commanding, it's thrilling. Until Levi, I never thought I'd be this turned on by a man telling me what to do.

"I aim to please, sir."

I don't know where that came from, but when I'm around him, I lose all my inhibitions.

His lips curve up in a self-satisfied and sexy grin. "And you do it so well."

The urge to beg him to kiss me overwhelms me. But that might fall in the romantic bucket, which he has no interest in.

A wicked thought blooms inside my head.

I look over my shoulder.

With our backs facing most patrons, no one is paying us any attention. They're too busy devouring their delicious meals.

I pull my lower lip between my teeth as I weigh the pros and the cons of my wicked idea.

Levi cocks a brow. "What's going on in that pretty little head?"

With lust leading my thoughts, I glide my hand down his chiseled body until it lands on his muscular thigh. I caress the length of it a few times before my hand slips between his legs and brushes against his hard-on. *The devil made me do it.*

His body tenses and his eyes close.

I hesitate.

Perhaps that was too forward.

"If you're going to touch me, do it for real or not at all." His voice is like gravel. He repositions my hand, guiding it so it drags up every mouthwatering inch of his cock. He closes his hand over mine, pressing my palm against his erection. "Yeah, like that."

I shift against my seat to alleviate the tension building between my legs.

"Feel how hard I am for you."

He stares down at me with hooded eyes and I lose myself in the deep-blue ocean framed by long dark lashes.

My head clouds with lust and it leaves me disoriented.

He's like a potent drug, at least I assume, as I've never done drugs.

That's the only explanation.

Here I am palming a guy in the middle of a restaurant.

What's with me?

A faint smile teases his lips. "For the record, I like Dirty Jules."

It's like he could read my thoughts.

"You bring her out to play." Fuelled by a burst of confidence, I rub his thick cock over his suit pants.

God, the man is packing.

I still can't believe I was able to walk after multiple hard poundings, which resulted in multiple heart-stopping orgasms.

"Fuck, Jules."

I can't tell if it's a warning or a plea.

He grabs hold of my wrist, moving my hand away. "Let's get out of here before Carmela calls the cops on my ass for lewd behavior. I'd much prefer spending the night inside your sweet pussy than inside a jail cell."

To underline his point, he clasps the back of my head and pulls my face to his for a fiery kiss so passionate I can feel his desire all the way to my toes.

Chapter 11

Levi

Half past seven marks the tail end of the afternoon romps at Dark Compulsion. Since the majority of members don't show up before ten, there's a nice window in between that's perfect for impromptu hookups. Since this wasn't planned, I don't have my member's ring or card with me, but Larkin made sure to give the green light to the bouncers. Since Jules is in the system, security was a non-issue. I guide her by the hand to the elevators. It's a short ride, and it's just the two of us.

When we arrive to the sixth floor, we step out of the elevator, our fingers still intertwined.

"Have you been a member long?"

I glance down at her. "Four years."

"Oh, wow. That's a long time."

"The three guys you saw me with on Saturday are members. I blame them." I chuckle.

"It seems members are part of the top echelon."

"Yes. A lot of Hollywood heavy hitters are members. It's a drama-free zone for a hookup. Everyone is on the same wavelength. Outside of the club, no strings attached can be miscon-strued as, *no strings attached for tonight, but ask me tomorrow and I'll probably have changed my mind.*"

"I see."

"The Continental Rule, which prevents members from mixing business with pleasure, ensures your partner is here to play and not use sex as a gateway to pitch the next blockbuster or to launch into a falsetto worthy of a Broadway production, just before showcasing their dancing abilities."

Her step falters and burst out laughing. "Oh, my God. That was hilarious."

"Made you laugh." *And God, if the sound isn't infectious.*

"You did," she says. "It's a sound I barely recognize."

"Keep hanging out with me, kid."

"I'd like that."

"So would I." I wink.

"Did the Continental Rule come to be for a reason?" She circles back to our conversation.

"A member fell asleep, and when he woke up, his wrists and ankles were roped to the bed. He was forced to listen to a talentless wannabe actress audition for a movie he was casting. The actress didn't know there was a panic button on the wall, right behind the bed. Security barged in to save the poor guy and drag her ass to the street. She was banned from the club forever."

"*Excommunicado.*"

I nod. "*Excommunicado.*"

"I gather from the guys you were hanging out with, aka the rock gods and band members of Random Misconception, you're in the Hollywood industry."

Rod, Jace, and Beckett rarely go unnoticed.

"I am."

"What do you do?"

"I'll tell you all about it later," I say as we stop in front of our suite.

"Okay," she says. "Do you come here often?"

"Like I told Carmela, lately, business has been my sole focus. You're my first victim in a long time."

"Lucky me."

I wink.

"You don't date?"

It's a loaded question, one that always brings back sad memories.

"I haven't in a while." That's all I'm willing to share right now. Going down that road is a guaranteed mood killer.

"I'm sorry, Levi."

I guess my tone was clipped.

"It's a long story." *And a painful one.*

"I have a few of those myself."

"We're here to forget. Remember?"

"I'm totally on board with that plan."

I swipe the keycard and push the door open, holding it for her as she steps inside.

I drop the keycard on the console table next to the door, reach for her waist and pull her to me, a sense of urgency guiding my every move.

My fingers brush up her face before cradling it. For a few breaths, my eyes bore into hers.

Her long, dark eyelashes flutter like crazy.

"Fuck, you're beautiful, Jules."

She lifts her chin up, offering me her lips.

"What do you want?"

"Kiss me." Her breath comes out in a soft sigh. "Please."

"I had my lips on you half an hour ago."

"That's a lifetime ago." She pouts.

"I agree."

Putting an end to her torment, and mine, I lower my lips to hers.

The kiss is hot, possessive.

I grip her face between my palms and slip my wet tongue into her welcoming mouth.

Fuck.

I could kiss her like this all day long.

My hands travel from her face, to her shoulders, down her back until they're cupping her firm, bouncy ass.

I groan and so does she.

Fucking perfection.

Squeezing her ass cheeks tight, I bring her body close, and she whimpers so sweetly as I grind the evidence of my desire against her.

God, what is this woman doing to me?

"You're such a great kisser," she says against my lips.

I pull away from her. "You too, sweetness."

"I'm responding to your lips," she says. "Kissing is a bit of a mess of tangled, probing tongues, and noses smashing together, but kissing you, Levi... is a soul-stirring experience."

"I'm happy to kiss you anytime you beg for it."

"I'm moved by your generosity."

"You should be."

"Cocky much?"

"A lot cocky, but you like me that way."

"You're lucky I can't argue."

I chuckle.

"I want you to head to the bedroom, remove your shoes, suit and underwear, but keep the white shirt on. Then, I want you to find the blindfold in the drawer of the nightstand, put it on, and sit pretty on the bed. Got it?"

She grants me a flirtatious smile. "Absolutely."

She sashays to the bedroom, shedding off her blazer on the

way. She looks over her shoulder. Sin flashes in her hazel-green eyes.

My dick swells against the fly of my pants. I palm it, willing it to calm down.

It's ridiculous how much she turns me on.

I give her a few minutes.

I toe off my shoes and remove my socks. I slip off my suit jacket, fold it, and drop it on the couch before removing my belt. I head to the bar in search of an ice bucket. It doesn't take me long before I spot one. I grab it and fill it with ice. I stride to the bedroom and reach the threshold.

The last time, my desire for her was so jacked up, I couldn't take my time. Now, I can. I allow my eyes to travel the length of her body, all the way down to her toes, painted in a sexy raspberry color.

I want to slide my cock deep into this sweet little distraction so bad I can taste it.

Patience.

"I sense your presence," she says. "What's that noise?"

"You'll soon find out."

I approach her, place the bucket on the floor, and join her on the bed.

She peeks inside the bucket. "Ice?"

"Yes."

"We're going to have a drink?"

"Not quite."

"Why bring ice in the bedroom, then?"

"Do you like when I tell you what to do?"

She nods, her teeth worrying her bottom lip.

"Do you want me to show you all the forbidden things you don't know?"

The hands on her thighs clench into small fists.

"Relax," I say.

She does as she's told.

Her hands splay open against her tanned thighs.

My fingertips trace her long, delicate fingers.

"Come on, sweetness, you admitted to liking being bad," I say. "Let's push your boundaries and unleash more of the Dirty Jules that's desperate to come out. There's more of the bad girl trapped inside." I tap against her chest.

Her chest rises and falls with her rapid breathing.

She nods. "Okay."

Her innocence is intoxicating, her willingness is my drug.

"What was that?"

"I want you to show me all the things I don't know yet."

Satisfaction blooms inside me as she smiles.

"Sounds like you're ready to play?"

"I am."

I place a hand behind her back. "Lie down."

She drops her weight against my palm, and I guide her until her body rests on the bed.

"I love how you relinquish control. It allows me to offer you pleasure like you wouldn't believe," I say.

"The taste I got the other night was mind-blowing. I had never experienced pleasure like that before."

"There's a lot more to come..."

Her breath hitches every time I undo a button. I'm unrushed. I push the fabric open, exposing her heavenly body. Unable to resist, I drop a flurry of soft kisses against her taut stomach. Her heady scent tickles my nostrils.

Fuck.

I travel from her bellybutton up her body until my face is nestled between her perfect tits. Her skin is as soft as silk. I cup both breasts in my hands and squeeze tight as my thumbs circle her hard nipples.

"Are you getting wet? Is your tight, little pussy aching for my mouth, fingers and cock?"

"Oh God, Levi. I've been wet since we were at the restaurant."

Music to my ears.

I shift on the bed so I can reach for an ice cube.

I place it against her bellybutton.

Her body quivers and she yelps, bowing her back against the mattress.

"Oh shit." She sucks in a breath. "That's so cold."

Starting at her bellybutton, I trace a line all the way up to her chin.

Her body shivers, soft plaintive moans dropping from her lips.

I circle each nipple, round and round. Her hard peaks pebble even more as her chest rises and falls. I hold the ice cube over her body to allow droplets of cold water to drip along her skin.

She groans.

"Open your mouth."

She does.

I bring the ice cube a couple inches over her mouth and let a few droplets drip onto her lips.

She catches on and extends her tongue.

I tease her with the ice cube, relishing how she plays along.

I slide the melting ice cube into my mouth and lower my body, so I can feed it to her. She accepts my gift.

I grab another ice cube and repeat my naughty game.

Her reddening nipples and the streaks of red marking her skin are so fucking seductive.

She holds her breath as she anticipates my next move.

"Breathe," I say.

She exhales.

"Open your legs for me."

She does.

"Feet flat against the bed."

"Oh God," she says as she raises her knees and her thighs fall open.

I'm momentarily paralyzed, in awe of the wondrous view before me.

Time to take it up a notch.

I stick my hand inside the ice bucket. I curse under my breath as I wiggle it around, sloshing ice cubes to the wood floor.

She pants. "What are you doing?"

"I want to make sure our second time together is as memorable as the first."

"Being with you makes it memorable."

After a few torturous, long seconds, I pull out my hand, my skin pink from the coldness. "That's sweet, but I don't mean it quite like that."

"What do you—"

My icy fingers plunge deep inside her.

Jules's back bows from the mattress, and her arms lift above her head as she lets out a strangled noise.

I take away the discomfort by lowering my head to her pussy and soothing her with my warm mouth. Her cold juices drip against my tongue, coating my throat.

Fucking sweet.

I do it again.

And again.

And again.

I alternate between warm and cold, not allowing her time to catch her breath.

I'm so hard, my cock threatens to rip the zipper of my suit pants.

I plunge both hands in the icy cold water, but this time she doesn't get my mouth.

"You like that?" My voice is rough as my cold fingers fuck her sweet pussy. The thumb of my free hand moves in a languorous caress over her hard clit.

As I build up her arousal, I ratchet mine.

"Oh— Dear God— Levi—" She grips the sheets hard.

"I want an answer."

"It feels so good." Her hips move in rhythm with hard thrusts, begging for more. "So, so good."

"I love the way you respond to me."

"The things you do to me..."

"You mean like this?"

I pinch her clit.

She gasps.

I close my lips around her clit and suck hard.

She whimpers.

I pull away.

"Wh— What— Why did you stop? Please don't stop."

"What do you want? You want my icy fingers fucking you? Or my lips wrapped around your clit, sucking it hard?"

"Yes."

"Yes, to which one?"

"I want it all," she says. "I need your fingers and your mouth."

"You're a greedy girl."

"Yeah. Sure. Whatever. Just don't stop."

I chuckle in amusement.

"You're making me lose my mind and you think it's funny?"

"No, sweetness, I think it's sexy as fuck, and I'm not going to lie, I love hearing you beg."

"Please, please, please, Levi."

How can I refuse her?

I pull my fingers from her pussy.

"No—" The cry of complaint dies on her tongue when I slide the fingers that were inside her pussy into her mouth.

"Suck."

Her lips twists to the side.

"You've never done that before?"

She shakes her head.

"I'm honored to be your first. Now, suck."

I don't have to repeat myself.

She sucks my fingers clean.

The muscles of my jaw clench, my nostrils flaring with desire.

My balls ache and I'm hard as steel.

I swear, I could embarrass myself by coming in my pants because right now, my cock is fucking raging.

"That was hot, Jules. So fucking, hot. Do you like being *my* bad girl?"

"I do, Levi." She smiles.

I part her pussy lips. The tip of my tongue swipes over her pussy in one long, teasing lick.

Once.

Twice.

Three times.

"What about the ice?" She presses against me, demanding more.

"Like heroin, one hit and you're hooked."

She giggles.

I plunge my hand in the bucket, swirling it around before pulling out an ice cube. I slide it against my tongue and suck it to smoothness. As I close my cold lips around her clit, allowing the ice cube to nudge against it, I slide my icy fingers inside her pussy.

She writhes under my assault.

I hold her clit captive between my lips, sucking, toying, allowing the ice to melt through her folds as I take her higher and higher.

She wails and clasps both hands over my head, holding me tight between her legs as she rides my face.

My breathing becomes rapid and uneven and the icy cold soon changes to scented heat as she bucks against me. I'm half out of my mind with lust and desire for this woman.

"Oh, Levi, I— I'm coming, I'm coming, I'm coming."

I curl my fingers inside her and press against the soft spot.

She groans in satisfaction.

I caress that soft spot inside her without ever letting the pressure on her clit subside until her body trembles, and then she goes still.

But only for a beat as I flick at her clit for one last time.

She lets out a long wail, mixed with prayers and curses as I push her off the cliff and she chants my name over and over, bucking at my buried fingers.

Her labored breaths fill the room. Only the soft, sexy, jazzy beat playing in the background trumps it. I catch the lyrics.

Touch me slowly. Slowly.

Jules is still riding her climactic wave.

I don't rush her.

I pull my fingers coated with her juices out of her pussy, bring them to my lips, and clean them with my tongue. "Damn, I love your taste."

She yanks the blindfold off. Pleading eyes bore into mine.

"Fuck me, please. I need your cock inside me, Levi."

She doesn't have to ask twice.

I push from the bed and make quick work of shedding my clothes. I fumble in my wallet for a condom and place a packet between my teeth. Stroking my hard cock, I approach the bed.

She pulls herself up, resting her weight against her folded elbows.

"I've never seen a body like yours." Her eyes are fixed on my chest. "And that eye-catching tattoo... your ink is amazing. Is it just art, or does it have a meaning?"

I rip open the condom packet and wrap up.

"You asked for my cock."

She smiles wide.

She forgot about her question. Good.

When I land on top of her, it's in a tangle of limbs, lips, and tongues. I groan as I feed her each inch of my cock and she exhales a stuttering breath when I'm buried up to my balls. I fuck her silly, as if it's the first time I've dipped my needy cock inside her warm pussy. I come so hard, I fear I may pass out.

I have no words to explain this undeniable magnetic pull between us that seems to have just as strong of a hold on her as it does on me. Fucking her again only intensified it.

Chapter 12

Jules

Sydney can be stubborn sometimes. This time, it paid off in spades for yours truly. She refused to take no for an answer when I tried to wiggle my way out of Saturday night by hiding behind my mountain of responsibilities. Had she not pressed my hand, I would never have met the dangerously sexy man who single-handedly redefined everything I knew about sex.

Syd is going to die when I tell her I bumped into Levi. And I'm pretty sure she's going to freak out when she finds out I ended up visiting the club for a second time without her.

After a series of toe-curling orgasms, we're catching our breath. Levi is on his back, holding me in his strong arms.

Sigh.

I relish the warm, safe, fuzzy feeling I get from being close to him.

I'm becoming addicted to this man. It's crazy, considering I've known him for a short time.

My gaze moves to his gorgeous face.

His eyes are closed so I can ogle to my heart's content.

I bite my lip to prevent drool from dripping down my chin as my eyes run down his naked torso... all that smooth tanned skin on display over bulky arm muscles.

Yes. Yes. And, hell yes.

Levi has a mouthwatering, lean build, where oversized muscles would look odd on him—even if he's quite tall. His chest is a masterpiece. He's ripped, but his proportions are just right. As a personal trainer I've seen my fair share of muscle heads. He doesn't live at the gym. I like that. My gaze drifts to his abs that flow down, disappearing beneath the white sheet, covering his beautiful cock.

You're magnificent.

"Your gaze is burning my skin."

Busted.

He opens one eye and turns his head to the side. "What's going on in that pretty little head of yours?"

I quirk a small smile. "I think you broke me." Okay, it's not what I was thinking of, but nonetheless, it's the truth. "I don't think my legs are going to be able to function, so I can't drive home. I don't have any strength left to press the pedal."

He chuckles. "Is your car safe at your office?"

"It's a beat-up car, but yes, it is."

"Good. I'll drive you to your house. I'm booked solid in the morning, but I can pick you up in the afternoon and I'll drive you to your office. That way you can show me the smart bikes and the other exercise equipment your dad invented."

"You'd do that?"

He drops a soft kiss on the top of my head. "Yes."

"I might have to take you up on your offer. I can work from home in the morning."

I'm sure I could manage behind the wheel, but the invitation to spend more time with Levi Aldridge is too tempting to turn down.

"So... when you're not luring innocent women to a swanky suite of a kinky club to have your way with them, what do you do?"

"Oh, you're back to being Jules the innocent?"

I shift in his arms. "You're the long-time member of this club. This is only my second time. So, yes, I'm innocent."

He shoots me a suspicious side-glance, his lips pursed.

"It's true."

"I assume you want to know what I do for a living?"

"Yes. I'd love to know more about you... if that's okay."

He reaches out, stroking a sweaty lock of hair back from my face before tucking it behind my ear. "I don't mind telling you more about myself."

"Well, it's only fair since my life is an open book to you."

He chuckles.

"My brother and I own a stage design company. He builds the stages and I'm the light show guy."

My eyes widen in surprise. "I've never met anyone who does that as a profession."

"When it comes to concerts, people are excited about seeing their favorite artists and musicians live. Most don't think twice about the group of invisible people working in the background to make them look good on stage."

"You're right. I've been to a number of concerts and I've been dazzled by the elaborate stage and light show, but I don't think it ever occurred to me to Google to find out who was behind the creations."

"A concert wouldn't be a concert without our contribution."

"You're right again."

"I tend to do that a lot."

I swat his chest. "Cocky much?"

"You already know the answer to that, sweetness."

I smile at him.

He tells me all about his brother Linc and how he acquired his company. He also tells me about their employees and contract tradesmen and tradeswomen who help bring their creations to life.

I'm thoroughly impressed.

"That's fascinating. Is that why you get to hang out with rock gods like the members of Random Misconception?"

"We designed the stage for their farewell concert, and we've been tight ever since."

"You've accomplished so much at such a young age."

"Our father and uncles paved the way for us. I've been working part-time in industry since I was sixteen. Same for Linc. I never saw myself doing anything else."

"So, you don't have any musical talent?"

"I didn't say that."

"You sing?"

"No."

"You're a musician?"

"Wrong again."

"I give up."

"I rap."

That's the last thing I expected. "Seriously?"

"Yes, seriously."

"Are you any good?"

"Thanks for the vote of confidence, sugar plum."

"I didn't mean it like that."

"Sure." He shoots a skeptical sideways glance at me.

"Honest to God." I do a sign of the cross over my chest.

"I wish I had Beckett Christensen's voice, but I don't. It would take me years to train my voice to sing, and even then, there's no way I'd sound anything like Beckett. His voice is a gift. I've learned to control mine to rap. I have no desire to switch careers, but I can hold my own with word play and rhyme... especially when it comes the old school rap music."

"You have many talents, Levi Aldridge."

"Many, many talents." He winks.

"I meant talents *outside* of the bedroom."

He pulls me closer.

My eyes drop to his chest and I reach out to trace his eye-catching tattoo. Black ink adorns his chest. Not that I know much about tattoos, but the juxtaposition of skulls—one on each pectoral muscle—and butterflies is interesting. The addition of long hair clues me in on the feminine gender of the skulls. Levi's ink is contained to his chest—nothing on his arms, stomach or legs.

Three words are tattooed along his collarbone—*Fortunes Always Hiding*. He also has a fairly elaborate tattoo on his back of a woman, her face has similarities to the skulls on his chest. Also, this tattoo has vibrant touches of red on the woman's lips and the roses pinned in her hair. It's almost as if the ink is telling a story. I could study these tattoos all night long and not fully appreciate all the beauty of the artist's work, or the meaning.

"You never told me if this is random art or if it has any significance."

He grabs my hand, pulling it away from his chest.

The movement is so swift, you'd think his skin was on fire.

He stares at me.

Okay, I stepped on a landmine.

"I'm sorry. I shouldn't have asked..."

He closes his eyes for a beat, his nostrils flaring.

When he opens his eyes again, they're not the sparkly aqua-blue I'm used to. They're stormy-blue.

"Levi—"

"When you told me about losing your mom, I alluded to losing mine," he says.

"Yes, I remember."

"My mom was a nurse." He swallows. "One day, during one of her shifts, she ended up on the receiving end of a rusted knife."

I gasp, my hands flying to my mouth.

"An addict, high on God knows what, weaseled his way inside the hospital Mom was working at, in search of drugs—"

"There were no security guards?"

"There were, but they weren't posted at every entrance."

"Of course."

"From what the police told us, Mom was the first person the druggie encountered. From the video footage, the guy was threatening from the get-go, and then, he plunged the rusted knife into her heart."

"Couldn't they save her?" *After all, she was in a hospital.*

"That's the irony." His lips twist, almost to curtail a sharp pain. "After the guy stabbed her, he dragged my mother's body outside. I guess he was using her as a shield or bargaining chip. He dumped her bleeding body right outside the doors to the hospital, jumped into the parked car of a guy who had the motor running as he was wheeling his wife and newborn son to his vehicle—"

"He got away?"

"He didn't get far. As he was making his getaway, he ran through a red light. A transportation truck slammed right into him, on the passenger side, dragging him for half a mile until his vehicle slammed into a Jersey wall. He died on impact."

"Oh my God, Levi, I'm so sorry for the tragic way you lost your mom."

"No one should die like that."

"I agree." What a senseless and macabre way of dying.

He lets out a long-suffering sigh. "My mom died on November second."

I'm still uncertain how that relates to his tattoo, but I'm not brave enough to ask. Not after what he shared.

"I was twenty when she died. My father, my brother, and I were devastated. The days that followed Mom's funeral, I cried so much, I thought I wouldn't have any tears left—" His voice breaks.

"You don't have to continue. I understand your pain."

He caresses my cheek. "I know you do. That's why I'm okay telling you. I don't talk about Mom's death to many people. I'm quite guarded about that part of my life. It's too hard to relive."

"I get it."

"I look back sometimes and I wonder how Dad, Linc, and I were able to function because we were so lost in our sorrow. My uncles, aunts, and cousins were instrumental. So were mom's parents—they're dead now—and our parents' friends."

"Those pillars of strength are everything when you're grieving."

He nods. "They really are."

A long beat passes between us.

He doesn't talk. He keeps staring at the ceiling.

I remain quiet.

When memories claim my mind, it does a number on my heart. I'm sure it's the same for him.

"Life goes on." He blows out a breath. "I finished school, joined Linc's business, and I started dating. Annmarie and I were right for each other. It didn't take long before I popped the question. We were young, but for me, she was it. Not long after the engagement, my fiancée surprised me with a life-changing announcement—she was pregnant."

An uneasy sensation settles in the pit of my stomach.

"On a scorching hot day, Annmarie stopped at a convenience store to buy a bottle of water on her way to work after being trapped for God knows how long in LA traffic. Innocent enough, right?"

"Right."

"My fiancée was at the wrong place, at the wrong time. She stepped out of the convenient store, as two cars were barreling in, screeching tires and all. The police told us witnesses said everything happened in a blink of an eye. The cars parked. Doors flew open. The passengers stepped out, fumes shooting out of their nostrils. And then, fury rained. One of the drivers pulled out a gun and started shooting at the other guy. He got him in the chest. A bullet went astray, and Annmarie was shot in the kidney."

My hand goes to my chest, and I gasp.

"As she crumbled to the ground, her head hit the cement parking block, and that pretty much sealed her fate. There was no chance of survival for our little girl since Annmarie was only four months pregnant."

The poor man. That's beyond tragic.

My lips part in shock, but no words come out. I'm stunned.

He heaves a deep sigh. "Annmarie died five years ago on November second."

"I'm sorry for your loss."

He nods and continues. "Rod Wolfe was getting his life back on track after one too many visits to rehab. He had a lot of time on his hands back then, so he checked up on me a lot to make sure I was holding up." Levi traces the tattoo etched on his chest. "The tattoos were his idea. In Mexican culture, November second is the Day of the Dead—*Día de los Muertos.*"

"Was your mom Mexican?"

He shakes his head. "No. She wasn't. Neither was Annmarie." He answers my next question. "As Rod pointed out, I lost two women I loved—and my unborn child—on the same day—a day that's significant in Mexican culture. He's way more into tattoos than I'll ever be. He suggested these tattoos as homage to my mom, my fiancée, and the little girl I'll never know."

A tear trickles down his cheek.

And another.

I wipe them away.

I bite my lower lip hard in my attempt to keep my own tears at bay.

"Linc followed my lead. He has a stunning *La Catrina* tattooed on his back—an exact replica of mine." He sighs. "The pain was excruciating. Every needle point hurt like a bitch, but now, Mom, Annmarie, and the baby are with me forever."

"Oh, Levi..."

They say you don't know what it's like until you walk in someone else's shoes. I've walked in Levi's shoes. When people find out I lost both my parents, they're quick to extend their condolences. This is the first time I find myself in a position where I take on someone else's sorrow as my own.

Guilt squeezes at my chest. "Maybe I shouldn't have insisted so much."

"My tattoos are hard to miss," he says. "This being LA, a lot of people assume it's random art. You were willing to dig deeper. And I didn't mind telling you because it's something we share in common."

I nod.

"I became a club member at Rod's insistence," he says. "Dark Compulsion..."

The silence that stretches is awkward, damn near deafening.

"The club allows me to keep things simple with zero expectations," he says. "It's what I needed at the time. I couldn't offer more. After losing Mom and Annmarie, I closed the door to anything that could bring me that much pain. I don't date because nothing lasts forever. Getting close to someone and then losing them is unbearable."

His words are like an arrow to my heart.

He made me no other promises than to help me forget this dreadful day by giving me a few orgasms. Mission accomplished. He never promised more. My mind—and my heart—conjured more because it's never been like this before with any other man. It's just my luck it happens to be with a man who's closed his heart.

Chapter 13

Levi

My hand keeps stirring the liquid in my cup, but I'm miles away.

A hand waves in front of me.

"Earth to Levi." A man's voice snaps me back to reality.

My eyes bounce up at a familiar face, staring at me, puzzled.

"Rod." I blink, scouring around the coffee shop from where I'm standing at the prep station. It's as if I forgot where I was for a moment.

My buddy's eyes shift from mine to the large latte. "Is everything okay?"

"Yeah, everything is fine."

"Fine?" He scoffs. "You've been stirring that thing forever, lost in space. I had to call out your name three times before you heard me."

Shit.

"So, spare me the bullshit, Levi."

Rod isn't one to mince his words.

I sigh. "I had a rough night."

He frowns. "Want to talk about it?"

I consider him.

"Sure."

He points to my cup. "I'm pretty sure that coffee isn't hot anymore."

I close my hands around the cup. "You're right. It's luke-warm now."

"I'll get you another. I'll get myself one as well."

"I appreciate it."

"Grab that table over there and we'll talk."

Rod Wolfe wants to talk?

I must be in worse shape than I think.

After stepping out of the limelight—and rehab—Rod stepped into a successful new career. He and his business partner are behind the production of music videos of countless chart-topping singers and bands. Like us, their studio is also in Culver City. There are other great coffee shops in the area, but for some reason, I always end up at But First, Coffee. It's the same for Rod.

In no time, he struts back with more than just coffee.

I catch a woman staring at Rod, biting against her lower lip as if she's having a moment. He's what women call, tall, dark, and handsome. Rod Wolfe never enters a room unnoticed.

"I figured you might be hungry." He drops the tray containing coffees and an assortment of breakfast pastries on the table before slipping into the seat across from me.

"I'm starved. Thanks for this." I pick up a muffin and take a welcome bite.

"So, what's this about a rough night?"

I drop my muffin on the tray, grab the napkin to wipe my hands, and my mouth before crumpling it into a ball. "I spent most of it thinking about my mom and Annmarie."

"Sorry to hear that," he says. "What triggered it?"

"Remember my match from the *Ruined* party?"

Rod frowns. "Wild Strawberry? The sexy blonde with legs that wouldn't quit? The one you were lucky enough to be paired with? That match?"

I guess she made an impression on him.

"Yeah, her."

"What about her, other than she was perfect?"

You have no idea.

"I bumped into her yesterday as I was coming out of a meeting with my lawyers."

"No shit."

"I couldn't believe it either."

"She's one sweet little thing."

"She is. Her name is Jules—"

"Oh, you're on first name terms now?" His tone is mocking.

"Club names sound a bit weird in the real world."

"I wouldn't know," he says. "The few times I've bumped into a woman I hooked up with at the club, I kept walking. You didn't."

"I couldn't walk away from her."

"That sounds heavy."

"She was crying when I bumped into her."

Rod's head jerks back. "Why?"

I give him a quick summary of Jules's situation.

"Oh, man." He shakes his head. "Her stepmother is a raving bitch."

"Don't get me started." I twist my lips. "I'm meeting up with Jules this afternoon so I can understand her father's business a bit more."

"Do you think you can help salvage it?"

"I don't know yet. If I can't, chances are, someone in my circle has the means or contacts to help her."

"Good point."

"If that fails, I'll go straight to Larkin."

"He knows everybody."

"Fast forward. One thing led to another, and we ended up at Dark Compulsion again."

"So, you weren't lost in space. You were flashbacking to last night," he says with a shit-eating grin.

"Idiot." I chuckle. "She had questions about my tattoos."

He considers me for a beat. "I'm guessing you didn't give her a generic answer."

"I didn't."

"What's different about her?"

"Everything."

His eyebrows shoot to his forehead. "That's quite telling, Levi."

"From the moment I saw her sashaying towards us, there was this crazy, intense connection." I rub the back of my neck. "I didn't think twice last night. I wanted her again. I can count on one hand the number of club conquests I wanted to get to know more. Once we both come, I don't climb into bed with a woman afterward for a round of Twenty Questions. I'm not an animal. It's not like I'd kick a woman out right after coming inside her, but I don't hang out afterwards—"

"Jesus, no." Rod grimaces. "After a courtesy cuddle, I'm out of there."

"Exactly. I never have a conversation that doesn't revolve around the sex or mundane things. And I certainly never delve into anything personal."

"I hear you."

"It was different with Jules. She's working her way into my head..." *And into my heart.*

Rod tilts his head to the side. "In what sense?"

"After I was done making her scream out my name God

knows how many times, I laid in bed with her in my arms. Time passed, and I was unrushed to leave."

Rod's eyes widen. "Whoa."

"I don't know who the fuck I am around her, man," I say. "Instinct, logic, and self-preservation want to push her away. Why the fuck would I go down that road again? I should back away, I want more of her."

Rod's expression is unreadable.

I keep talking.

"She was curious about my tattoo. I opened up. A part of me was compelled to do so because she understands what it's like to lose your mom. I can't remember the last time I talked about Mom or Annmarie to anyone." For so long, grief stole my breath and tore me apart. Most times, I felt like a drowning man fighting to remain afloat in the middle of a riptide. "After driving Jules to her house, I went back to mine and sat in the dark for hours, reliving it all, whiskey as my only companion. After downing half a bottle, I dragged myself to bed, but I couldn't sleep a wink. I stared at the ceiling for a while until I gave up. I jumped into my workout clothes and headed to my home gym in the hopes of exorcising the ghosts. I guess at some point I must've sat on the floor because the next thing I knew, I woke up face flat against the floor."

"Why didn't you call your dad or your brother? Heck, why didn't you call me?"

"It was late. Chances are, I was going to end up waking them up. The same applies to you."

"Fair enough."

"I'm torn."

"About what?"

"Dark Compulsion makes it convenient to avoid intimacy—"

"Who the hell needs intimacy when you can have a good

time, no strings attached?" He sneers. "The only drama I want in my life is the one attached to the plot of a music video."

I chuckle.

Rod had a rough beginning in life. He doesn't trust many people, and you're lucky if he considers you a friend. As far as I know, the only woman he's close to is his best friend, Dominika. All the other women come and go, but she's his pillar.

"I know I'm speaking German when I say this, but when you meet the right woman, you welcome intimacy. In fact, you crave it."

"You're right, you *are* speaking German. And it turns out, I don't understand a word of German. Thank God for that."

"Fucker."

He grins.

"So, what are you saying? You want more with Jules?"

"Like I said, I'm torn." I let out a long sigh. "I told her I avoid relationships, and although she didn't say anything, everything between us shifted afterwards. By the time I was ready to drive her back to her place, it was tense and awkward between us." I rake my hand through my hair. "The hurt in Jules's voice when she wished me a good night, stabbed into me. I like this woman, but fuck, I'm not equipped to give her more. Annmarie's death broke that part of me." Another pause, followed by a long sigh.

Rod doesn't press me.

"Nothing in life is guaranteed, but I can't go down the road of getting close to someone and then losing them."

"Levi, now it's my turn to speak German. I can't spell the word relationship *with* the help of a good old-fashioned dictionary *and* Google. I wouldn't be able to spell the word with a gun pointed to my head. It's not in my DNA. However, you're wired differently. Jesus, you were willing to put a noose around your neck at twenty-two. I'd rather jump off a tall building before I let that happen to me—"

"Your point, Wolfe?"

"If you're torn about this girl because you're undecided about wanting to take it further, that's one thing, and entirely your prerogative. But if you're torn about Jules because you're afraid the second you get close to her, she'll be taken away from you, that's different. Granted, I never met your mom, but I knew Annmarie." His eyes study me. "Levi, neither of them would want you to avoid relationships for the rest of your life because of their tragic death."

With those words, he exposes my biggest fear.

Chapter 14
Jules

I push open the heavy door to the warehouse.

"Here we are." I invite Levi to go in first.

This is my second trip back to the office this morning.

Since my car was still at the office and I was dying to get an early start on things, I asked Syd to drop me off at the warehouse. I texted Levi to meet me here instead of picking me up, just to text him again when I returned back to my place, telling him there was a change of plan. A string of upsetting texts from Hillary—and her stupid lawyer who was enquiring about my legal representation—had me seeing red. I hurled my phone at the couch in anger. As I was still fuming, Syd honked to let me know she was outside. I ended up having to hop in my car and drive back home to fetch my phone since Levi doesn't have the office number. He told me to stay put and he'd pick me up.

Fun morning all around. Not.

"I don't think so. Ladies first," he says.

"Thank you, sir." I step inside.

He's been quiet during the ride from my home. He was nothing like he was yesterday when we were at Zia Josefina.

I'm guessing opening up about his mom and fiancée opened up the floodgates of heart-wrenching emotions. Been there, done that. Poor soul.

I turn on the lights and guide Levi to the back of the warehouse where the fitness equipment is stored. I drop my handbag and phone on one of the tables and turn my attention to him.

"Talk to me," he says.

"Let's do a show and tell instead."

"Sounds good to me."

I press the start button to power up one of the bikes. When I do, the large screen mounted between the handlebars turns on, but it's displaying a distorted image.

I curse under my breath.

This is embarrassing. This guy is so successful. I hope he doesn't think I'm wasting his time.

Pushing those thoughts aside, I hop on the bike. I dressed for the occasion, choosing a comfortable outfit—yoga pants and a turquoise tank top. I opted for a pair of Converse instead of heels. The only way to understand my father's creation is to show it in action.

I pedal at a slow pace.

"So, this is the main problem." I point to the screen. "The bike is top-of-the-line-everything. Daddy refused to cut corners, but without the app, it's just another stationary bike, albeit an expensive one. When the app works, it opens up a whole world of possibilities. Daddy's vision is for riders to be able to find a riding partner with just a few taps. There are different circuits and each competitor would be able to see the overall progress of the ride. There're four levels of rides—the quick twenty-minute workout, a half hour one, a forty-five minute one and an hour-long ride. Everything is customizable. There are music options, but there are ways for you to upload your favorite tunes. If let's say there isn't anyone online when you need to get a workout, you can recall your last best ride so you can try to match the result or beat it. This way, you always keep your workout at optimum levels. Also, because you're interacting with the app, you're not tempted to watch a TV show. It's supposed to be exercise, not channel surfing."

"You weren't kidding when you said these were smart bikes," Levi says.

I shake my head. "Daddy spent years on the concept before he had the first bike manufactured."

Levi circles around the bike, checking out all the features.

"Can I hop on this one?" He points to a bike next to me.

I guess great minds think alike.

So far, I've only seen Levi in perfectly cut suits. This is the first time I've seen him dressed casual. He's wearing a pair of fitted dark wash jeans, a red t-shirt with an artful design on the front that clings to his muscular chest, exposing his muscular arms. A pair of colorful red and black high top Converse adorn his feet. His Chucks are custom. Yep, he's sexy as all hell in whatever he wears.

I extend a hand. "Be my guest."

He hops on the bike.

As he pedals, he pushes different buttons.

He keeps nodding his head, his lips pursed.

I'm not sure if that's a good thing or not.

He meets my gaze. "I'd like to see the other equipment."

"Not a problem."

We hop off the bikes, and I guide him to the other smart equipment.

I power up each one of the prototypes, and as expected, the screens display distorted images.

Levi meets my gaze. "The app is the only issue?"

"Yes, it is."

He walks back to the bikes and crosses his arms over his chest. It's clear from his serious expression, he's taking everything in.

"Should I abandon ship?" I brace myself for his verdict.

"That would be a huge mistake, Jules," Levi says. "You're sitting on a multi-million-dollar business."

Wh—what?

"If you play your cards right, this is the kind of business you could sell for an eye-popping number to a whale company with deep pockets."

I can't believe my ears.

"This isn't a losing battle?"

"The only way you can lose this battle is if you give up. You're at the cusp. Your dad created a pretty ingenuous concept right here."

Chapter 15

Levi

Myriad emotions play out on Jules's beautiful face. Surprise. Shock. Dismay. Relief.

"Are you kidding me right now?"

"I'm not," I say. "I'm dead serious. You had me at Esports."

She frowns. "When did I say that?"

"You didn't say that, but your dad's app is based on the same concept as Esports."

"You're going to have to translate that for me."

"There's a bevy of online party games so you and faraway friends can play from the comfort of your respective homes."

"Really?"

I nod. "You can even play Monopoly remotely."

"Oh wow."

"If you want to take it up several notches, there's Esports, aka, virtual video game competitions," I say. "You wouldn't believe how many people watch virtual game competitions. It's a billion-dollar business. Since the age of the gladiator, us humans thrive on competition. In the digital age, we no longer have to be at the same physical location. If we parallel this to your smart bikes, you're about to revolutionize the industry. Regardless if it's at home or at a gym, indoor bikes are monotonous. Your dad nailed it. An app that allows you to plug-in and ride against someone else online—despite of their location or time zone difference—is fucking ingenious."

"If only I could get the app to work properly and sync with the bikes. That's the bone of contention right now."

"Like I said yesterday, it's a question of finding the right coder." I tap the screen. "The potential behind this bike is huge. Think of stay-at-home moms—or dads—who have a limited time to work out. By competing against someone else, you can amp up your workout by a thousand fold. The same applies to the other fitness equipment."

"Oh, wow." She's dumbfounded. "The price tag of these bikes is fairly steep, I thought boutique gyms were my main customers. That was Dad's vision."

"You have a much wider market than that," I say.

She frowns her confusion.

"Other than stay-at-home parents and boutique gyms, you also have condo gyms and home gyms. I'll go as far as to say, the number of actors on location for long stretches of time would jump all over this." I pause. "I couldn't sleep last night. After tossing and turning for a while, I decided to hit my home gym. With a bike like this one, I would've been able to find someone to compete with even in the middle of the night instead of pedaling alone."

"That's it. You got it."

"Come to think of it, a lot of five-star and boutique hotels would also want this type of bike in their gyms instead of the basic ones."

"Talk about dreaming big." She shakes her head. "I knew I was way over my head, but hearing your ideas, it solidifies what

I thought all along—I don't have what it takes to turn this business around."

I place my hands on her shoulders. "I disagree, Jules."

"How can you say that, Levi? You walk in here and in no time, you lay out expansion plans I was blind to."

"You were trying to keep your head above water," I say. "You stepped into the role of CEO of a company while you were grieving and adjusting to your new reality. Not to mention, you had to contend with your despicable stepmother. Since you only worked here part-time, and your father didn't have time to prepare you for his succession, you were at a severe disadvantage. A lot of people would've folded. You didn't. You persevered."

Her shoulders slump. "I love your take on things, but that's not how I feel."

"Why don't we change that?"

"What do you mean?"

"What if you had what it took to turn this business around?"

"But I don't," she says.

"You need a solid partner—not your flighty stepmother. You also need a good and loyal team."

"And right now, I have none of those things."

"You *have* a business partner."

A puzzled look flashes on her pretty face.

"You're looking at him. Now, we just have to find us a good team."

Her mouth opens and closes a few times.

She shakes her head.

She's processing.

"Really?" Her voice is high.

"Really. Let's do this together."

She blinks up at me. "Okay." One word, but it's still laced with hesitation.

"My brother and I have this affirmation for when we're about to start working on the concept for a new stage."

"What is it?" She's wide-eyed.

"Let's go fuck some shit up."

She laughs.

"It's our way of stating we're about to shake up the status quo... that's why our business is built on word of mouth. Thinking outside the box sounds cliché, but that's how great ideas come to life. That's how you turn lemons into lemon tart."

"You mean, lemonade," she says, playing along.

"Stretch your mind beyond the mere beverage."

"So, how do we think outside the box to save Daddy's company?"

"I'm glad you asked." I grab her by the arm. "Let's go back to your office and sketch out a plan."

Jules's office is tiny and bare, such a contrast to our offices. I suggested we sit in the small conference room instead.

"Let's start with the most pressing issue." I sit next her. "Remind me again who's the majority share holder and what's the split."

"I am. Daddy left me fifty-one percent of the shares."

"Do you have an accountant?"

"We use a firm," she says.

"Is your accounting up to date?"

She averts her gaze.

"I wanted to make sure the employees were paid. That was my priority."

Yet, the fuckers jumped ship on her.

"Okay, that's the most important thing right now," I say. "Then, we're going to get them to evaluate how much it would cost for me to buy out Hillary's shares—"

"Absolutely not," she says, glowering at me, her eyebrows pinching as she folds her arms over her chest. "I can't let you do that, Levi."

"Why not?"

"It's like you're betting on the horse that has the best chances of reaching the finish line last. I don't want you to lose money."

"Did you forget what I told you in the warehouse?"

"What if you're wrong? So far, any attempt at getting a meeting with owners of the boutique gym chains has been an epic fail."

Doubt and fear roll off her.

I take her hands into mine. "Do you trust me?"

She averts her gaze. "This isn't Dark Compulsion. This is real life." She shifts in her seat.

"Eyes on me, Jules."

Her hazel-green eyes meet mine. "Do you trust me? Club or no club."

She ponders on my question for a beat.

I let go of her hands and make to stand up, but she grabs hold of my wrist.

"Wait," she says. "I trust you. But you'd be taking on a huge responsibility—and risk. I don't want you to be disappointed."

I sit back down. "I'm going to do more homework, but like I said earlier, you're so close to the finish line."

She considers me for a long stretch.

I cock a brow. "We're doing this or not?"

"Okay, partner." She offers a small smile.

"I'll buy out Hillary, but I want you to hold the majority of shares. I'll only be a partner at twenty-four percent."

"That's not fair. If you're helping me turn things around and you're using your own money to buy out Hillary, we should be equal partners."

I shake my head. "I'm probably going to need another partner. I want to make sure you're the majority shareholder with fifty-two of the shares."

"Oh," she says.

"About this office—"

"I can't afford it now, so it makes no sense to keep struggling to pay for it now that I'm a one-woman show. Though I'll still need a place to store the equipment."

"Linc and I have numerous warehouses in Culver City, but for insurance purposes, I think it's best if you rent a separate location—"

"I can't afford the monthly rent on a warehouse in Culver City," she says.

"I'll rent it for you, *partner*."

She doesn't argue.

"Let's talk about the house." I move things along. "You said your father pulled out as much equity as he could to keep the business afloat?"

"That's correct," she says.

"So once the bank gets what they're owed, you'll be splitting whatever's left with Hillary."

"I guess so." Her mood is somber.

"You can't contest your father's will."

"Unfortunately," she says. "Everything is a mess, and I have no clue where I'll live once the house is sold. I guess I could stay with Sydney for a few weeks..."

"A lot of actors and wealthy people use house-sitting companies when they're out of town for a long stretch of time. Even with the most sophisticated home security service, having someone in the house is a deterrent to would be burglars. I'll ask my friend Collin Dennison—"

"What?" Jules's eyes go wide. "You know Collin Dennison?"

"I do. And I know his brother—"

"You know fitness model Collin Dennison *and* renowned fitness guru and chef extraordinaire Shane Dennison?"

"I do."

"How do you know them?" I open my mouth to respond, but she interrupts. "Sorry. That's too personal. You don't have to answer."

I cringe.

I'm sure this has to do to with how I handled things last night.

"It's not too personal," I say. "I met Collin and Shane through Rod. The Dennison brothers are tight with the guys from Random Misconception. Back then, Collin was transitioning from acting—"

"Why?"

"According to him, it's more rewarding and far more lucrative to be a fitness model and social media celebrity than being a C-List, if not a D-List actor. Once a household name as a successful teen actor, Collin's star had been fading as he became an adult, relinquishing him to a status he hates—the easy-to-remember, but hard-to-name character actor. This is the kiss of death in Hollywood. When he did get roles, he was too often typecast."

"Wow, you know people in high places," Jules says.

"It's an occupational hazard." I wink. "Going back to what I was saying, Collin and Shane travel on location to shoot their annual calendar of hot men." The Dennison brothers sell an obscene number of them every year. "When they're away from

LA, they go through an agency to find a house-sitter. In LA, it's as common as burger joints. You'll have to store your belongings, but by becoming a house-sitter, you'll have a multimillion-dollar roof over your head, located in one of the best ZIP codes in the city."

"This is far beyond what I could've ever expected." She places a hand over her heart. "I was drowning and you're my life jacket."

I grab her by the neck, lacing my hands through her long, blonde, silky hair. "I'm committed to seeing you through this, Jules."

"Thank you, Levi."

The temptation to kiss her is overwhelming, but I pull away. "It varies, but if you're able to find a six-month housesitting contract, you'll have time to breathe."

"Something I forget to do these days."

"Let's remedy that," I say.

"I like the sound of that." She offers a warm smile. "In many ways, this works well because I don't have much to my name. Just the things in my bedroom. Hillary used most of the money she received from Dad's insurance to update all the furniture in the house." She sucks in a deep breath. "She was tired of living with my mother's memory looming over her head. She invested the rest in her daughters to transform them into Hollywood star material."

"You've got to be kidding me."

"I wish I was."

"Some people are real assholes. I guess I should say, *Twatts*."

"Your timing was impeccable."

"Not bad." I wink.

"I assume Hillary will either sell her new furniture or have it shipped to New York, unless her duke boyfriend is taking care of furnishing their new home."

So far, so good. "Let's talk contracts."

"You mean the one we'll be drawing for our partnership?"

"No. Not that one. I'm talking about contracts your ex-employees signed."

"Oh. Daddy was a stickler. Everyone had to sign a ten-year non-compete contract and a non-disclosure agreement. He even had Hillary—and her girls—sign one when they were first dating."

"Where are those contracts now?"

"Daddy's lawyers have the originals and scanned copies. I also have copies on my laptop, stored on a cloud, and copies in a safety deposit box at the bank."

Smart.

I consider her for a long while.

"Is something wrong, Levi?"

"On the contrary. Your father knew what he had in his hands."

She flashes me a beaming smile. "I guess you're right. I never thought about it that way. I always teased him and told him he was paranoid."

"You're only paranoid when you know you're holding gold in the palm of your hand."

"Hillary always thought the company was never going to amount to much."

"We don't care what Hillary thinks. You're about to give her twat ass the boot."

"Amen to that." She lifts her hands above her head and does this little sexy little dance on her chair.

I much prefer this version of Jules than the frightened woman I bumped into yesterday.

"We need your dad's lawyers to resend a letter to your former employees—including the Twatts—to remind them they signed a legal document."

She frowns. "Not that I can afford their fees, but why do we need them to do that?"

"Greed," I say. "As for the fees, I'll cover them."

"Thank you."

"It's clear from the way the last three employees dropped you like a hot potato, they don't think you have a hope in hell of turning a profit. When you start turning out millions in monthly sales, they'll be kicking themselves for abandoning you. We want to make sure they don't get any twisted ideas and start running their mouths to a competitor."

"I didn't even think of that," She nods. "What do I tell Hillary? She knows I don't have two pennies to rub together, she's going to be suspicious as to where I found this avalanche of money to pay for lawyers."

"What did I say earlier about Hillary?"

Recognition dawns. "We don't care what Hillary thinks. I'm about to give her twat ass the boot."

"High five!"

She claps my hand, laughter spilling from her gorgeous lips.

"Can you show me your cost of production numbers?" I keep things on track.

"Yes. I have all that on a spreadsheet."

"Good. We need to start from the ground up," I say. "Pull the data out and anything else you have. In the meantime, I'll step out to make a phone call. I think I have the perfect business partners—"

"As in, more than just one?"

"Yes. I think these two guys will be all over the Cycle-Thonix and the rest of the Thonix family. I'll get my lawyers and accountants to go over the numbers, but since you were transparent, I know where you're starting from."

"God, you move at lightning speed, Levi."

"For months you were in way over your head. It's no longer

the case, Jules. The faster we move, the faster we can bring the bikes to market, the faster you can start making money. There's a lucrative market for the CycleThonix. There are other smart bikes on the market, but none of them allow you to ride with a virtual partner in real time."

"Okay." She nods, still soaking in my words. "Fast, it is."

"Glad you're on board. While I'm making a few calls, why don't you make an appointment with your dad's lawyers and your accountants? Make sure you get a few options so I can see what works best in my schedule."

"Got it."

I stand up. "Let's go fuck some shit up."

"I'm onboard." She flashes me a wide smile.

Chapter 16

Jules

Excitement bubbles inside me, threatening to burst like a champagne cork on New Year's Eve just when the clock strikes midnight. I'm so giddy, I'm bouncing off the walls.

Daddy, I'm not going to let you down.

I choke up with emotion.

It takes me a few seconds to find my composure. When I do, I'm itching to share the good news. Sydney is not only responsible for changing the course of my sex life, but it appears my best friend put me into the path of a savior who's about to transform my whole existence. I snatch my phone off the conference table and dial her up.

"Hey, Jules."

"Hey, Syd, can you talk?"

"Austin and I are working at a massive Beverly Hills property—"

"Aren't they all massive in that zip code?"

"You're right." She giggles. "In any case, we're taking a break. It's so hot today. Fuck, I hate boob sweat."

I laugh.

"What's going on?"

"You're never going to believe what I have to share."

"Hit me!"

I give her a quick rundown of my conversation with Hillary. I tell her about bumping into Levi right after. I share the highlights of our sexy night at the club. I conclude by telling Syd about Levi and me going from a one-night stand to a partnership.

"Hillary is such a twat." She shouts so loud on the other end, I have to pull the phone away from my ear. "The woman is a stupid cow. I swear to God, once you have her out of your life for good, we have to go out and celebrate."

"Deal!"

"Now, let's talk about that fine piece of man candy that's doubling as your knight in shining armor."

I giggle like a silly girl.

"Thank God for sending him your way," she says.

"I couldn't agree more. He's not only dreamy, he's also a phenomenal lover. Thank you for dragging me out that night."

"I played a tiny part in it. This is all fate."

"After so much bad luck, I can see a glimmer of hope."

"From what you described, it's a hell of a lot more than a glimmer."

"I prefer to err on the side of caution," I say. "But it's undeniable, Levi is a savvy businessman. His vision is so huge, it gives me goosebumps."

"I'm so glad your dad's business won't weigh so heavily on your shoulders anymore. As for the house, I can't imagine what it's like to have to leave your home—and you know you could've stayed with us—but your hands are tied if Ms. Twatt wants out. On the bright side, you'll be living in enviable zip codes as you work on turning the business around."

"It saddens me to leave my childhood home, but since Hillary, Petula, and Olive moved in, it stopped being the safe place it once was. Bouncing around from one strange home to another will feel weird, I'm sure, but at least, I won't have to live with my evil stepsisters and their bitch of a mother."

Chapter 17

Levi

I step out of the conference room and roam around Jules's office. Only empty desks and workstations greet me. I still can't get over the stunt Hillary pulled. The nasty bitch rarely showed her face at the office, but she decided it was her responsibility to make such a detrimental announcement.

Un-fucking-believable.

I stop in front of a window overlooking the parking lot, pull out my phone and dial a guy who will see the opportunity in CycleThonix.

"Levi, my friend," Collin says. "What's up?"

"Hey, Collin. Am I catching you at a bad time?"

"No. I just got back home. Man, my boxing trainer whooped my ass. I doubt I'll be able to feel my arms tomorrow."

"It's your fault for being one of the top fitness models out there." I chuckle.

"Blame my fans," he says. "These muscles sell the calendars we produce and a long list of luxury brands." I can imagine him flexing his biceps. "Women have certain expectations when they see my perfect body on display. It's my duty to make sure I don't crush their fantasies."

"You're delusional."

"Jealous?"

"Moving right along."

"Beckett came over my place on Monday night for dinner," Collin says, changing the subject. "It sounds like my big brother and I missed a good party at the club. That was a hell of a theme. I won't lie, I cursed our prior engagement in Miami. Word has it, you scored."

"Beckett talks too much."

"There's no smoke without fire, Levi. That girl must've been something else. Beckett couldn't shut up about your match. I hope you enjoyed the leggy blonde."

"She's the reason I'm calling." I cut to the chase.

"You connected with her again? You lucky dog."

"Collin, you don't even know what she looks like."

"I'm telling you, Levi, Beckett had stars in his eyes. That girl made an impression on him."

"I'll give him that much, Jules is breathtaking."

"I doubt Jules is her club name," Collin says. "Did you break protocol?"

"I didn't. I bumped into her yesterday afternoon. Outside of the club, it's fair game."

"And you're calling me so I can give you some pointers?"

"Fucker."

He chuckles.

"This call is strictly business, Dennison."

"I don't follow."

"I'm calling you first, but I intend on calling Shane right after."

"Don't keep me in suspense, Levi."

I brief him.

"Oh, that's a killer concept for a stationary bike," he says.

"You should see it."

"Do you have any photos?"

"You should come and see it in person," I say.

"Why do I feel you have something up your sleeve?"

I tell him about becoming Jules's new partner. "It's going to take more capital to bring the product to market. That's where you and Shane come in."

"Why us?"

"Simple, the Dennison name is synonymous with fitness—you and Shane are kings in the arena. Same for many of your cousins. Your brother is still considered one of the top personal trainers in the country. And he's a top Food Network chef. He might not have as many personal training clients as before, but Shane's roster of former A-lister celebrity clients is legendary. He's shaped the bodies of the biggest stars in Hollywood. You might be too cocky for your own good, but it's undeniable, you're an influencer and a trendsetter."

He laughs.

"I still have to dig deeper, but from my initial assessment, once the app works, Jules is off to the races. She's going to need solid marketing and a face to represent the brand."

"And you were picturing my face," Collin says.

"I was picturing Jules's, Shane's, *and* yours."

"Why the three of us?"

"Jules is the CEO of the company, she's stunning, and she's fit. She's the embodiment of the brand. The same for you and Shane. I don't believe in reinventing the wheel. The way to sell fitness products is by *showing* attractive, fit people *using* the product. If they happen to have name recognition, it's a bonus."

"You're thinking infomercial?"

"Exactly."

"Okay, this sounds interesting."

"I want to enlist Dominika as the video producer and creator," I say.

"This is quite the departure for someone who specializes in music videos."

"I know, she's one of the most sought-after video producers and creators in the industry. At the price point these bikes will fetch, the commercials need to hit the bullseye without clobbering the viewer over the head with cheesy tactics. The ideal client isn't someone who needs to be convinced of the virtues of working out. It's someone who wants to take their workout to the next level."

"You're sure this has legs? After all, you don't have numbers yet."

"Like I said, the app is the hold up. I'm convinced Jules is sitting on something huge."

"You're pretty confident about this." He's not onboard.

"I'm telling you, Collin, you have to see it to believe it."

Silence stretches on the other end for a beat.

"How long will you be at Jules's office?"

"I take it you're coming down?"

"You've piqued my curiosity. I want to check out the bike with my own eyes. Feel free to call my brother, but I have no doubt it'll be the same for Shane."

Chapter 18

Jules

Collin and Shane Dennison are standing in my warehouse. *Oh. My. God.*

Someone pinch me.

I'm doing my best to maintain my cool and not come across like a silly fan girl. The Dennison brothers have the kind of over-the-top presence that commands attention. Sure, they're gorgeous, but it's much more than that. Like Levi, the tall, blue-eyed, brown-haired hunks ooze confidence. I'm not used to being around men who strut around, dripping with that much cocksureness. And that's the operative word. These guys are men. Not boys.

Talk about an upgrade.

When Levi said he had a couple of candidates in mind as business partners, never in a million years did I imagine it would be Shane and Collin Dennison.

I mean, these two are celebrities.

Much to my surprise, the Dennison brothers showed up in appropriate training gear, which made it easy for them to jump on the bikes and give them a good run. They also inspected and

tested the other smart equipment. I was biting my nails, antici-
pating their verdict. The words that came out of Shane's mouth
nearly landed me on my ass.

"Jules, Levi is right, you're sitting on a gold mine."

Just when I had lost all hope, these men show up in my life.
Hillary expected me to drown. On the contrary. I'll end up
with a trio of kickass business partners to the rescue.

Hillary is going to be forced to eat her words.

After giving the Dennison brothers a tour of the warehouse,
we're back in the small conference room. For the past three
hours I've been taking the three men through our operations.
We've been poring over spreadsheets, contracts, patents, and a
slew of other documents related to the production of the bikes.

"Between the three of us, we should have the funds to kickstart this," Shane says. "But what about creating a crowdfunding campaign? This would be a massive flow of upfront
cash."

I frown. "We can't produce thousands of these a week."

"Your dad produced a hundred CycleThonix bikes, right?"

"Yes, Shane."

"That's more than enough to get the buzz going," he says.
"To sweeten the pot, we could offer personalized training and
rides for the core group of one hundred who snatch the first
round of equipment. One of my former clients won the Tour de
France twice. Imagine if people were able to tap into his
training routine from the comfort of their home?"

"Oh."

"On top of that, I can offer meal and diet plans." Shane is
on a roll. "Plus, Collin and I can share one of his typical
workout sessions—I'm still his personal trainer."

"What's a great idea," I say.

"I agree," Collin says.

"That's a killer idea, Shane," Levi says.

"Here's one more." Shane's blues eyes bounce around the table. "I've been playing around with different smoothie recipes that offer optimal workout fuel, like my s'mores protein shake, Aztec chocolate protein shake or root beer float protein shake."

Those sound sinful.

"As I perfect the recipes, I can post them on my site," Shane says. "The end goal is a self-published recipe book. I'm nearly there. Once published, our crowdfunders would receive a signed copy."

"Holy smokes, Shane," Levi says. "You're on fire."

"I know, right?" Shane nods, a sly smile stretching his lips. "Not all smoothies are created equal. Many are a sugar dump in your system without giving your muscle the proper nutrients."

"Shane is right. Not all smoothies are created equal," I say. I might not know much about running a business, but I know what fuels the body.

"On top of that, we should get paraphernalia and create some cool swag bags," Collin says. "People love that shit."

"We should consider branded clothing—t-shirts, hoodies, sweat pants, socks, and caps." Shane piggybacks on his brother's suggestion.

"Yes, to all of the above," Collin says.

"And towels, water bottles, and blender bottles." Shane keeps adding to the list.

Levi claps his hands together. "Perfect!"

"Since this is an app, we should also consider creating an online community," Collin says. "Those things are powerful for retention. Shane, that's where you should post your smoothie recipes."

"Good one, Collin," Levi says.

Collin pumps his chest out and grins.

"What about the Fit Thonix VIP 100 Club?"

Shane's suggestion is on fire.

"Now, you're talking." Levi slams his hand against the table, making me jump. "Oh, sorry, sweetness, I got carried away."

I brush it off and smile.

This meeting is going so well, it's like my brain is about to explode. I would've never come up with all these phenomenal ideas. Gosh, I was thinking way too small.

I lift my eyes to the ceiling and send God a huge thank you.

"What a perfect way to brand our first one hundred buyers as VIPs," Levi says. "Exclusivity is a huge selling feature."

Collin lifts a finger in the air. "If we're going to have an online community and the Thonix's value proposition is all about challenging yourself via virtual competitive workouts, let's wrap it up as a 90-day challenge. Some people will want to lose weight. Some will want to increase their fitness level. And some will want to get more ripped. Regardless, people love attainable goals."

"Collin is right," Shane says.

"So, our Fit Thonix VIP 100 Club gets a 90-day challenge on top of everything," Levi says.

"Once the challenge is over, we want our early adopters to show off their transformation." Collin says. "We do it Holly-wood style with a big fucking party. I'm talking red carpet, photographers, the press, fitness bloggers and an army of celebrities. After a night like that, you'd have to be living under a rock not to know about Fit Thonix equipment."

Levi and Shane nod.

Wow. Just wow.

"We'll create so much buzz with the crowdfunding *and* we'll create a second wave when we have our graduation party," Collin says.

"People are going to be throwing money at us," Shane says.

"This will send our pre-orders through the roof," Levi says. "This ensures we get the product to market with a minimum out-of-pocket investment on our end, which means we can be profitable in a blink of an eye."

I'm too stunned to add anything of value to this conversation.

Yesterday at this time, I was on the verge of despair. Now, I'm so overwhelmed I don't know if I should be screaming, fainting. or giving these lovely men thank you kisses.

Chapter 19

Levi

I tap Jules's nose with my finger. "I bet you didn't suspect your day was going to end this way when you woke up this morning."

"Err... that's the understatement of the century." Her voice trembles. "I still haven't been able to pick up my jaw from the floor. I can't believe what transpired in the conference room."

I brush her long hair behind her shoulders. "I told you, your dad was close."

"Wow." She shakes her head. "Shane and Collin Dennison are going to be my business partners."

"Hey, what about me?"

She laughs, reaching out to cup my cheeks. "You're more than a business partner. You're my guardian angel." She drops a soft kiss on my lips.

I wrap my arms around her, tightening my hold as I pull her body close to mine. Our tongues dance together, and she moans into my mouth.

For a few long beats, we're both lost to this blazing kiss.

I break our embrace. "We need to celebrate."

"I agree," she says. "It's too bad Shane and Collin can't join us."

"Something tells me there will be many, *many* opportunities for us to celebrate. However, you're right, it would've been great to hang out with them."

I never expected the Dennisons to be here for five hours. The second they tested the CycleThonix and understood the concept behind the app, they were hooked. Our brainstorming session was so all-encompassing, I had my executive assistant order a late lunch and lots of coffee from one of our favorite caterers and had it delivered to Jules's office. The energy was too high for us to take a break. Given how incredible this afternoon was, I would've invited the guys to celebrate with us, but they had prior engagements. They're emceeing a charitable gala.

"Why don't I drive you back to your place so you can pack an overnight bag," I say, "and we'll go to my place? I have some superb prime Angus steak. Collin and Shane hooked me up with friends of theirs who have one of the top grass-fed Angus ranches in Summerville, Texas. I order a couple dozen at a time and freeze them. It's expensive, but worth it. Once you taste that meat, you'll never want another steak in your life. I can marinate the steak and throw them on the barbecue. I'll also throw in large shrimp I have in the freezer. Kind of like a surf and turf. I have an incredible bottle of vintage champagne we can pop open. On the way to my house, we'll stop to buy dessert. There you have it. Celebration for two."

Jules stares at me. "You want me to come back to your place and have dinner with you?"

"Yeah. Spend the night with me."

Her eyelashes flutter like crazy.

"I don't invite women to my place—"

"I heard you last night."

The hurt in her voice stabs me.

"You don't do relationships. I get it." Her words are as cold as ice.

I let out a long sigh. "About that—"

"It's okay, Levi—"

"Let me finish, Jules."

"Okay." She crosses her arms over her chest before resting her back against the seat.

Her defenses are up.

"I didn't see you coming, Jules Salinger. I couldn't stop thinking of you last night and the attraction I feel towards you is unsettling. It might not have come across that way last night, but you make me reconsider so many things."

"Like what?"

"Like the reason I closed my door to relationships," I say. "Until you came along, I never wanted more with a woman. You've thrown me off my axis."

"Is that a good thing?"

"It is. I love fucking you, but I also love *being* with you."

She blushes. "You have a way with words, Mr. Aldridge."

"You know you love my dirty mouth."

"Guilty as charged." She laughs. "But, now that we're business partners, shouldn't we keep it platonic?"

Hell, no. "Is that what you want?"

She shrugs. "I want to give you a way out."

"I don't need a way out. I know what I want." I bore my eyes into hers. "And that's you."

She blushes.

"Let's see where this goes," I say.

"What do you mean?" The words come out is breathless gust.

"I don't want to put the brakes on, Jules. Let's explore this to the fullest. I'm not interested in seeing anyone else."

"Oh my God, Levi." She brings a hand to her chest. "I feel the same way. I was devastated last night——"

I drop two fingers against her lips, silencing her. "I know."

"Maybe I shouldn't say this, but I've never fallen this fast for someone in my life."

Fuck if those words don't do something to me. "It's the same for me."

She offers a warm smile.

"You wanna be my girlfriend?" I wink.

She shakes her head.

"You don't want to be my girlfriend?"

She doesn't answer.

"Jules?"

"This is the most incredible day of my life, Levi."

I tip her chin up. "We're good together, sweetness."

Her eyes blink wide and turn warm. "We are."

Chapter 20

Jules

The ride from my office to Silver Lake is excruciating. No surprise at this time of the day. When Levi pulls off the highway and starts gunning down the road towards my house, butterflies flutter in my tummy.

From time to time, I shoot him a furtive glance.

He responds with a wink.

God, he's so gorgeous it's almost criminal.

He was amazing before, but now as my boyfriend, he's pretty fucking perfect.

I still can't get over it.

What a difference a day makes. Twenty-four little hours that can turn your whole world around. And for once, it's for the best.

"I can't wait to have you in my bed," he says in a voice that drips with desire.

"Are you going to tie me to it?"

Where the hell did that come from?

I blame this man's intoxicating presence for that bold question.

"You like it when I restrain you," he says with a mixture of awe and pride.

"It's sexy."

He shoots me a sideways glance before returning his attention to the road ahead.

"I haven't decided what I'll do to you yet."

His words unleash a craving in me.

"It doesn't sound like I'll sleep much tonight."

"I wouldn't count on it."

The warning travels straight to my clit.

The sexual tension in the Audi SUV is so thick, you could slice it with dental floss.

Still drunk on whatever brazen serum I ingested, I push my seat belt off my shoulder without unbuckling it, and turn in my seat to face him.

His aqua-blue eyes shift. The lust I read in them is my undoing.

My eyes lower to his crotch and I lick my lips.

He considers me with interest.

A wicked thought surges.

I teeter at the edge, unsure if I should recoil or go all the way.

Decisions, decisions.

Fuck it.

I reach out and set my palm flat against the zipper of his jeans, running it down the length of his bulge. "So, what are we celebrating tonight?"

His eyes drop to my hand for a beat.

Excitement swirls in me when he doesn't ask me to remove it.

"We have a lot to celebrate," he says.

"Where to start?" Being bold like this doesn't come naturally, but he brings it out of me.

"You seem to have already made up your mind."

"Your menu sounds delicious, but there's something else I'd love to have in my mouth tonight."

He does a double take, shock written all over his gorgeous face. "Is that so?"

"Yup." I pop the P.

"What exactly?"

"You know..."

"Don't be vague. Ask for what you want point-blank, little girl."

I'm a ball of nerves and anticipation.

The good girl in me cautions I'm walking a tightrope, but the bad girl tells me to ignore the sensible Jules.

I unbutton and unzip his jeans.

"What are you doing?"

I steady my breathing. "You told me not to be vague." My voice wavers. "I want to start the celebration early."

I slide my hand inside his jeans. He doesn't demand I stop.

His cock swells and thickens beneath my slow-moving grasp.

He wipes a hand over his mouth, as if considering his options.

Fuck, this is so hot.

I'm so wet, I'm sure I'll leave a stain on the seat.

He glances in my direction for the briefest of moments, and it's long enough for my heart to jackhammer against my chest.

"Fuck, I love when you're a bad girl."

So do I.

His eyes devour me, amplifying my desire a thousand fold.

I keep rubbing his erection through his boxer briefs.

"You want this cock inside your pretty little mouth?"

I nod.

"Now?"

I nod again.

It's like another woman is occupying my body. A daring one.

His eyes hood, leaving only a sliver of blue peering at me.

With my past two boyfriends, sex was an in and out thing. Most times, I was responsible for my own orgasms. Everything is so hedonistic with Levi. He knows my body better than I do. I want to pleasure him with my mouth the way he pleasures me with his.

But, hell, if he looks at me this way every time I step out of my comfort zone, I'm game to do it more often.

He drops a hand onto mine, pressing so hard against my palm it's almost painful.

A small, bemused smile touches his lips as he gazes at me. "You filthy slut."

Slut?

I should be offended, not turned on.

I shouldn't be grinding against my seat, my clit seeking relief.

He tilts his hips. "Pull my cock out."

Okay.

I asked for it, but now, I'm not so sure.

"You don't have the right to go shy on me, Jules. It's so fucking sexy when you ask for what you want."

Well, when he puts it like that.

I muster all the courage I have and do as I'm told.

My body vibrates with need when his thick erection is freed through the open fly of his boxer briefs.

"You got me all worked up. Take care of it."

I don't have time to register his words. He fists my hair and yanks my head down, putting my face in his lap. His hard cock is an inch from my face.

Oh. My. God.

Panic courses through me.

It's after seven and the sun is still shining bright in the sky. "What if someone sees?"

"It's only now it's a consideration?" There's an edge to his voice.

"Err... I guess so."

There's an art to being a bad girl. I'm not there yet.

"We're in the SUV, which means we're elevated. Unless we're flanked by transport trucks, your secret is safe with me," he says.

I'm sure that was meant to comfort me, but the panic doesn't subside.

Being bold is one thing. Public indecency is another.

I should've thought this through.

"Think of how thrilling it would be if someone caught you sucking me off? We both know there's an exhibitionist in you."

The idea of someone watching sends tingles to my clit.

The center console makes things a bit uncomfortable, but I ignore it. I fist his cock, and wet my lips by licking them.

My pussy can stretch way more than my mouth...

"You're thinking too hard," he says. "Close your lips around my cock."

God, I love when he's this domineering.

He gets off on the power.

I get off on handing it to him.

I stick my tongue out and lick the tip of his cock. His cock is warm, his flesh silky smooth against my tongue.

He lets out a low groan.

There's no saving my panties now.

"Take me in deeper."

I slide my lips down his length, swallowing several inches of him.

"Fuck, I love your mouth."

Bursting with confidence, I bob my head, swirling my tongue over the bulbous mushroom head of his cock.

He lets out a feral grunt.

Up and down.

Up and down.

With each head bob, his breathing picks up.

It's exhilarating.

He clasps a hand over my head, forcing me to take several more inches of him. "Deeper."

His assertive voice lights me up and compels me to obey.

I widen my mouth and struggle a bit when I attempt to swallow a few more inches of his cock.

"You'll get used to my size." Amusement colors his words.

I doubt it, but I don't argue.

"Relax as much as you can. It'll make it easier."

I respond with a nod.

"I want words."

"I will."

"Get back to it," he says.

My eyes scour around, trying to figure out if any of the passengers in the surrounding cars are clued in on our raunchy and risqué play. No one cares.

Back to the program.

His body trembles when I skim the tip of my tongue over the slit of his cock. I wrap my lips around it and suck him off like it's my mission in life. My phone rings at the bottom of my handbag, sitting next to me. I ignore it.

I bob my head up and down with such determination, I bump it against the steering wheel as I try to move at a faster pace.

Ouch.

"My cock is that good?"

I nod.

I slide my lips over his cock so I'm swallowing nearly every inch of him. If I take him in any deeper, I'll choke.

Up and down.

Up and down.

"Such an eager girl," Levi says.

Satisfaction courses through me at his words.

I bore my eyes into his.

His intense gaze shifts to mine, setting me on fire.

I'm a mess inside, desperate for this man.

Yeah, I'm a hopeless addict.

For a few breaths, his eyes bounce from mine to the road, one hand firmly on the wheel, the other caressing my hair.

"Fuck, you look hot with my cock between your lips."

Pleasing him gives me such a thrill and I crave more.

A moan of delight slips out from me, filling the quiet interior of the Range Rover. It's only then I realize he turned off the music.

What happens next, takes me by surprise. It's like something snapped in him. He fists my hair, guiding my head, forcing me to go faster.

Mother of God.

I had a tiny bit of control over him, but now it's gone. Levi is in full alpha mode, as his hips move at a steady rhythm, pumping in and out of my mouth, feeding me every inch of his cock.

He's unleashed.

He fucks my mouth. Hard, fast, and unrelenting.

"Your fucking mouth..."

I gag when his cock hits the back of my throat.

He loosens his grip.

"Shit," he says.

I pull back abruptly, letting his cock drop out of my mouth.

I pant, struggling to catch my breath.

"You're okay?"

I wipe the saliva from my lips. "You're huge."

He chuckles.

It's only when I peer up at him, I realize we're no longer moving.

We're parked on the side of the road.

When did that happen?

Cars and trucks whiz by, unaware of our transgression.

My watery eyes flicker up to his.

He studies me from behind his hooded gaze.

"Where is the shy girl now?" His tone is teasing.

"When I'm with you, I do things I'd never dream of doing otherwise."

"I'm a bad influence on you."

"You love that, don't you?"

A devilish grin stretches his lips.

He clasps a hand behind my head, pulling me closer until our foreheads touch. "Damn right I do." He drops a soft kiss against my lips. "Let's get to your place so you can finish what you started. I can't drive and come at the same time."

"And I can't wait to make you come," I say to my beautiful man.

Chapter 21

Levi

The rest of the drive to Jules's place is a cruel exercise in control.

I never suspected she would be bold enough to go all the way.

Fuck, that was hot.

My cock is still as hard as steel and desperate for relief.

"It's the house right up front." She points. "You can park in the driveway next to my car."

I slide next to a set of wheels that's seen better days. She wasn't joking when she said it was beat up.

We both get out of the SUV and stroll to the front door, hand in hand.

Her phone pings as we step into the house. She closes the door behind me and locks it before digging inside her handbag.

She groans.

"Who is it?"

"Hillary. Again. It's her sixth text message reminder of the day. I bet all those missed calls are from her." She lets out a frustrated sigh. "I have no intention of talking to her." Jules drops her phone into her bag and places it on the console table near the door.

"Jesus, is she going to keep pestering you until you cough up the money?"

"Seems like it," she says. "And since nothing is official yet between the four of us, I can't assure her she'll get her for money on time—"

"Make her squirm. Wait until the last possible minute to give her a clue you'll come up with the money."

She shoots me a devilish smile. "Oh... that's devious."

"Tit for tat, baby," I say. "Hillary pulled the rug from under your feet, leaving you stranded. And that's after burning through your father's insurance money. It's not like you have a garden of Benjamins growing in your backyard. She knows that. The evil bitch wanted to make you suffer."

Jules nods. "I don't know why she hates me so much."

"It doesn't matter anymore."

"You're right."

"The only thing that matters, is booting her out of your life. You want to keep quiet about everything that will transpire over the next weeks. If Hillary catches wind you secured three investors and there's hope for your father's business, you'll never get rid of her. She'll continue to be the leech that sucks everything out of you."

She considers my warning.

"Mum's the word." She runs a zipper across her pretty lips.

"Exactly." I nod. "Now, let's not waste another second talking about that witch."

"Agreed. Do you want the tour?"

That's not what I had in mind.

I scan the small house. The brand new furniture Hillary bought lacks flair. The same for the reproduction paintings adorning the walls. I doubt that's a real van Gogh.

"Maybe after." I grab her by the waist, pulling her to me until we're chest to chest, her wide hazel-green eyes staring up into mine. "I'm a breath away from a severe case of blue balls. The house tour can wait."

Her hand lands on my chest, balling my t-shirt into her small fist. "And you want me to take care of your *little* problem?"

"Watch your smart mouth, *little* girl. We both know there's nothing small about my cock, and yes, I expect my girlfriend to take care of my big dick."

"You're so demanding." She rolls her eyes.

"You're singing a different tune than you were earlier," I say. "I much prefer when you're more *agreeable*... with my cock between your lips."

Without giving her a chance to respond, my mouth slams against hers, swallowing her smart retort. My tongue parts her lips, delving deep and claiming her with urgency. She clings to me as if she's unable to stand on her own and might crumble to her knees any second. The more I deepen the kiss, the more she sinks into me, returning my passion with as much fury.

Fuck, yeah.

I pull away, place my hands on her shoulders and turn her around so she's facing the living room.

"I want you naked and bent over the back of the couch."

Her head whips around, astonishment written all over her beautiful face.

"I—I have a bedroom."

"I'm not particularly interested in your bedroom."

"But—"

"It's unlikely your stepmother and stepsisters will show up."

She looks at me from over her shoulder.

The wheels in her head are churning.

"You're a study in contrast, Jules Salinger. It doesn't take much convincing for you to suck me off on the road, but fucking you in your living room is a problem?"

She turns to face me.

She cocks an eyebrow as if saying, *Game on.*

With her eyes on me, she strips.

As she removes each item of clothing, she flings them around the room. It's not meant to be provocative, but goddamn is it ever sexy.

I stop her as she reaches for her panties. "I'll do the honors."

I fist the stretchy pink underwear with yellow trimming, and with one hard tug, rip the thong off her body, leaving her completely naked to me.

She gasps, her eyes snapping to mine. "You didn't just do that."

"I needed quick access to your pussy."

"I could've removed them."

"Not the same thing. Not as fast."

"Barbarian caveman."

"Oh, baby, stop kidding yourself. You enjoyed it as much as I did."

She flashes me a wide grin.

"I want you over there." I jerk my chin.

"Aren't you going to get undressed?"

"I gave you an order, Jules."

She turns on her heel.

I slap her fine ass, and her body jolts.

Her frown is firmly in place when she glances at me from over her shoulder.

"If you're itching for a proper spanking, you're on the right track."

She purses her lips and sashays to the couch. The view of

her phenomenal, bouncy ass is nearly enough to make me come.

Damn.

I undress at light speed.

With quick hands, I rummage through the pocket of my jeans, pull out a condom packet from my wallet and take my time admiring her in this wicked position before approaching her.

I lean forward so my chest rests against her back. My lips flirt with her earlobe. "Your ass in the air like this is pure sin."

"I've never had sex like this before," she says. "I mean, I did it a few times with an ex on the couch, but it was on the cushions."

"That's so predictable."

"Before you, that's all I knew."

"Good thing I came into your life."

She wiggles her ass against me. "Can't argue with that."

"For the record, I like being the one to introduce you to all sorts of debauchery."

"You're doing a bang up job of it, Levi Aldridge."

We laugh.

I drop the condom onto the couch cushion.

"You don't want me to finish sucking you off?"

"I'm too impatient for your pussy," I say. "If you wrap your lips around my cock, I'll come down your throat. I'd rather shoot my load deep inside you."

My hands grip her firm ass cheeks, parting them.

She gasps.

"Levi, please, wait." Her voice trembles.

"Wait for what?"

"I'm not ready for anal sex."

"You're not. I want to slide right here..." I angle my body and nestle my hard cock between her ass cheeks, relishing her warmth. The skin-on-skin sensation is heart-stopping and my eyes roll to the back of my head. "This is fucking amazing."

"Oh, yes... it is." Her voice is like a purr.

I shove two fingers inside her pussy.

She hitches a breath.

"Always so fucking wet for me."

She nods.

"Your juices are practically running down your legs, sweetness."

"I want you so much, Levi."

"I want you too, baby."

I pump my fingers inside her and skate my thumb over her clit while I work my hips back and forth, grinding against her magnificent ass.

My bad girl rides my fingers slow and steady.

"Jesus," she says, panting.

When her hips start swinging faster, I pull my fingers away.

"Please don't stop, I'm close," she says.

"I don't want you to come over my fingers."

I reposition my cock, sliding into the hollow space between her legs, rubbing the tip against her hard clit.

"Goddamn."

"Sweet baby Jesus," she says.

I toy with her, working both of us into a frenzy.

My balls contract in an almost painful way, reminding me I need to fuck her before I waste a good load.

I reach for the condom, tear it open, and wrap up.

Fisting the monster between my legs, I grip her hip with my free hand, repositioning her body. I press my hungry erection at her entrance, then plunge deep inside her in one powerful thrust.

A feral grunt escapes my lips.

A whimpering one escapes hers.

I let loose between her legs, pumping in and out of her almost violently.

Her pussy clenches, gripping my cock like she never wants me to withdraw.

I tilt my hips back, before slamming right back into her with unwavering force.

Adrenaline pumps through my veins, pushing me to fuck her like an animal.

She takes what I have to give her. She submits fully to me.

The sound of slapping skin on skin takes over the room.

Jules's moans and pleas soon turn into something incomprehensible.

We're wild, wholly consumed by passion.

My eyes drop to where our bodies join in the most intimate way, and I swear it's like my soul is merging with hers.

I fist her long, blonde hair, wrapping her silky mane a few times before pulling her head back.

Our eyes meet.

"Who do you belong to?"

"Oh, God, Levi."

I slap her again.

"That's not the answer I'm looking for."

And again.

"Who do you belong to?"

"You," she says. "I belong to you."

"Fuck, you're perfect."

"Fuck me harder, Levi."

That's her answer?

I'm keeping her.

I don't hold back.

I pump in and out of her with an ever-increasing tempo. My hips work at a frantic pace, slamming deeper inside her with every punishing thrust.

Her back bows, and she lets out a long wail of pleasure.

I slide a hand around her waist and down her tummy until I find her clit.

"I fucking love your cock. I fucking need it. I fucking need you." She rides my cock faster and faster.

Not that I needed an incentive, but that's my undoing.

With one hand, I clasp her hip to keep her in place, as I fuck her senseless.

Like a fool, I chant. "Yes, fuck. Yes, fuck. Yes, Jules."

Somewhere past the overwhelming sound of my heartbeat, I hear Jules, chanting my name. The strong staccato pulses with which she clenches around me, milking everything she can from me, vibrate all the way down to my goddamn toes.

Jesus fucking Christ.

I'm too far gone to allow her the courtesy of a respite.

I need to come.

I fuck her at unprecedented speed and follow right behind her.

A primal, aching cry tears from my throat as my orgasm hits.

"Holy shit, holy shit, holy shit. Fucking hell, I'm coming. Oh, Jules, baby, I'm *fucking...*" I release my hot seed deep inside her, shouting loud enough to be heard in Hawaii. "*Coming...*"

I come, and I come, and I come.

Stars dance across my vision as potent pleasure fills me to the point where I'm unable to discern pain and pleasure.

For several long beats, I don't move. I can't.

Neither does she.

My breath comes out labored. Like hers.

When my legs stop trembling and I'm certain I won't collapse to my knees, I lean my chest against her back and trail soft, languorous kisses across her shoulders.

She purrs like a satisfied kitten.

With a sigh of contentment, I bury my face into the crook of her neck, kissing her there gently. "You belong to me," I say between kisses, my hands roaming over her spent body.

"I belong to you."

Hearing those words in the heat of passion was as hedonistic as fuck, but now, when we're no longer chasing after our climax, the words take on a whole other dimension. Once, fear and trepidation would have me bolting out of here like the house was on fire, but not today. The words feel right. She feels right. I can't seem to get enough of her and no way am I putting the brakes on.

Chapter 22

Levi

Jules is sleeping in my arms. It's seven in the morning, and I can't find it in me to wake her up. I'm relishing this moment. It's been such a long time since I *slept* with a woman, I forgot how good it was.

Her mane of long hair fans across my chest. In the morning sun, the honey-blonde color is almost golden. I brush my fingers along her arm, flashing back to our many, many hot as fuck trysts since she boldly wrapped her lips around my cock in my SUV.

Damn.

My cock swells as she stirs beside me, sliding one leg in between mine as she cuddles even closer.

Great.

Now, her warm, damp pussy rubs against my thigh.

I'm doomed.

A lazy hand caresses down my stomach and settles against my hipbone, making my cock swell even more.

I adjust myself, but it does little to bring me salvation.

My sleeping beauty groans, making things worse for me.

Fucking her would solve my problem, but that might be pushing the envelope. She'll need a few hours to recover from our sex marathon. I worked her hard throughout the night. It's her fault. She told me I couldn't make her come more than three times in one night. Challenge accepted.

Jules cracks an eyelid open. "What's that?" Her fingers trailing up my cock.

"Morning wood."

"Is your girlfriend expected to do something about it?"

Fucking tease.

I shift my hand from where it's resting on her shoulder and stroke a strand of blonde hair behind her ear. Her mane is wild, like a woman well fucked and fully satiated. "Since you're here... we might as well put your mouth to good use."

She swats my stomach.

"I mean, I'd love for my girlfriend to take care of my morning wood."

"You're lucky I'm agreeable."

"You don't have to beat around the bush if you want my cock. You can be upfront about it."

She rolls her eyes.

I untangle myself from her, reaching to the nightstand where there are only a couple condoms left and grab one.

"Hey, Levi, you still in bed, you lazy bum?" a voice says from somewhere in the house.

"Shit." I drop the condom like it's on fire.

Jules's eyes widen. "Who is it?"

"My brother," I say.

"And he just let himself in?"

"He has a key."

"It makes sense." She blows out a breath. "Too much fucking affects my brain."

I chuckle.

"Your place is a mess, little brother," Linc says as he approaches my bedroom. "I guess the cleaning lady didn't—Holy shit, you're not alone."

He discovered the trail of clothing, and God knows what else we left in the hallway.

"Daddy, that's a bad word," my nephew says.

"Sorry, buddy," my brother says. "You're right."

I rub a hand over my face. "Linc, please go downstairs. I'll come join you in a minute."

"I'm sorry about that. Don't take too long, I have to take Micah to school."

"You didn't have to come over."

"You were MIA. It's unlike you. You should've warned me, that way I wouldn't have showed up unannounced. Sue me for caring."

I rub my hands over my face. "Wait for me downstairs."

"Got it," my brother says. "Come on, champ, Uncle Levi has to conceal the evidence." The amusement in Linc's voice is unmistakable.

"What does that mean, Daddy?"

"You'll understand when you're an adult, son."

I shake my head.

"Good morning, Uncle Levi."

"Hey, Micah, I'll be right out."

"Daddy bought you muffins from your favorite bakery. He says I can't have one until you do. I *really, really* want one, Uncle Levi. Can you hurry?"

I try hard not to laugh.

"You were supposed to keep that between us, buddy," my brother says.

"Oh," Micah says. "Forget I said anything, Uncle Levi."

This time, I can't hold back my laughter.

Linc clears his throat. "We'll wait downstairs."

"I didn't mean what I said, Uncle Levi. You don't have to hurry."

I put the little guy out of his misery. "I'll be right out, Micah."

"I already know which muffin I'll have."

"Message received loud and clear," I say.

He giggles.

"It's a family affair?" Jules says in a low voice.

She looks terrified.

I cup her beautiful face in my hands, and kiss her lips. "It's not."

"Your brother knows you're not alone," she says.

"I'm okay with that, Jules."

"What is he going to think of me when I try to sneak out of here?"

"You're not sneaking out."

"Fine. I'll wait here for your brother to leave." She crosses her arms under her naked chest, lifting her tits in a tempting way.

Focus.

"You don't get it," I say.

Confusion tugs her eyebrows together.

"You're not my dirty little secret, Jules."

A rosy shade of pink blooms on her cheeks.

"This isn't how I was going to introduce you to my brother, but hey"—I shrug—"it is what it is."

"You want to introduce me to your brother?"

"You're my girl."

She blinks.

She blinks again.

"You're a part of my life now," I say.

She takes a deep breath and blows it out. "This is still so

new..." There's a thread of uncertainty in her voice that gives me pause.

She's right. This is new. I'm out of practice and, true to form, I'm putting the pedal to the metal.

I place a finger under her chin and tilt her head up. "So?"

She bites her lower lip. She's considering. "So nothing, I guess."

"Good." Taking her hands into mine, I bring them to my lips and drop a soft kiss. "I have an extra toothbrush you can use and you can borrow one of my t-shirts. Let's get freshened up, then we'll go meet the family."

The smile on her face speaks of relief. "Okay. I'd like that."

We walk hand in hand down the stairs.

My t-shirt swallows her, and her long hair is piled up in a messy bun on the top of her head. Her beautiful face is devoid of any makeup. She radiates. If it weren't for my brother's unplanned visit, I would be balls deep inside her right now.

I curse under my breath, shaking my head.

"What?"

"Nothing."

She frowns, but doesn't press.

When we reach the threshold to my kitchen, she squeezes my hand tight.

I squeeze back, reassuring her.

She responds with a crooked smile.

Here goes nothing.

Linc is busying himself with the espresso machine. Micah is sitting at the kitchen island, his iPad clenched in his little hands, his attention laser focused on whatever he's watching.

Linc got sole custody of the nine-month-old Micah. It took a DNA test to confirm Micah was his son. His bitch of a wife wasn't sure. She'd been cheating behind my brother's back for a little over a year, fucking not one, but two different men without condoms.

"Good morning, guys," I say.

Micah lifts his head up, greeting me with a beaming smile. "Good morning, Uncle Levi."

"Someone got a haircut."

"I got one yesterday afternoon before soccer." He brushes a hand over his sandy blond hair. "I wanted to let it grow, but Daddy said it was getting too long."

"It looks good," I say.

He beams, grinning wide at me.

His big blue eyes shift to the woman standing next to me.

"Good morning," he says. "What's your name?"

"Good morning. My name is Jules."

Micah drops his iPad on the counter, jumps off the high stool, and rushes towards us. He's all decked out in his school uniform.

He assesses Jules with a critical eye, scanning her up and down. He spends a little too much time fixated on her dainty toes, painted in an orangey coral shade.

He meets her gaze and waves. "Hi, Jules. My name is Micah Alexander Aldridge. And I'm six. And it's Micah. Just Micah. Not Michael."

"My name is Jules Madeleine Salinger." My girl plays along. "And I'm twenty-three. And it's Jules. Just Jules. Not Julie."

"That's funny." Micah giggles. "You said the same thing I did."

"I like the way you introduced yourself," Jules says.

"I like you," Micah says.

She laughs.

He giggles.

"That's my daddy." Micah points behind him. "His name is Linc Aldridge. And it's Linc. Just Linc. Not Lincoln. He's older than you. He's older than Uncle Levi, too."

Micah only recently became particular about names to stand up to a name-bully at his school. After hearing my brother's name when a parent called him out, this kid made fun of Linc's name, stating only lazy—or dumb——people gave their kids a nickname instead of a proper name.

Jules laughs. "Good morning, Linc."

"Good morning, Jules," my brother says. "It's a pleasure to meet you." He crosses the kitchen with a hand extended.

Jules takes it in a two-handed handshake.

He towers over her. Barefoot, she barely reaches his chest.

At six-four, Linc has two inches on me.

"You're drop-dead gorgeous." The words fall out of my brother's mouth, surprising us all.

"She's *really* pretty." My nephew nods. He's staring up at her, grinning from ear to ear, his eyes twinkling with delight.

"Thank you," Jules says in a shy voice.

"No wonder my brother forgot I existed last night." Linc's eyes bounce from hers to mine. "Let it be known, I would've been in the same boat." His words drip with admiration.

Well, that was easy. He's camp Jules.

"Oh... um... I don't know how to respond to that," Jules says.

"You don't have to." Linc's attention shifts to me.

It's subtle, but one eyebrow crawls up.

Watching him process the information is oddly touching and quite amusing. I don't have to give him a long, drawn-out explanation. If Jules spent the night at my place, and I'm introducing her, it's more than a passing fling.

"Did you have a sleepover with my uncle, Jules?" Micah breaks the silence.

"Something like that, buddy," I say.

Jules's wide eyes snap up to mine.

I wink at her.

"Oh." Micah nods. "I see." He turns to my brother. "Daddy, I want to have sleepovers with girls."

"You have to wait until you're your uncle's age," Linc says.

"But that means I have to wait a long, long time," my nephew says.

"Micah." My brother frowns.

"Okay, I'll wait a long, long time," he says.

I chuckle.

Linc shakes his head.

Jules still looks like she stopped breathing.

I rub a comforting hand up and down her arm, coaxing her to relax.

"Hey, Linc, how long do you have before you have to take Micah to school?"

"Since he got up well before his wake-up call, I figured we'd get ready early and spend some time with you. I have half an hour before I have to hit the road."

"Good." I nod. "That's enough time for you to get to know my girlfriend."

Linc's eyes widen.

"I want a girlfriend who does sleepovers, too." Micah pushes a small fist in the air.

We laugh—even my blushing girlfriend.

Chapter 23

Levi

My to-do list was already bulging, but the addition of the Thonix line of products is making my head spin. The last three days have been a whirlwind of meetings, conference calls, video calls, and brainstorming sessions.

Since there's so much to do and so little time, Jules cajoled her dad's former assistant to come work for us. Alice Blanchard was one of the last three people still holding the fort until Hillary opened her bitchy fucking mouth. Once we quashed any insecurity around her paycheck, Alice signed the new employment contract.

I'm glad she did.

The woman is a machine. Our deadlines are aggressive. A newbie wouldn't be able to keep up.

When Linc surprised us with his early morning visit, there wasn't much time to go into the nitty-gritty details surrounding my new business venture with my girl over breakfast. He invited Jules and me to his place that same night. Once Micah was tucked in bed and sound asleep, we filled him in over a nice bottle of red and more dessert. I was expecting my brother to be polite and wait until it was just two of us to chew me up for my brash decision. To my surprise, Linc was blown away. In fact, he congratulated me for jumping in with both feet. Like Shane and Collin, he believes Jules is sitting on a gold mine. She was floored all over again.

So now, it's all systems go.

It's going to be a fine juggling act spearheading two businesses, but sometimes in life, you have to burn the candle from both ends.

After spending a morning with Jules and Alice, we spent the afternoon with her dad's lawyers. By the end of the week, all her former employees—including the Twatts—will receive a reminder to keep their mouths shut. Then, we were off to meet with her accountants. Tomorrow, we're meeting with my lawyers to create a new business structure with the Dennison brothers. Thank God, we secured a kickass coder for the app. The other thing that can make or break the launch of our crowdfunding program and the Fit Thonix VIP 100 Club, is marketing. It's imperative for the rapid growth of the business. Buying TV spots would be prohibitive. And I don't think it's a gamble that would pay off. Social media is more within reach. The key is to produce an entertaining video that gets shared over and over again.

My phone rings.

It's like telepathy.

I snatch it from my desk, eagerness bubbling inside me. "Hey, Dom, I was just thinking of you."

"Hey, Levi," she says. "I'm sorry I'm only now calling you back." I called her at nine o'clock this morning. "I had to finish editing a video to meet a deadline."

"Don't worry about it. I got back to the office not long ago. Had you called earlier, I wouldn't have been able to talk to you. Your timing is perfect."

"Good. Word has it you're wearing a lot of hats these days," she says.

"How did you hear that?"

"Collin dropped by Rod's studio yesterday as we were wrapping things up, and the three of us went for drinks."

I chuckle. "Collin is so excited."

"He is. He couldn't stop talking about the CycleThonix bike that's going to revolutionize the way people work out at home."

"I hate to say this, but I have to agree with Collin. Once we figure out the technology, there's no stopping us from being industry leaders."

"So, it's true? You're going into business with Collin Dennison?"

"*And* Shane."

"Yeah, but Shane is the sane, levelheaded one. It makes sense you'd want to join forces with him. Collin, on the other hand, is a loose cannon." She laughs.

I join her.

"It's a façade, Dom."

"I don't buy it." The amusement in her voice is audible.

"Collin is a great businessman. He brought some incredible ideas to the table. He's one hundred percent invested. He has name recognition and a face—and body—women love. Along with Jules—the CEO—and Shane, he'll be a great representative for the brand."

"What about you? Are you going to be representing your brand?"

"You know me, Dom. I'm more of a behind-the-scenes kind of guy. It's a professional hazard."

"Good one." She laughs. "From what Collin describes, this sounds like quite the project."

"It is. You'd think I didn't already have enough on my plate."

"No rest for the wicked."

"Something like that."

"I got an earful from Collin, but tell me more about the bike and how I can help."

I start from the theme party night at Dark Compulsion. Dom isn't a member, but she knows what happens there.

"One illicit night that turns into more," she says when I finish giving her the rundown.

"Much more."

"Wow, Levi. That's... a big step for you."

"Businesswise and relationship wise."

"You've been reluctant..."

"To get involved long term with a woman after Annmarie's tragic death. Yes. Yes, I have. But I want a relationship with Jules."

"Congratulations, Levi," she says. "Contrary to your buddies, you don't view relationships as a death sentence."

That's a loaded statement. "Are you talking about my buddies in general or one in particular?"

"I plead the fifth."

Rod and Dom have been best friends since they were teenagers. They're stuck in a friend zone status quo that expired a long time ago. They're just too blind to see what the rest of us see. *Fools.*

"Let's go back to the reason I called you." I veer the conversation. "Video is the way to go to promote these bikes—"

"Collin alluded to that last night."

Collin and his big mouth.

"I'm kind of partial to video, so I thought it was a good idea."

"Collin wasn't supposed to let the cat out of the bag—"

"We're talking about Collin Dennison here."

"True. At least he held back and didn't divulge everything."

"What do you mean, Levi?"

"We'd like to hire you as our video producer."

Silence greets me on the other end.

"Dom?"

"I'm still here," she says. "I shoot music videos. I don't think I'm the right person for the job."

"I could hire a company that specializes in infomercials, but we're not selling a get-fit-quick-for-only-twenty-nine-ninety-nine-when-you-order-today type of product."

She laughs.

"We're going after a specific audience, willing and able to dish out a small fortune for exercise equipment. I don't think a rah-rah video is going to cut it. We need something slick and memorable... hence why we're knocking at your door."

She lets out a loud sigh.

"Was that a yes or no?"

Dominika's boundless creativity is exactly what we need to kickstart this project.

"It would be challenging in a good way to step outside of my box," she says. "I'd have to look at my schedule, but I'm sure I can find a spot for you."

"That's great news, Dom."

"I must say, Levi, this project sounds intriguing."

"Wait until you see the equipment. You're going to be blown away."

"I have a question."

"I'm all ears."

"Not that I have any experience, but if I'm not mistaken, crowdfunding campaigns can be tricky."

"Those campaigns require a certain level of expertise or else it can be an epic fail."

"Is Jules going to manage your campaign?"

"No. Shane was able to convince one of his former tech clients—who leveraged crowdfunding to kickstart his last venture, which he sold for several billions of dollars—to help us out. The guy is now retired at the tender age of thirty-five and living in Ibiza. He'll manage the whole thing for us. It just so happens he's in LA, visiting family. He wanted to check out the bikes. He's on board. In fact, instead of a fee, he wants a cut of the profits. He's so certain, he's even agreed to take care of the marketing for the first six months."

Her head jerks back.

"It's wild, Dom. When a guy at that level wants a piece of the action, you know it's good."

"It's damn good."

Jules was convinced by my positive outlook of her business. She was excited by the Dennison brothers' reaction. She was beside herself by Linc's verdict. But Shane's guy put dollar signs in her eyes. It's sinking in. As long as Hillary doesn't change her mind and decide to keep her shares, it should be smooth sailing.

Chapter 24

Jules

I'm high on the euphoria of the last two weeks.

Not long ago, Levi Aldridge was a stranger. Now, he's my boyfriend and one of my incredible business partners. As much as I'd love to spend my days and nights wrapped in his arms, I can't. In between our hot fuck sessions, I have a business to run. He has two. Speaking of my sexy boyfriend and formidable lover extraordinaire, he's been in New York for the past four days. Our nightly video chats pale in comparison to being with him—even if they're dirty as fuck. And, sure, I'm tickled pink by his daily text messages reminding me I'm his filthy girl and he's thinking about me, but I long to kiss his lips. He should be landing at LAX any minute now.

Thank God.

I'm not ashamed to admit, I miss him like crazy—far more than I expected. I'm counting the minutes until I see him. I have so many indecent thoughts in my mind, and I can't wait to get him all to myself. A wave of desire prickles through me, pooling in my belly.

God, I'm addicted to the man.

Since our first meeting in my conference room, it's been two weeks of brutal work. Thank God Alice agreed to come back. I wouldn't have been able to do it without her. That's what happens when you're well connected. My three business partners tapped into their circles to secure the experts we need to see the crowdfunding through. I have wings knowing I'll be able to do Daddy's memory justice.

The expertise of Shane's consultant is mind-blowing. There's no way I would've been able to hire someone with that kind of pedigree. Things are moving so fast, it gives me whiplash. Working side-by-side with these savvy businessmen is a huge eye-opener. For the longest time, it was just me. Now, I understand why it always felt like I was walking in quicksand. The constant doom and gloom voice that was my only companion is quiet. Not being around Hillary also helps a lot.

After a quick bathroom break, I trail back from the small kitchen to the conference room, latte in one hand, a large peanut butter cookie in the other, singing a happy tune in my head. Since I scarfed down my lunch, I take a few minutes to enjoy my coffee and indulge in the sugary treat. Once I get my sugar and caffeine high, I get back to work.

So little time, so much to do.

I'm immersed in my work when a key slides into the door.

I told Alice not to come in on weekends.

"Oh, yoo-hoo, Jules," an annoying voice singsongs.

Hillary?

"Your car is in the parking lot."

God. What does she want?

I do a double take when she appears.

She's a redhead now?

Hillary's hair is eerily similar to the Jack-o'-lantern

pumpkin bucket kids use to go trick-or-treating on Halloween. The color is nowhere near Sydney's beautiful shade or sexy salon shades I've seen other women sport.

"Oh, there you are," she says, stopping in front of the conference room. "Working hard?"

Her voice sets me on edge.

"You came to check up on me?" I purse my lips. "I'm touched."

Even though it's Saturday and it's as hot as Hades outside, Hillary is decked out in a head-to-toe neon green pantsuit. The sheer blouse she's wearing is in the same screaming shade. So is her bra. The in-your-face color against her red hair is jarring.

What the hell?

She comes and stands in front of me, hovering over me like a witch about to pounce. She curls her lips up in a smug smirk. "Some of us have lives, Jules," she says. "While you're slaving, wasting your youth, the duke and I are attending a yacht party in Marina del Rey. This"—she waves her finger up and down the length of her body—"is designer. A gift from my boyfriend. I even got my hair done for the occasion. Being a blonde in LA is *so* cliché."

Which is why you spend an exorbitant amount at the salon to get Olive and Petula's hair dyed every six weeks like clockwork?

She smooths down her flame-colored hair, a smug smirk perking her lips. "This hair color is much more New York, and the duke says I look much better as a redhead."

Eye roll.

"It makes me stand out and gives me an air of sophistication."

The duke doesn't grasp the meaning of sophistication.

"Do you want me to organize a ticker-tape parade?"

She glares at me.

The tension between us is suffocating.

I have my issues with Hillary, but I still struggle to understand what my father saw in this woman. Her only redeeming quality is she'd beg, steal, and die for her daughters. However, I doubt she ever cared about my father. And from what I've observed since his passing, I'm certain she never loved him. Daddy was a kindhearted man who was lonely when Hillary came crashing into his life. The thing is, Daddy didn't fall in love easily, and once he did, love is blind, as they say. Hillary used that to her advantage. Until his last breath, he was oblivious to her faults.

"That won't be necessary," she says, checking her manicure. "I thought I'd stop by to talk about the next steps. Given it's Saturday, I knew I'd find you here."

"What do you want?" I bother to hide my annoyance.

"You've been ignoring my text messages and calls all week."

"I've been busy. Remember, you gave me an ultimatum."

"Yes, and that's why I'm here. I'm glad you came to your senses about the house." My jaw clenches. "I might not get much out of it once we sell it, but at least it'll be lunch money for when I move to New York."

Condescending bitch.

"It's so important to be seen at the right restaurants."

Blah, blah, blah.

Hillary wanted to work with a real estate agent she knows. I put my foot down. Levi found me someone he trusts. That's good enough for me. Hillary was fuming, but in the end, her greed won over. She's desperate for her half of the money.

"Have you found a way to buy out my shares from this sinking business?" She straights her shoulders and adjusts her blazer.

God, that color is offensive to the eye.

I stare down at my clasped fingers as a foreign emotion seizes me—rebellion. "Hillary, I have two weeks left." I meet her gaze. "So, calm the hell down."

Her expression shifts to amusement. "You know, it would be much easier if you left me the house. Your half can make up for my shares in this company."

I shake my head. "Not going to happen. My father left me half of the house. It's mine. Not yours. In fact, that other half should've never been yours to begin with."

Her hand curls into a fist and she draws in a harsh breath. "Grudges are petty and immature, Jules," she says. "I'm Hamilton's widow"—I don't need the reminder—"therefore, I'm entitled to half of the house. Not much you can do about it now."

I glower at her.

"It's so convenient how Daddy is sometimes your husband and sometimes he's the guy you leeched."

"Where are you going to find that kind of money in only two weeks?" She ignores my snide comment.

"As long as I come up with it, why do you care?"

Levi and I have talked about this at length.

Hillary is oblivious to everything that's transpired in the last two weeks, and we're determined to keep it that way. If she catches wind of our progress, I'm doomed.

"Did business pic up all of a sudden?" She looks around the conference room before letting out a demented laugh. "Oh, God," she says, clenching her stomach. "That was a funny joke."

Bitch.

"Business is still a flatline... as always."

Fuck off.

"Unless you win at the lottery, there's no way you're going

to come up with the money. Instead of wasting everyone's time, give me your half of the house and let's call it a day."

Over my dead body.

I shoot to my feet, anchoring my splayed hands against the conference room table, because God knows if I don't, I'm liable to slap this woman across the face. "Keep dreaming."

An evil smirk slides across her lips, and her gaze sharpens on me, slivers of disdain darting back at me. "Cut the act. You're on borrowed time. We both know it."

"This isn't an act, Hillary. I'm as serious as a heart attack. You've taken enough from my father *and* from me. I'm not handing you my half of the house." I have to coax myself to keep my boiling rage in check. "You're going to get your share of the company. I. Will. Buy. You. Out."

Since meeting Levi, I silenced the straight and narrow girl inside me, and a new woman emerged in her place. Daring, brazen, and willing to embrace her sexuality. It's the same for business. Now that I know what I have in the palm of my hand, nothing this despicable woman says can affect me. I'm ready to fight for what's mine.

She crosses her arms over her chest, lifting her chin. The gesture drips with disdain. "You may act like a tough girl, but I won't hesitate to sue you—"

"You can take your empty threats and stuff them where the sun don't shine."

Hillary's overdrawn eyebrows shoot to her forehead like elevated apostrophes, her dark brown eyes widening like saucers. For a few beats, she stares at me in shock. It doesn't look like she's breathing. I swear, she's turned into a living statue.

"You have no ground to stand on." I keep talking. "We're selling the house. And, at the risk of sounding like a broken record, my time isn't up yet. You'll get your money. Now, if you're done wasting my fucking time, I'd like to get back to work."

She considers me for a long stretch, her eyes sliding up and down my body, as if it's the first time she sees me.

That's right, bitch, take a look at the new me.

She pulls the strap of her obscenely expensive designer bag—a gift from the duke, I'm sure. "Well... I thought we could have a civilized conversation, but I was wrong."

Lady, you're wrong about a lot of things.

I glare at her.

"This was a courtesy reminder, Jules."

"We both know you're lying. You came here to rub my face in it."

A second ticks by.

Then another.

And another.

We're staring at each other like two bulls in a ring.

"I'm starting an exciting, new chapter of my life, Jules." Her eyes scan the room before landing on me. "You're stuck here."

I cross my arms over my chest, mirroring her defensive stance. "I'm okay with that."

"Good luck with your pathetic life," she says.

"Let's see how long it takes before the duke gets tired of you and your whiny, ungrateful daughters."

Her lips pinch.

She drops the set of keys to the office on the table. "I won't need these anymore."

"That's one thing we can agree on."

With that, she turns on her heel, exiting the conference room in a puff of sickly-green rage.

My exasperated sigh chases after her as she barrels down the hallway before storming out of the building. Her stomping footsteps come to a halt, and then the door slams shut, leaving me alone.

Buh-bye, bitch.

Hillary expected her sudden—and spiteful—life-altering decision to sink me. It only made me stronger. I, Jules Salinger, am a survivor, and I'm no longer alone. For the first time in a long time, I don't feel defeated.

Chapter 25

Levi

We were supposed to have dinner first. I dropped by Zia Josefina's on the way back from LAX and selected Jules's favorites. Those plans went up in smoke the second I opened the door and laid eyes on her. She looked like a fucking vision in her white maxi dress. I couldn't resist. I all but dragged her by the hair to my bedroom to fuck her senseless. After two steamy rounds, we stuffed our faces silly with succulent Italian food. Now, we're chilling in the backyard, contemplating the beautiful night. We're on the outdoor couch under the gazebo. It's made of a wooden frame, a steel slope roof and tempered glass. It's a bit of an extravagance, but the success of our company has allowed me the luxury of buying a house on McKinley Avenue in Venice—an upscale and coveted Los Angeles neighborhood. My brother doesn't live too far. It's a far cry from the modest home we grew up in.

I'm proud of this house, but I'm mostly proud of the backyard, which I had designed as my little getaway. In our business, the hours can be punishing. The expansive pool, lush greenery, pit fire and full outdoor entertainment area make up for it.

I'm lounging in nothing but a pair of shorts. I didn't bother with a t-shirt. Jules's sexy body is adorned in nothing but the black shirt I was wearing when she arrived at my place. Her pretty white dress was a liability around tomato sauce. Her head is rested on my lap as I caress her long blonde hair, both of us admiring a dark sky dotted with twinkling stars.

"It's probably because I'm always in such a rush when I'm in New York—my days are so crammed—but I never notice the stars," I say. "Here, in LA, I do. I'm glad to be home."

"I'm glad you're home too," she smiles up at me, her fingers walking about my abs.

My eyes travel the length of her bare legs before meeting her gaze. "You say that because I made you come three times."

She swats my stomach. "Hey."

I wink.

"I hope one day I'll be able to visit New York," she says, changing the subject. "I've never been."

"Our little project is going to do so well, you won't have a choice but to travel to New York to promote the hell out of the Fit Thonix line of products."

Her eyes sparkle with wonder. "Oh, I love the way you think."

"It's in the cards, baby."

She smiles before pulling her lower lip between her teeth. She does that when she teeters between belief and disbelief.

"Everywhere I turned, I could see dollar signs—so many possibilities. I predict, we'll have a billboard in Times Square or outside Penn Station within a year." Even though I was in New York for the business I share with Linc, our venture was always at the back of my mind.

"You're crazy, Levi. It must cost a fortune to get a billboard ad anywhere in New York, let alone Times Square."

"It does. The cost is prohibitive. I checked. Within a year we'll be able to afford it. If all goes better than planned, then we might cut that timeline in half."

"You're shitting me?"

I shake my head.

"In no time, we assembled a dream team—you, Alice, Collin, Shane, Shane's venture capitalist former consultant, Dominika, and yours truly. Everything is falling into place. There's nothing stopping us from dreaming big, Jules. Really big."

Her long, dark eyelashes blink a mile a minute, her mouth gaping open.

"It's a lot to take in?"

"I was thrilled by the prospect of getting into the black and not having to dodge creditors all the time. What you're talking about isn't even on my radar." For a few beats, it seems like she's having a conversation with herself. "But now, it is. New York City, hear me roar." She lifts her hand into a fist over her head.

"You're stepping into your boss lady role."

"I am and I like it."

"You're sexy when you're bossy." A hint of red touches her cheeks. "I didn't know boss ladies blushed."

"Well, this one does," she says, squirming in her seat.

"I got some good news on the ride back from the airport."

"Do tell."

"The leasing agent called. One of the warehouses we visited last week in Culver City has free space. It's the one that has a glass door and a large glass paneled window that looks like it's a garage—"

"Oh, the light-gray building with the window decorated with funky wrought iron bars?"

I nod.

"That building is perfect. What a treat to have an office space in a safer neighborhood. I won't have to look over my shoulder anymore when I leave the office."

That's one of the reasons I was so eager for us to get started with the search. Jules's current office isn't located in the most crime-infested neighborhood in Los Angeles, but lately it's been going downhill. Jules has been taking defense classes for a year now and she carries a can of mace anytime she leaves the office at night, but it's not enough to deter an asshole looking to do her harm.

"It's a decent size space to store one hundred bikes plus the prototypes, with plenty of room to grow," I say.

"This is so exciting." She claps.

"It's like killing two birds with one stone. You can have your workspace at the front, near the windows. It's spacious enough to fit a small, growing team comfortably. You can move in the first of next month."

She shakes her head. "I can't."

"Why not?"

"I gave my thirty-day notice at the current office, but I still have six weeks to go."

"You'll tell your landlord you're leaving in two weeks," I say. "I'll cover next month. You don't want to miss out on this kind of opportunity. Finding space in Culver City is like looking for a needle in a haystack. Not to mention, it's going to be challenging if you're in another neighborhood and I have to drive back and forth between the two locations. At least this way, you're close by."

"You're my guardian angel, Levi Aldridge." She smiles up at me.

I tap the tip of her nose. "Things are lining up in your favor, sweetness."

"I'm buzzing with excitment," she says. "Speaking of things lining up for me, guess who paid me a visit today?"

"Hillary?" I say.

"How did you know?"

The glee of malice shining bright in her eyes was a dead giveaway.

"She leaves you God knows how many messages every day, looking for update," I say. "I guess she got impatient."

"She did. And she was pretty vocal about it."

"Hillary loves to run her mouth."

"And she gave her mouth a good workout today."

I give Jules a onceover. "Since I don't see any scratch marks, I assume you were the one left standing."

"Damn right."

"She's itching to know how you'll come up with the money to buy her out?"

"Right again." She smiles. "You're good at this game."

"Hillary Twatt is predictable."

She nods. "I put her back in her place."

"This, I have to hear."

Jules shares the highlights of her meeting with her money hungry stepmother.

"That woman is a piece of work," I say when Jules finishes.

"On a happy note, she's still clueless about our plans."

"Good."

"She left her keys behind right before vamoosing on her broom."

I laugh. "The imagery... especially in that hideous color suit."

"You weren't the one forced to stare at it." Jules's body quivers, her face contorting in disgust. "The only positive outcome from that meeting is she can't wait to be done with me."

"Two weeks from now, this woman will be an unpleasant, but distant memory."

"I'm counting the days," Jules says. "There was something nagging at me about our altercation, though."

"What?"

"It became blatantly clear Hillary's ultimate plan was to cheat me out of what was rightfully mine."

"What do you mean?"

"She gave me an impossible deadline. Shy of a miracle, she knew I wouldn't be able to come up with the money to buy her out within thirty days. She was counting on that. She was going to sue me to get the half of the house that's mine. Without you, I would've ended up with nothing."

"What a piece of shit," I say. "That's what a lowlife like her would do."

"After she left my office, I was consumed by our conversation, replaying it in my head over and over again. There was something about her reaction that caused me to pause. She seemed upset I'd found a way out of this thorny situation—"

"How dare she talk about what your father and mother worked hard to acquire as lunch money."

"Belittling me and making me feel inferior are her favorite pastimes," she says. "This time, it didn't work. Instead, I saw red when she spat those words in my face."

"You're a saint for not slapping her."

"Trust me. I really wanted to, but I didn't want to give her any more ammunition. I'm sure she'd sue me like this." She snaps her fingers together.

"Good for you for keeping a cool head."

"She didn't make it easy. She kept pushing my buttons, but I didn't give my wicked stepmother the upper hand." She lets out a dramatic sigh. "The only sad thing about all of this is I'll never be able to see the expression of mortification on her face when everyone—and their grandmother—starts talking about the kickass CycleThonix bikes. I wonder what she'll have to say about, and I quote, *The useless piece of metal shit your loser of a father wasted years tinkering with.*"

"Even if you never witness it, the day will come when she's forced to eat her words," I say. "She's walking away on the eve of a major turnabout." A diabolical smile stretches my lips. "It's going to hurt like a motherfucker when realization hits her right smack between the eyes."

Jules laughs.

I snatch the bottle of champagne from the ice bucket. "Let's drink to that."

She leans forward to grab her flute.

I fill her glass, then mine.

I lift my flute. "Here's to the end of your forced partnership with Ms. Hillary Twatt."

She does the same. "Hear, hear!"

We chill out for a few long minutes in a comfortable silence, listening to the stillness of the night, while sipping on our champagne. From time to time, she eyes me from over the rim of her glass.

"What are you dying to ask me?" I drop my flute on the table.

She mimics me.

"I still can't believe you bought champagne," she says. "I would've been happy with wine."

"We have a lot to celebrate."

She frowns her confusion. "You only found out about the warehouse on your way back to your place and you didn't know about Hillary, yet you brought this bottle of champagne with you from New York. What am I missing?"

"A crazy thought took root in my head when I landed in New York, and I haven't been able to shake it off."

She shoots me a suspicious side gaze. "I'm afraid to ask."

It was only a fleeting thought when I left LA. Five hours and twenty-three minutes of flight later, and I couldn't shake it off, no matter how much I told myself I was nuts.

"Why's that?"

"Because every time you open your mouth, you rock my world."

"Oh yeah?"

"You know you do."

"Come here," I reach out for her, lift her and drop her on my lap so she's straddling my thighs.

I bring my hands to her face, resting my palms on her cheeks, forcing her attention on me. *God, those hazel-green eyes.* "You're so fucking beautiful, Jules... and you're mine." I growl.

Her eyes are enormous.

"What aren't you telling me, Levi?"

"Relax."

Untrusting eyes stare back at me.

"It's nothing bad," I say.

"Okay." She offers a slow nod. "Why do you look all serious all of a sudden?" Her fingers trace a line along my stubbled jaw.

"Move in with me." The words come flying out of my mouth. I was planning on delivering my message with more finesse, but my impatience won over.

Jules's hand tenses on my skin and her jaw drops.

Myriad emotions flash back at me.

"Wh—what?"

"I said, move in with me."

She swallows a breath. "We've only been dating for three weeks."

I didn't want to admit to myself how strong Jules's power

was over me. I couldn't bring it into words, but with each passing hour in New York, it became clear words weren't as important as action.

My fingers walk along her arm. "The deeper I get in with you, the harder it is to get out."

She blinks.

"But here's the thing. I'm not itching to get out. I want more, Jules."

She stares at me

"Talk to me, Jules."

Her eyes close, not giving me a response.

Shit.

Am I moving too fast? "This isn't the reaction I expected."

Her eyes pop open and she looks bewildered. "I didn't see that coming." Her voice drops to a hush. "I—" She cuts herself off and shakes her head.

"Finish that sentence."

"I never thought you could feel this way about me."

"Believe it, Jules. Fuck the house-sitting agency and fuck finding a storage locker for your belongings. It's a waste of time. I want you here with me. I don't want to be driving all over LA to see you at night and I don't want you bouncing from my place to someone else's."

"Wow."

"Is that a good wow?"

She nods.

"Good."

"I can't get enough of this"—she gestures a finger—"of us. It's like I'm addicted to you, Levi."

My heart threatens to bloom out of my chest. "It's the same for me."

We exchange a warm smile.

"You still haven't answered me," I say. "Are you going to move in with me?"

She reaches out and combs her fingers through my hair. "That's a big ask." There's a hint of amusement in her expression.

"It is. Do I get an answer?"

Her hands latch onto my face, gripping me with force. "I want to move in with you. I want to be here with you."

I expect a feeling of sheer terror to seize me, but it doesn't. All I feel is certainty. I'm taking a huge leap. And everything about this feels right.

I crush my mouth to hers, letting the warmth of the night envelop us. The world seems to sway when my tongue slips into her greedy mouth. Kissing didn't ever arouse me until her. Her hand curls, grabbing a fist of hair at the base of my neck, pulling me closer to her.

Goddammit.

We allow free rein to our passion for several long beats until she starts gyrating her hips back and forth, gliding her naked pussy against my growing bulge, coating me with her dripping juices.

She picks up the pace and her breaths quicken.

My brain stops working.

My cock throbs, threatening mutiny. It's like I didn't fuck her before dinner.

I pull her away from me. "I want dessert now."

"Oh." She looks confused. And vulnerable. And needy.

A trio of emotions that fans the flames of pleasure inside me.

My lustful gaze lingers for a few long breaths on her. "I'm talking about your pussy, silly."

I don't know what I expected as a response, but certainly not this.

Jules undoes the buttons on my shirt, exposing her gorgeous body.

I arch a brow. "What's going on here?"

"You said you wanted dessert... feast on this," she says.

"My filthy girl wants me to fuck her right here?" My fingertips dancing over the exposed skin of her neck.

She moans, sending tingles of desire dancing through my balls.

"What if we get caught?"

"I won't remove the shirt," she says. "It's so huge on me, it'll hide any... wrongdoing."

I can't help grinning at her. "You're playing with fire, little one."

The truth is, with the trees, shrubs and tall gate surrounding my property, it's unlikely we'll bother the neighbors. As long as we keep quiet, no one will know.

Her lips part in a sensual smile as she lifts off my lap. She makes quick work of lowering my shorts before grabbing my hard cock. She lines it at her entrance and impales me.

I groan. "Oh, God."

"I'm okay throwing dignity out the window," she says, wrapping her arms around my neck and pulling herself closer.

We both groan as she lowers herself, swallowing every inch of my cock.

My eyes meet her heavy gaze. "You're going to ride me until I come."

She bows her back so her chest presses to mine, her hard nipples scratching my chest as they brush against me.

Jesus Christ.

I swallow a moan before sliding my fingers into her hair and pulling tight. "You heard me?"

"I intend on doing just that," she says with a wry smile.

With a groan, I claim her mouth and stroke my thumb over her clit.

Sucking in a deep breath, her head lolls back, breaking our kiss.

She starts moving her body up and down my solid cock.

There are no words to describe the incredible sensation—

I grip her hips hard, halting all movement. "Shit! Condoms!"

She looks at me bewildered.

"I'm clean," she says.

"Me too. We have to get tested regularly to maintain our membership at Dark Compulsion."

"We don't need a condom, then."

I consider her.

"You're sure?"

She silences me with an all-consuming kiss.

"Fuck the condom," I say against her lips.

We begin to move together in perfect harmony.

Her cadence is almost timid.

I catch her a good one on the ass. "Ride me like you mean it."

I don't have to ask twice.

I grab her by the waist, slamming her body against mine. "Harder."

She yelps in surprise.

Soon, she takes over.

Up and down.

Up and down.

With no barrier between us, I have the staying power of a teenage boy.

I gasp, my fingers flexing against her bare ass as she rides me like I'm a thoroughbred. "Jules— This— Shit— I— I'm—"

I can't even think straight.

"Not yet," she says. "Not yet. I need to feel you inside me a little longer."

I groan my frustration. "You're killing me."

She responds by riding me harder. Faster. Like a woman possessed.

I try to contain the straining climax, but I'm fighting a losing battle.

"Oh, fuck. Fuck. Fuck. Fuck," she chants.

Her pussy clenches hard around my cock.

I grunt.

She's close.

And so am I.

Her pace is frantic.

She's practically bouncing off my balls.

A primal, aching cry spills from her throat as her orgasm hits.

Her pussy pulses, gripping my cock, even as she writhes on top of me, and I can't hold back any longer.

I'm done.

My body tenses and my hips buck and my beautiful girl cries out as I spurt hot cum inside her.

My orgasm is so strong, I'm seeing damn stars as her pussy still clenches my cock, milking everything I have to give.

Goddammit.

"My God." She falls into my arms.

I rest my forehead to hers as we both draw in long breaths, our hearts pounding together as one. "You okay?"

She nods.

"Good." My hands clasp her hips, holding her still as she tries to move. "I just need a second..."

"For what?"

"Another round."

"Excuse me?"

I flash her a wicked grin. "Fucking you without a barrier is fucking incredible."

"God, I created a monster."

"A monster that serves you well," I say. "You unleashed the beast inside me. I get to fuck my hot girlfriend bare and outdoors. You better believe one round isn't enough. I only need a moment to recover before I'm locked and loaded again."

Chapter 26

Jules

Sydney and I are on a video call, and judging from the sparkle of excitement in her eyes, she's as giddy as I am.

"Oh my God, your new office is amazing. Love, love, love the wrought iron on the large window." A hand waves all over the place. "When I'm not working in the boonies, we're totally going to have to savor a bottle of expensive champagne at my place. A French charcuterie board and a French dessert board are a must."

I couldn't wait to show her my new space, but since her and Austin are trapped working on the landscape of a ritzy estate located near El Matador Beach, this is the next best thing. I just stepped back into the building. So far, I've only showed her the exterior, and she's already jumping for joy. I can't blame her.

"Champagne and fancy food boards? Isn't that a bit much?"

She shakes her head, a strand of red hair falling in her eye. She brushes it behind her ear. "You're stepping into the big league. We have to up the celebrations."

"I have to be honest though, I'm still a little nervous, Syd. Fingers crossed everything goes better than planned."

This space is far more expensive than the other location, and since Levi is footing the bill for now, there's a lot of pressure.

"It will," she says. "Your father left you something precious. It was just a question of finding *the right* business partner... I guess in your case I should say, partners."

"And kicking the old useless partner to the curb."

A devilish grin curls her lips. "It's about time you no longer have to carry that monkey on your back—I mean, I'm so happy you no longer have any financial ties to Hillary Twatt and her bratty offspring."

"Free at last, free at last, thank God, I never have to see that woman ever again." I raise my hand, waving over my head as if I'm in the front pew at church, praising the Lord.

We laugh.

"Bravo for keeping Hillary guessing—and stressing—by not wiring the money to buy her out until the last hour," Syd says.

"My boyfriend came up with that devious plan."

"He's a keeper."

"Damn right."

We laugh again.

Levi was right. With the help of a home staging company— they removed Hillary's fake masterpieces from the walls—and a few cosmetic touchups here and there, we were able to sell the house in a blink of an eye. Once the bank was paid on the second mortgage, Hillary and I split the rest. After the bank took their share, there wasn't much left for me. I'm okay with that because I don't have to see Hillary ever again. The landlord to the old office space was happy to get paid, even though we had vacated the space.

"New boyfriend. New partners. New zip codes for your home and your business. You're on a roll," Sydney says.

"I never dreamed of living in Venice Beach. As for Culver City, it's such a departure from the old location. That area was heading south fast. I'm glad to be out of there."

"Thank God for Levi," she says.

"Thank God for Levi."

That man is my lifeline.

"Austin is going to kill me if I extend my break too long. Even with the team we hired for this colossal job, we have so much to do. But there's no way can I go back to work until you finish the tour."

I love her enthusiasm.

"Check out the rest of office." I move my phone around the workspace to give her a panoramic view.

"It's a good size."

"Let me show you the warehouse." I navigate through my new office with my phone extended in front of me. You got to love technology. "It's a bit of a mess, but you get an idea," I say, turning the phone around so we're looking at each other. I frown. *Shit.*

"Is everything okay?"

"My battery is running low," I say. "I have to plug it when I end this call."

"I have to go soon, anyway. But not before saying this... You're too hard on yourself. You moved in yesterday. You have one hundred bikes, and God knows what else to unpack and organize. I can imagine the mountain of bubble wrap you'll end up with."

Alice and I spent all afternoon yesterday and today unpacking, but it seems we haven't made a dent. Since she was on the verge of exhaustion, I sent her home. Levi is meeting with a vendor for drinks and dinner tonight, so instead of waiting for him in his huge house, I decided to keep at it. Speaking of huge house, we've been living together for two weeks now. He would scold me for calling it *his* house as opposed to *our* house. I still can't wrap my head around it. I had a moment of hysterical deafness when he suggested the crazy idea because he was moving at lightspeed. In the end, I'm thrilled I accepted his offer. I doubt I'll call it *our* house anytime soon, but waking up in his arms is a dream come true.

"There's no time to waste," I say. "I have two weeks to get this place in tiptop shape *and* hire a handful of new employees before I have to devote all my time to the crowdfunding campaign."

"You can't wait to crack the whip, huh?" Syd winks.

"I have a lot of deadlines to meet."

"You, my friend, are sounding like a boss lady."

I toss my hair with a dramatic flair, owning the title.

We dissolve into giggles.

"On a serious note," Syd says, "we're being silly and juvenile, but I can't tell you what it means to me to see you smile again. You haven't sounded this lighthearted in so long, I almost forgot the sound of your laughter." Her words tug at my heart.

I go from elation to sadness, as the weight of the last nine and a half months washes over me. "It's been a long road out of hell."

"But look at you, rising from the ashes."

"I never thought the day would come where I would stop stressing over Dad's business. Gone are my constant anxiety attacks. I knew it was never Daddy's intention, but there was so much out of my control."

"And here you are fighting back like the heavyweight champion of the world."

"Yeah, I'm still throwing the punches," I say. "In a little

over a month since bumping into Levi, I've had to pinch myself daily to make sure I wasn't sleepwalking."

"This is as real as it gets."

I nod, emotions making it hard to speak.

"I only have a few more minutes left on the clock, babe." Sydney breaks the silence. "Before I go, show me what I'm supposed to transform into a little oasis."

"Good idea." With quick steps, I cross the office, enter the warehouse and head to the back of the building. I exit and walk the short distance to a patch of land attached to the building. "I was hoping to create a cool little seating area with greenery over here for my mighty team," I say before turning my phone.

"Move your phone from left to right so I get a better view."

I do as I'm told.

"That's totally doable," she says. "That shouldn't take more than a weekend of work with a small crew."

I turn my phone so we're looking at each other. "Really?"

"Yup! I'll come by to scope things out first. Trust me, I'll make it super nice for you and your employees."

"You're the best, Syd."

"You deserve this, Jules," she says. "Okay, I have to go. Thanks for the virtual tour."

"Talk to you later." I blow her kisses through the phone.

She does the same.

I end the call.

"I should also get back to work."

I tuck my phone into my back pocket and return to the warehouse.

An hour later and I'm sitting in a cloud of bubble wrap. I managed to unpack three steppers and two treadmills. After giving them a good wipe, I moved the equipment to the side so they're no longer in the middle of the space.

Yay me.

"I need a break. And a boost of energy," I grumble to myself as I admire my work. Famished and desperate to stretch my legs, I dust off my jeans and head to the tiny kitchen to wash my hands. I open the fridge and laugh. Other than the bottles of natural energy drink Alice bought, it's pretty bare. I grab a bottle, crack it open, and take a sip.

Crap. I didn't charge my phone.

I drop the bottle on the counter and head to the warehouse. It takes forever to find the stupid thing under all the bubble wrap.

"There you are." I sigh in frustration, holding my phone up in victory.

I head to my office to fetch my cord.

Pop. Pop. Pop.

I stop dead in my tracks.

Pop. Pop. Pop.

A violent sound assaults my ears, causing me to drop my phone. I try to catch it before it hits the cement floor, but it's in vain.

Fuck.

Tires screech against the asphalt.

Engines gunning angrily.

What the hell is going on outside?

A loud bang follows, suggesting two vehicles colliding into each other.

An accident?

Voices echo in the distance.

The shouting match is frightening.

Pop. Pop. Pop.

I was so preoccupied with saving my phone, it's only now it registers.

Gunshots?

An explosion of shattering glass follows.

I jump in fright.

My heart is beating at the same infernal rate as my temples.

Just when I think it can't get worse, it does.

The deafening cracking sound of gunshots pierces through the night and it makes me scream.

Culver City is supposed to be a safe neighborhood.

What the hell?

Fearing I've drawn attention to myself, I drop to the floor and clamp both hands over my mouth.

Oh my God, oh my God, oh my God.

My life flashes in front of my eyes and I can only think of the man I love.

Levi.

I love him.

What a moment to have an epiphany.

It takes this for me to see the light?

What follows can only be described as a rainfall of gunshots.

Holy shit, I'm going to die.

I'm going to fucking die.

My body trembles from the anxiety rushing through my veins, adrenaline twisting my gut.

The shooting seems to last an eternity then, everything stops.

The night is as quiet as it was several minutes ago, before the nightmare started.

Is it over?

I need to call for help.

I need to get out of here.

I reach out for my cracked phone. I try to power it, but it's a lost cause.

Fuck. Fuck. Fuck.

I asked the phone company to transfer the old office's

number to my phone until we buy corded phones, which Alice planned on doing tomorrow. So right now, I'm screwed.

Panicked, I belly-crawl, tears streaming down my face.

I need to turn the lights off. I don't know who's out there, and I sure as hell don't want them to know I'm in here. They have guns. I don't.

Fuck, I'm shaking like a leaf.

Once the office is immersed in darkness, I crawl to safety, praying to God and all the saints up above.

Chapter 27

Levi

After a promising meeting with vendors vying for our business, I'm standing in front of the Quintus Hotel, waiting for the valet to bring my car. I'm wearing multiple hats these days, but tonight's meeting was all about the stage production businesses. Linc is on daddy duty, so it's just me. When my white Porsche Carrera approaches, I can't help but grin. Going back home to my girl is my favorite time of day. We've had a few rocky moments adjusting to each other, but overall, asking her to move in with me is the best decision I've made in a long time. The valet hands me the keys to my car. I'm about to slip behind the wheel, when my phone rings.

"Hey, Linc," I say, answering the call. "Calling to find out how the meeting went?"

"No." I expect him to elaborate, but he doesn't.

"Linc?"

"I'm heading to the studio."

I frown at the phone. "Everyone is versed on what they're supposed to do, and if anyone has questions, Stephen is there to answer them. He's the supervisor on duty tonight—"

"Stephen called in a panic—"

"Why?"

The guy is unflappable even under the most stressful deadlines.

My brother lets out a long sigh. If I didn't know better, I'd say it was a long-suffering sigh. The team must've hit a wall.

"Levi, there's been a shooting—"

"At the studio?"

"No. Somewhere in Culver City. The neighborhood is under police lockdown."

My heart sinks. "What the fuck are you talking about, Linc?"

"I didn't waste time gathering details. After Stephen called, I jumped into my car, drove Micah to Dad's place and now I'm gunning down the streets towards the studio, praying the cops don't stop me. I tried calling Jules... I can't get hold of her."

Thank God I insisted on them exchanging numbers. Other than Sydney, Austin, and me, Jules doesn't have anyone in her camp.

"Wh—what?"

"Stephen is pretty freaked out. So is the rest of the team. I thought for sure Jules would still be working since she just moved in—"

"She's at the office. She texted me after she sent Alice home to let me know she was sticking around for another couple of hours."

"Why isn't she picking up, then?"

"Jesus." I rub my hand over my face. "I'm on my way."

"I'm sure she's safe, Levi," Linc says.

I'm surprised I can hear anything over the blood hammering in my ears. "You don't fucking know that."

"Whoa, little brother," he says. "I understand where you're

coming from—trust me, I do—but you losing your shit isn't going to help anyone."

"I'm going to go find Jules." I ignore his comment. "Keep me posted on what transpires at the studio."

I end the call.

Fuck. Fuck. Fuck.

I flashback to the day Annmarie's tearful dad called me. His words wouldn't come at first, but I knew from his broken voice it was pretty bad. I died a little that day when he told me what happened to my girl and our unborn child. And I died a little when Dad received the call letting us know Mom had been stabbed in the heart.

I can't go through this again. I might not recover.

"Is everything okay, sir?"

I stare at the valet, a little lost.

"I'm not sure," I say.

It's only when I look around, I remember where I am.

"I can hail you a chauffeured car and take care of your car," he says.

Mortification must be written all over my face for him to suggest that.

I'm just about to open my mouth to thank him and tell him not to bother, but think better of it.

"Yes, please."

During the drive to Culver City, I call Jules numerous times. Each time, it goes straight to voicemail. As worry takes root in the pit of my stomach, I turn to Google for answers. Other than a smattering of amateur videos posted by passersby on news sites, this is still a developing story. One thing is certain, there was a shooting. And fatalities.

Fuck.

This is my worst nightmare. The thing I feared the most, and the reason I've avoided a relationship for so long. With each passing mile, bile rises in my throat. The beat of my heart, keeping time with the pounding in my head.

As the Benz zooms down LA's streets, I flash back to the last two weeks with my girl.

I grab hold of my shirt, fisting it as if it's enough to contain the pain.

This cannot be happening to me again.

I can't lose another woman I love.

I bring a hand to my throat.

I can't breathe.

My phone pings, forcing me back to the moment.

It's a text from Linc.

> **LINC**
>
> FYI – everything is barricaded. Police everywhere. I had to park a few blocks from the studio and walk the rest of the way. You might have to do the same.

> **LEVI**
>
> I left my car at the Quintus Hotel. I'm in a chauffeured car.

> **LINC**
>
> Smart. I'm too far. From what I can see, whatever happened wasn't around our studio.

> **LEVI**
>
> Everybody is safe, then?

> **LINC**
>
> No shakeups around here. Okay, I just got to our studio. I'm going inside. Text me when you connect with Jules.

If she's still alive.

I hate that's the first thought that surges.

When I don't answer, he sends another message.

LINC

Text me **when** you connect with Jules.

The addition of stars doesn't go unnoticed.

I know what he's saying.

When. Not if.

I repeat the mantra in my head over and over again before responding.

LEVI

I will.

LINC

Catch you later.

As I close the app, my eyes lift to the action ahead.

Linc wasn't joking.

Even with the warning, I'm baffled by what I see. Swirling blue and white lights slice the sky.

What the hell?

An army of police forms a wall, blocking the area. Ambulances are standing by. It's a chilling scene straight out of a crime drama TV show. There are a few passersby, but not many. It's no surprise at this late time.

I dial Jules again.

Still nothing.

Shit.

A cop directs the chauffeur, forcing us to make a right.

Fuck.

The detour is excruciating, and I curse under my breath. We inch down a street lined with cars. The police presence is more prominent as we approach the area where Jules's office is located. The garlands of yellow and black police tape paint a disturbing picture.

What in God's name happened?

There's no crime free zone in LA, but Culver City isn't subject to this level of anarchy.

Goddammit.

I need to get to her.

"This is taking way too long," I say to the driver. "At this rate, we'll never get there." My impatience boils over.

"I'm sorry, sir."

"This isn't your fault," I say. "It'll be faster if I walk."

"Are you sure?"

"Yes."

I drop a wad of cash on the passenger seat and get out of the car. I hurry, dialing Jules one more time.

Dread grips my throat, as fear sets in my heart when she doesn't answer. Again.

As I make my way to her warehouse, I take in the scene surrounding me, baffled. Two cars are fused together. One of them rear-ended the other, full force. The one with all the bullet holes looks like a cheese grater. There's shattered glass everywhere. And then there's the pool of blood. It's gruesome.

I avert my gaze when two EMTs pushing a stretcher pass me by. It's carrying what I can only assume is a dead body, covered with a bloody sheet.

Dear God.

I pick up my pace.

"You, over there!"

I glance in the direction of the voice that yelled at me.

"This area is restricted," a cop says.

"My girlfriend is in there."

"You have a hearing problem? I said, this area is restricted.

Unless you have a business in the area, you need to keep walking."

He just handed me my opening.

I approach him.

"As a matter of fact, I do. Our office is located right over there." I point.

"I'll need to see some ID and proof."

I pull out my driver's license and pull up a copy of the leasing agreement on my phone, showing my name and Jules's. I hand both to the officer.

He inspects them.

Hurry up, hurry up, hurry up.

He hands them back.

I place them in my wallet. "What happened?"

"I'm not at liberty to say," the cop says. "It's still under investigation."

"Can I go to my office now and check on my girlfriend?"

"You're sure she isn't over there." The police officer points to a group of people huddled not too far. "A bunch of people came rushing out after the incident."

I search the small grouping.

"No, I don't see her."

He nods. "Make it quick. We're going from building to building. We want to keep the area clear and we're searching for witnesses."

"I understand."

I run as fast as my legs can carry me.

This is a fairly isolated part of Culver City at night, since the buildings surrounding us are all old warehouses converted into offices and studios. The sophisticated security system and cameras were huge selling features to the building we leased. Considering the value of our high-end exercise equipment, it's a must. I thought we had all our bases covered in preventing any possible theft. I never thought we'd need protection against the carnage I just witnessed.

When I reach Jules's office, my panic kicks up several notches.

A quick inspection of the building fills me with dread.

Some of the windows are shattered.

The sight snaps my heart into two.

Please, God, no.

Then it hits me.

I left the set of keys to her office at my studio. I didn't think I'd need them tonight.

Panic assails me all over again. My airway cuts off and I stare at the doorknob, helpless. I jam my fingers through my hair and pull hard. My mind races as I hurry through my options. My blood pressure roars in my ears, right along with the alarming sirens telling me to get inside this goddamn office by any means necessary because Jules needs me. She could be injured, or worse...

Shit. Shit. Shit.

Something slams against the recesses of my stomach, and if it wasn't for my desperate need to make sure my girl is alive, I'd allow my fear to paralyze me. Snapping out of it, I search the area for a blunt object, but I'm out of luck.

Fuck.

A cocktail of fear, worry, and adrenaline make my head swim, but determination to get to my girl pushes me into action. I lift my foot and kick to the side of the doorknob, putting everything I have into it.

Nothing.

So much for testing the security. It works.

In my frustration, I grab the handle, ready to shake the hell out of it. When I do, it twists.

She didn't even lock it?

Jesus Christ.

She must've been too consumed with cleaning and organizing to even remember.

Goddammit.

With shaky hands, I push the door open and tiptoe inside.

I'm not a gun owner, but right now, I wish I were.

It's pitch black.

Going by memory alone, I tap along the wall until I find a light switch and flick it on.

My weary eyes adjust to the light.

On a frantic breath, I search the space.

There isn't a trace of my girlfriend anywhere.

"Jules?" I run from one office to the other.

No answer.

My feet carry me to the kitchen, my heart racing.

It's empty.

"Jules, where the hell are you?"

The storage room door cracks open, and she pokes her head out. She looks like a frightened little lamb. Seeing her sews my heart back together, a piece of her inside. I've never felt such relief in my life.

"Jules." I hold my arms out and she comes crashing into me.

She's crying so hard, I barely recognize her gorgeous face.

There's so much I want to tell her, but not now.

I grip my hands around her shoulders and practically shake the hell out of her, demanding an explanation, "What happened? Are you okay? Did someone hurt you?"

Her hazel-green eyes aren't the color I love. They're enormous and dark.

"Are you okay, Jules?"

She can't talk. She's too emotional.

I lift my eyes and search for the enemy.

It's just the two of us.

She's shaking in my arms.

"Take your time," I say.

She wriggles out of my grasp and slams into me. She's holding on to me so tightly, it's almost impossible to breathe.

"I'm here, sweetness. You have nothing to fear. I'll protect you no matter what," I say. "Tell me what happened."

"I— I—" She hiccups.

I don't rush her.

She clings even harder to me. "I was so scared I was going to die and never see you again."

Her words freeze my heart.

Chapter 28

Jules

It's a little past two in the morning by the time we walk into Levi's house. LAPD detectives wanted to question me before I was allowed to leave. Since I was inside the warehouse, I didn't see anything, but the gunshots and the pool of blood tell a horrific story. As I was waiting to be dismissed, I overheard someone mention something about rival gangs settling a score. Someone else speculated two MC clubs were going at it. Either way, guns were involved and people died. Given the area, it's surprising Culver City would turn into a war zone, but then again, violence knows no boundaries.

After giving my statement, and once the EMTs made sure I was okay, we walked to Levi's studio. My boyfriend's older brother was wearing an anxious expression on his handsome face when he saw us. I was taken aback by the way he crushed me in his big arms, hugging the hell out of me. I was a little confused at first by his intense reaction, then it hit me. He lost his mom and his almost sister-in-law to a violent crime.

"I'm too wired to sleep," Levi says. "Do you want a drink?"

He heads to the bar cart in the living room. "I need one," he says before I have a chance to answer.

"I do too."

"Wine?"

I shake my head. "Something stronger."

"Vodka and tonic on ice?"

I nod.

"Are you hungry?"

"I am," I say. "I haven't eaten anything since lunch."

"I'll reheat the leftover pizza from last night."

"That sounds good."

"Go change into something clean and I'll take care of the drinks."

"Okay."

I turn to leave, but stop.

It's on the tip of my tongue to say, but I hesitate.

Levi cocks his head to the side when I remain rooted in silence. "What is it?"

I bite my lower lip.

"Jules," he says.

I plaster a warm expression on my face so as not to give away the turmoil inside. "Thank you for everything."

So much has transpired tonight. So many emotions. The last thing I want is for him to run away screaming if I use the L word.

"You're mine," he says, his eyes like pools of blue ink. "I take care of you."

God, those words are like a cyclone, causing an intense experience throughout my body, bordering on electrifying.

He approaches me.

"Are we clear on that?"

I offer a shy smile. "We are."

"Now, go," he says.

I run up to his room—*our room*—to change and run back down.

As I reach the last step, a crashing sound has me jumping out of my skin.

I yell, my hands flying to my beating heart.

"Levi, are you okay?" I rush to the living room.

He's standing there, the pieces of a broken bottle of vodka shattered at his feet, his eyes closed, a hand gripping his chest.

His face is as white as a ghost, and the beads of sweat dotting his forehead are quite telling.

So is his labored breath.

Oh, no.

Since Daddy's death, I've dealt with enough bouts of extreme fear to recognize the signs.

I approach him and place a hand on his arm.

"Levi." My voice comes out in a whisper.

He opens his eyes.

He fixes his eyes on me, but it's as if he doesn't see me.

"Are you having a panic attack?"

He offers a small nod.

"Breathe," I say.

He lets out a single breath.

Then another.

And another.

It takes a few long seconds, but after a few beats, he regulates his breathing.

He reaches out for me, stepping on the broken glass.

He cups my face in his hands, boring his eyes into mine.

He doesn't say a word.

"Let's go sit," I say.

He nods.

I guide him to the couch.

He sits next to me.

He drops his elbows against his knees and stares at the space between his parted legs.

"Talk to me," I say.

Giving Linc's reaction earlier, I have a feeling I know what this is about, but I'd rather he tells me.

"Fuck," he says on the heel of a loud exhale. "I suppressed the bad memories as much as I could to make sure you were safe, but it's like the dam broke open while you were upstairs and it hit me all at once. I could've lost you tonight... like I lost Mom, Annmarie, and my unborn child." His gaze meets mine. "That would've been too much to bear."

His heavy words hang in the room.

My heart aches for him. "But you didn't." I caress his cheek with the back of my hand. "I'm here with you."

He takes my hand in his and kisses it. "Thank God."

A moment of silence passes between us.

"Something happened to me while there was a war raging outside the building," I say.

His eyes widen in panic. "You told me were okay. You even told the EMTs—"

"I'm okay, baby."

His gaze is skeptical. "You're sure?"

"Yes. I mean, something happened here." I tap two fingers against my heart.

He frowns his confusion.

I was debating whether to take the plunge or not, but to hell with it. I don't want to hold back anymore.

"Before this terrifying experience, I'm not sure I would've had the courage to be this brave. Levi..."

I exhale a shaky breath.

Okay, maybe I'm still a little scared.

His hand searches for mine, locates it, and tugs, prompting me. "What is it?"

"I love you." The confession comes flying out of my mouth. "I know this is crazy and we've only been together for five weeks and if you don't feel the same way—"

"I fucking love you."

"You do?"

He lifts me from the couch and drops me on his lap.

I straddle his legs.

"I love you," he says. "It hit me on the way to your office. Life is too short not to tell you."

I let out an enormous sigh of relief that shifts into amazement.

"Oh my God, I can't believe this. You feel the same way I do?"

"Believe it," he says.

His confession echoes in my ears, sending me soaring like an eagle.

Holy. Fucking. Shit.

He loves me.

Unimaginable pleasure bursts through me like a geyser of pure happiness.

"I foolishly hoped you would feel the same way, but hearing you say it—"

Levi silences me with a kiss.

When his mouth takes mine, it steals all the air from my lungs. His hand cups the back of my neck, to hold me better as his lips own mine, igniting blinding desire between us.

Fuck. He can kiss.

I'm woozy.

Nah. I'm drunk on this man.

He breaks our embrace.

"You ruined kissing any other man," I say.

"It's a good thing because there's no way in hell another man will ever kiss those lips."

My mega grin matches his. "I'm okay with that."

"Dinner and drinks can wait." His mouth carving a path along my jaw. "I need to feast on your heavenly body—one inch at a time."

He stands up with me wrapped around him like a koala bear.

I never want to let go of this man.

"I love you, Jules." He peppers kisses all over my face. "You're my whole world."

"I love you too, Levi." My voice catches over the words, and I give in to the intense elation taking over me.

Being with Levi feels like the missing piece of my soul I've been searching for has slotted into place.

Chapter 29

Levi

Since sealing the deal on our partnership, things have been fast and furious. We've been moving at breakneck speed in the last couple of weeks. We had so many things to knock off our never-ending to-do list leading to this monumental day. The long hours and intense work made it that much easier to put that scary night behind us. It took Jules a few days to recover. The rumors were true. That tragic, fatal night—when I thought I almost lost another woman I love—started as a bad case of road rage on San Diego Freeway and escalated when two rival gangs decided to use Culver City as a war zone to settle a score. All I know is, it was too close to home.

So here we are at Rod's studio, shooting our first promotional video we'll use for Fit Thonix's crowdfunding.

Dominika's small studio is annexed to Rod's, but she shoots videos here because it's fully equipped. Linc and I created a kickass set, complete with large screen TVs that showcase the results from pre-recorded simulated rides. As I suspected, fixing the tech glitch preventing the screens on the bikes from properly connecting with the app was child's play for a top coder. Our guy delivered in spades. Now, you can have a virtual ride with one or multiple riding partners—up to five in total. Dom hired three model-actors—two women and one guy. She had a specific concept in mind—six bikes placed in a triangle formation. Jules, Shane, and Collin rotated on the first bike throughout the shoot.

Rod and I are standing to the side, a little removed from the set. Dom dismissed the three models a half hour ago, but she wanted a few extra shots with my business partners.

"Watching her work, is something else," I say.

"It is," Rod says, his eyes never leaving Dom. "I could watch her all day long."

"Something about the way you said that..."

His eyes lock onto mine.

I cock an eyebrow.

He responds in kind.

I open my mouth to say something, but his gaze moves away from mine.

What the hell?

"And... cut!" Dominika shouts, peeking out from behind the camera. "We did it, gang." Her hands lift in victory.

"It's a wrap, people!" Dom's 1st Assistant Director's booming voice resonates throughout the studio.

I meet Dom's gaze. "We got it?"

"The sixth take was the charm." She smiles, her blue eyes sparkling.

"That's what I'm talking about," Shane says.

"I can't believe we're done," Jules says.

"We got the *'money shot'*," Dom says, a wide smile stretching her lips.

Jules returns her smile. "Thank you so much, Dom."

"My pleasure," Dom says.

"You're the best," Jules says.

"Yes. She. Is." Rod draws out the words.

All eyes are on him.

"What?" He shrugs. "It's true."

He's acting strange today, as if he lost his favorite puppy.

"Watch out world, here comes Fit Thonix." Jules leaps off her bike and comes running to me, her excitement boils over.

I wrap her in my arms, kissing the top of her head.

"For the record, I brought my A-game from the very first take," Collin says, getting off his bike.

No, he's not vain.

Rod shakes his head.

"Yes, Mr. Peacock, we know you can do no wrong." Shane takes a jab at his brother as he dismounts from his bike.

"I'm a professional," Collin says.

Shane narrows his at his brother. "And we're not?"

"That's debatable." Collin offers a shit-eating grin.

"The first take was great, Collin." Dom whips her long hair behind her back. "But you look even better in the last round. The angle showcases your ripped muscles and your ink to perfection."

Dom knows how to stroke the ego of the finickiest prima donnas.

Collin flexes a bicep.

The man has no shame.

"You're sure it was a good idea to go into business with him?" Rod jerks his thumb in our friend's direction.

"Sometimes I wonder." I play along. "But it's too late now. We're stuck with him."

Rod swings his gaze to Jules. "What about you?"

She laughs. "I plead the fifth."

"Good girl." I chuckle.

"You guys get off easy," Shane says, walking our way. "You don't share a last name."

"Hey, I'm still in the room," Collin says. "I can hear you guys."

"That's the whole point, Dennison," Rod says.

We laugh.

In the past month Cocky Collin has been an outstanding brand ambassador, using his Hollywood contacts to open doors for us. When he suggested throwing a fancy Hollywood party to introduce the concept early in the game to a few of his 'friends' instead of waiting, we jumped at the opportunity. Before the end of the star-studded evening held at his mansion last Saturday night, the first one hundred bikes were sold.

The next day, the internet was flooded with photos of celebrities posing with one of the three prototype bikes we had set up. Our hashtag is still trending.

Fueled by the demand and the media frenzy, we invested in another one hundred bikes—all made in the great US of A. We're cutting it close, but the bikes will be ready within the next three weeks. Forking out extra money for the enormous fee to expedite the process, will pay off.

"I may be a little anal, but I want this video to springboard the Fit Thonix brand and piggyback on the buzz you kick-started last weekend," Dom says.

"I'm teasing," Collin says. "I'm sure you'll make *me* look good."

"You're such a fucking conceited asshole," Shane says. "You couldn't stop while you were ahead. It always has to be about you."

Collin shrugs.

With all his faults, you can't help but love the guy.

"Like always, you nailed it, Dom," Rod says, changing the subject.

"Thank you." Dom tucks a strand of jet-black hair behind her ear.

A moment passes between them.

"I'm going to change," Jules says.

I give her a onceover. "Fingers crossed our new branded fitness gear flies off the shelves."

She smiles up at me. "They'll be big sellers. I know they will."

"I want to buy all the outfits Jules wore on set today," Dom says.

Jules grins wide. "See, we have our first client."

I tap the tip of her nose. "You're right, boss lady. Go get changed."

"We're going to do the same," Shane says. "We're still up for drinks?" His eyes bounce to each one of us.

"We're celebrating, so, yeah, we're all up for drinks." Collin is the first to respond.

"I thought I'd get a few hours of editing in while all these ideas are floating in my head," Dom says.

"No, you're not." Rod's response is quick, his tone unwavering.

Dom's brows shoot up. "Excuse me?"

"You're part of the team, Dom. You have to come out and celebrate."

"And... you're part of the team, how?"

"I own the damn studio, and Levi invited me," Rod says.

"Right." Dom nods.

There's a loaded conversation going on between these two we're not privy to.

Truth be told, Rod doesn't need to be here.

Dom is a professional. So is her crew. I'm pretty sure Rod has other things to do than to hang out on set. Yet, he's been hovering like a mother hen all day long.

"You've been working late for the past couple of weeks," Rod says. "Let's hang out tonight and have some fun."

She cocks an eyebrow.

"Come on, Dom."

She considers Rod.

For a few beats, they stare at each other, as if they were the only two people in the room.

Jules and I exchange a look.

Shane and Collin do the same before shifting their attention to me.

I shrug.

Lately, Dom and Rod have been hot or cold. There doesn't seem to be a middle ground.

Chapter 30

Jules

I stifle a yawn as I reach for my mug. It's only eight o'clock in the morning but this is my second latte since I got to the office. I'm a little tired after last night. What was supposed to be casual drinks, turned into a celebration when Jace and Beckett showed up at the studio. They received a text message from a proud Collin. Since Rod's business partner Loki returned from a meeting while we were still debating where to go, we invited him to tag along. Rod invited his brother Roark to hang out with us because he's certain he's a potential customer. In the end, the group was getting so large—and rowdy—Shane decided to have a huge cookout at his place. He insisted I invite Sydney and Austin.

It was ridiculous.

Great food, great wine, and incredible company. I've known Austin for a long time and I've never seen him starstruck. Then again, Random Misconception is one of his all-time favorite rock bands. Being around Rod, Jace, and Beckett was a little over the top for a longtime fan.

When we got back to Levi's house, he had another type of

celebration in mind. As if he hadn't fucked me ten ways to Sunday, Levi woke up this morning with a raging hard-on I just had to take care of. Now, I'm paying the price.

My life is going so well, it's unreal.

I drop my cup on the saucer, determined to shake off my sleepiness and power through my to-do list. This is the final stretch leading to the big day. I knew going into it, planning a crowdfunding campaign is hard work. I didn't expect it would be this demanding. Thank God for Shane's contact. No wonder Joseph Crane is a billionaire many times over.

The doorbell rings.

"I'll get it!" Alice's heels clack against the floor as she rushes towards the door.

Since my lapse in judgment on the night of the shooting, we triple check to make sure the front door and the back door are locked at all times.

"I'm sorry, Jules."

I shift my eyes from my laptop to Alice standing at my door. The expression on her face is unreadable, but if her fidgeting fingers are anything to go by, I'm not going to like what she has to say.

My eyebrows knit together. "What is it?"

She tucks a strand of highlighted hair behind her ear, shifting from one foot to the other. "A man in a suit, standing at the door—looking official and quite standoffish—says it's personal and I should get you."

"Okay." I get up. "Let's go find out what he wants."

I trail behind Alice to the door.

The man in question is standing outside, his back facing the building.

I open the door. "Good morning,"

He turns to face me.

"Good morning," the tall bald man says, whipping his sunglasses off his face. "Jules Salinger?"

Alice is right, he looks official.

"Yes, that's me."

He pulls an envelope from the inside of his suit jacket and hands it to me. "Miss Salinger, you've been served."

My stomach bottoms out.

"Wh—What? What do you mean I've been served?"

"It's all in there." His eyes drop to the envelope.

With that, he's gone.

"Wait—"

"My job here is done, Miss Salinger." He slips behind the wheel of a black Ford SUV and drives off, not even bothering giving me a second glance.

I close the door and turn around, my jaw still sweeping the floor, disorienting thoughts floating in my mind.

"You've been served?" Alice shrieks.

"Apparently."

"Who would sue you?"

"Beats me, but we're about to find out."

With shaky hands, I open the envelope, my mind racing, trying to figure out who I might've pissed off or wronged.

My head jerks back upon reading the first few lines.

What in the actual fuck?

My bewildered eyes drop to the next two paragraphs.

"You've got to be kidding me," I say.

"Who's suing you?"

I'm too shocked to answer.

My eyes scan the papers I'm holding.

Rage simmers inside my belly as I read the legal document. By the time I flip to the second page, I'm as worked up as a volcano ready to blow.

I meet Alice's gaze. "Hillary. That's who's suing me."

"What? Why?"

"The stupid bitch thinks I duped her."

"That woman needs to up her medication or get her head checked," Alice says. "I swear, she's mental."

"More like, greedy," I say. "I need to speak to my former stepmother."

"Give her hell," Alice says.

"Trust me, I will."

I stomp to my office, cursing along the way.

I slam the door shut so hard, I'm surprised the glass doesn't shatter. I snatch my phone from the desk and dial Hillary.

"Jules—"

"What the fuck is your problem, lady? Didn't you suck enough from my father?"

"You're just a dumb blonde, playing boss, pretending to know shit," she says. "Let me school you. You know nothing about nothing. If you did, you'd understand once you've been served, all communication goes through our lawyers."

With that, she hangs up.

Anger ripples across my skin like a bush fire. "Fucking bitch!"

It takes everything in me not to hurl my phone across the room.

Chapter 31

Levi

A month later

My eyes stretch out to the horizon, soaking in the majestic view. Even though the ocean is within reach, sometimes you have to leave Los Angeles to appreciate its beauty. And there's no better place than perched on top of the deck of the gorgeous Catalina Island house I rented for the next three days. I take a sip of my coffee, smiling around the rim of the cup.

This will be a hell of an extended weekend.

I move my eyes from the blue ocean to the iPad, re-reading the screaming headlines.

'FIT THONIX: THE CROWDFUNDING SUCCESS STORY OF THE YEAR'

'FIT THONIX BREAKS CROWDFUNDING RECORDS'

'CYCLETHONIX REDEFINES HOME FITNESS'

'CYCLETHONIX MERGES GAMING AND FITNESS TO CREATE THE ULTIMATE HOME WORKOUT'

'BYPASS THE GYM MEMBERSHIP: GET A CYCLETHONIX INSTEAD'

The list of glorious accolades goes on.

Three days later, and the press is still buzzing.

So is my head.

The excitement and high from our big day linger on.

My feet haven't touched the ground yet, and I doubt they will for a very long time.

When we all gathered at Jules's office and huddled inside the conference room, we were confident we had a stellar product. After all, my girl, Alice, Collin, Shane, and myself worked our butts off. Not to mention, one hundred high profile celebrities had snatched up our first batch of bikes. So many had done a spectacular job at being honorary brand ambassadors, fanning interest among their followers. Still, we didn't expect the crowdfunding campaign to take off like a rocket launching into space.

Joseph Crane didn't disappoint.

We watched, shocked, as the second lot of one hundred bikes sold in the blink of an eye. Collin's idea for the Fit Thonix VIP 100 Club knocked it out of the park. People were practically fighting over each other to secure spots at the different levels. It was wild. The comments were hilarious to read. But right in the middle of the crowdfunding frenzy, our website crashed. The site wasn't hacked or anything like that. People who couldn't get into the VIP Club were placing pre-orders at a mind-boggling rate. To our surprise, we have a large number of international orders. We didn't account for that. That's going to require a little extra legwork, but we're all up for the challenge. The six of us—including Alice and Joseph—lived at Jules's office to respond to the overwhelming demand. Even with the extra temp staff we hired, it wasn't enough manpower.

When things somewhat calmed down, I whisked my girlfriend away for a little break. Shane, Collin, and Alice are holding the fort. I considered a seven-day getaway in a tropical destination, but Fit Thonix is on fire. And, I have another company to run. I can't afford to be away from LA that long.

"Good morning," a sleepy voice says.

I lift my eyes from the iPad.

"Good morning, sweetness." I smile as my girl steps onto the deck.

I chuckle when my eyes land on the slogan across her chest. *'DON'T FUCK WITH THE BOSS LADY'* Her morning hair completes the look. When I saw those nightshirts online, I couldn't resist. I bought her one in every color. It's not only fitting for her new position, but it's also a fuck you to Hillary.

Jules saunters over to me, rubbing the sleep from her eyes.

I circle my arms around her waist, pulling her close.

I place a soft kiss between her breasts.

She giggles and places one on the top my head.

"Do you want breakfast?"

"In a minute. I need some vitamin D first," she says, pulling away from my embrace. She sits across from me, closes her eyes and salutes the sun. "Why did you let me sleep so late?" Her eyes still closed.

"It's only nine o'clock," I say. "That's hardly late. You've been working like a dog."

"I guess my body is still wired to get up before the crack of dawn."

"As the CEO of a successful multimillion-dollar business, poised to become a *multibillion*-dollar business in record time, you should be allowed to sleep in while you're on your mini vacation."

Her eyes pop open.

"So, we'll both be billionaires." She smiles wide.

"Seems like it." I return her grin. "Although, we won't be the only ones."

"No way we'll forget the Dennison brothers. They were my lifeline."

"Hey, what about me?" I feign being vexed.

She reaches for my hand. "You've been my knight in shining armor since day one."

"I can live with that."

"I guess this whole billionaire thing is old news for you," Jules says.

I frown.

"You're a paper billionaire, Mr. Early Investor."

"True." I laugh. "I'll enjoy every cent of the buyout money Gage's people will transfer to my bank account, but becoming a billionaire through our sweat equity will be so much more satisfying."

We stare at each other for a beat, a goofy smile spreading our lips.

"We did it." She shakes her head. That's been her go-to phrase every time realization hits. "It wasn't all a dream, right?"

"It's a dream all right, but we're fully awake." I wink.

"I know I sound like a broken record. Thanks for humoring me."

"That's what I'm here for."

We exchange a warm smile.

Within forty-eight hours of kicking off the crowdfunding campaign, we had sold a whopping twelve thousand bikes at four thousand dollars a pop. If the momentum keeps up, we'll be on track to double that many orders within the next two weeks. Joseph says we have everything required to become a unicorn—a start-up that goes from zero to billion dollars in sales rapidly. In Jules's case, she was deep in the red before I came onto the scene, making the turnaround even more noteworthy. This time around, Linc was in a position to invest. At this rate, Micah's *grandkids* will be set for life. Life is good.

"A couple months ago, I was certain I was going to end up bankrupt and homeless—"

"Look at you now."

"Look at me now," she says. "I can't believe how much money we made in a matter of days."

"It's all about having the right partners."

"We're a pretty kickass dream team."

"I won't argue with you. Joseph is so excited by how well things turned out, he'll stick around in LA for another couple of months to help before going back into retirement in Ibiza. He texted me this morning."

"God, that man knows a thing or two about making a boat load of money fast."

"Shane promised he'd blow our minds."

"He certainly did."

Jules reaches for the iPad.

"I wonder what's trending today," she says with feigned innocence.

I chuckle.

She scrolls the screen, an evil grin stretching her lips.

"Oh, look, the press is still persecuting Hillary. Poor her." She infuses the statement with enough sarcasm to choke a whale.

"She wanted the spotlight? She fucking got the spotlight."

"I don't know who's been advising her, but she should've focused her energy on suing them rather than suing me."

"I'm not sure what she spiked her Kool-Aid with when she thought she had a leg to stand on," I say.

If I wasn't living in LA and working in the entertainment industry, I'd be tempted to say Hillary Twatt's lawsuit was the most frivolous in history. After Jules was served, she texted the three of us, desperate for backup. Collin couldn't get out of a prior engagement, but Shane and I debarked at her office like soldiers ready to declare war. We hired the best lawyers money can buy. Once we had the peace of mind Hillary was delusional, we ignored her distracting antics and kept focusing on our goals.

The money hungry bitch wouldn't have it. She huffed and puffed and threatened to blow the house down. When that didn't work, she turned to the media as a last-ditch resort. The interview that aired yesterday was an aberration. I can't believe a network thought her flimsy lawsuit was newsworthy. Shame on them. I hope it tanks their reputation. It had more holes than a cheese grater. It goes to show what a good publicist can do. Collin suggested Jules retaliates with an interview on Wire News Network's Enews, but our legal team refused to give any substance to that deranged woman's accusations. Too bad. Jules would've pulverized her former stepmother on WNN's entertainment program, showing the world how much of a witch she is.

"I'm so happy it never slipped from my lips that I had found solid business partners," Jules says.

"I told you. One word, and you would've never been able to get rid of her. She's a bloodsucking leech. Plain and simple."

The bitch was suing Fit Thonix for five million dollars, claiming Jules conned her into selling her shares of a profitable business by lying about the potential. It's such bullshit, it's laughable. The woman is such an idiot, she forgot about how well she harassed Jules. The trail of text messages and countless voicemails are proof she was never coerced to relinquish her shares. The judge didn't waste any time throwing her case out of court.

"You're still suing you're stepmother, right?"

"I intend on giving that bitch a little of her own medicine. I'm suing her for defamation." My girl made the decision last night, but I'm glad she's standing firm.

"Even if you don't get a dime out of it since she's penniless now that her boyfriend stole the profits from the sale of the house, watching her sweat will be reward enough."

"Damn right," Jules says. "On the flipside, her little one-woman show was a coup. I always knew she was a fraud."

Hillary's fifteen minutes of fame is paying dividends. She was intent on playing the victim at all cost, but she forgot she has a shady past. She's been dodging her creditors and people she owes money to for years, moving around to keep a low profile. Now, they know where to find her.

"I always had my suspicions about the duke, but I didn't expect him to be a fraud as well," Jules says.

I cock an eyebrow. "Birds of a feather..."

"They deserve each other."

Since he was never able to cut it in Hollywood. the duke has been using his acting skills to prey on widows seeking the company of a handsome man. Hillary fell for the forty-year-old con artist. His relationship with her wasn't about her sparkling personality or kind heart. It was about cold, hard cash. To avoid waving a red flag by depositing a huge amount of money in her account after the sale of the house, Hillary used one of her boyfriend's offshore accounts. Duke Florian skipped town when the media scrutiny became too much. He crossed the border and scampered off to his hometown.

Duke Florian Thauvin de la Poutaille isn't a duke after all. His real name is Jersey Trudeau, and he was born in

Chicoutimi, Quebec. Not France. Surprise, surprise, he doesn't have any ties to the future king of France because there is no fucking future king of France. Hillary was so stupid, she bought his lies.

"Just like we deserve each other," I say.

Jules gets up from where she's sitting, circles the table, and comes to sit on my lap.

She grabs the front of my t-shirt and bunches it in her hand. "I love hearing you say that." She clasps her other hand behind my head, forcing my lips to hers.

Her grumbling stomach interrupts our heated kiss.

"Oh, shit. Talk about bad timing," she says before biting her lower lip.

I chuckle.

I stand up with her in my arms. "Why don't I feed you before you pass out on me?"

"I'll come and help."

"Nah. I'm okay." I drop her to her feet. "You stay out here and soak in the sun. While you were sleeping, I ran to the bakery and raided the place. I did the same to the little shop that sells quiches."

Her laughter follows me as I stalk towards the kitchen.

It only takes a few trips back and forth before I have a scrumptious feast laid out on the table.

Jules's stunned gaze bounces from mine to the spread. "This is a fancy breakfast."

"My queen deserves it," I say with a ceremonious bow. "The next three days are all about you."

Her attention moves to the table for a beat. Questioning eyes meet mine. "You even bought pale pink dahlias."

"They're your favorite."

"They are."

I snap my fingers. "I forgot something."

"You're full of surprises this morning, Mr. Aldridge," she says over my shoulder.

If she only knew.

I enter the kitchen and head to the pantry. I part boxes of cereal until I find what I'm looking for. I hid a little surprise in the last place she'd look. I tuck the small box in the back pocket of my shorts, a sly grin tugging my lips. I hurry to the refrigerator and grab a box containing a small cake. I plate it and place it on a tray. I pull out two mini bottles of champagne from the fridge and flank the plate with them. I grab a couple of straws instead of flutes.

Her inquisitive eyes are on me as I walk back on the deck. "Cake? Champagne? For breakfast? Haven't we celebrated enough?"

I shake my head. "Silly Jules. There's no such thing as too much celebration."

I place the tray in front of her.

She gasps and her hands fly to her mouth. "Are you—" Her eyes lower to the plate. "I mean— Oh my God. Oh my God. Oh my God." She shakes her head. "Levi, is this for real?"

I drop to one knee.

"It's as real as the love I feel for you, Jules."

"I'm the luckiest woman in the world to have found you."

"I think we found each other."

"Okay." She lets out a small laugh.

"When I said the next three days are all about you, I meant it. This wasn't about us taking a break from LA. I wanted to whisk you away to a place where it would be just the two of us."

I shared my plans with Linc because I thought I was moving too fast. He assured me I wasn't. Everything feels right with this woman.

"Jules, will you marry me?" I read the message that's iced on the cake.

She sucks in a breath and laughs as tears well in her eyes. "You crazy man."

"I'm crazy for *you*," I say. "I fucking love you, Jules."

She blinks.

"I want you to be my wife and the mother of my children. I want to love you forever."

A river of tears stream down her beautiful face.

I reach up and wipe them away with my thumb.

She grabs my hand in hers and peppers it with a flurry of soft kisses.

"I know it's fast, but I—"

"You had me at the cake, Levi," she says, through her tears.

"So, it's all about my ability to order the best cake on the island," I say.

A smile breaks on her gorgeous face.

"I love you so much, Levi. The last couple of months have been a dream. Becoming your wife is the icing on the cake."

"That darn cake again," I say.

She laughs.

I take her hands in mine.

"Jules Salinger. My girlfriend and the woman I love with every fiber of my being." Her lips quiver at my solemn tone. "We're going to have an amazing life together."

She tightens her grip.

I glance down at the delicate hands that are encased in mine and back up to her smiling hazel-green eyes.

"We're going to have a fucking amazing life," she says.

"Let me make it official."

She knits her eyebrows together in confusion.

I let go of her hands and fish for the little red box hidden in my pocket.

Her breath hitches when I pull it out.

I open the box and present it to her.

"Holy eye-popping diamond ring," she says. "That's gorgeous."

"I got a little help from a certain redhead."

"Well, said redhead knows me too well."

"You like it?"

"Levi, it's perfect."

Music to my ears.

I pull out the ring and take her hand in mine.

We're both grinning like fools as I slip the dazzling ring on her finger.

She lifts her hand to eye level.

"I'll need to walk around with bodyguards from now on," she says. "This rock is enormous."

I went all out. I got her an exquisite, brilliant round diamond center with a swirling halo of smaller diamonds, with additional diamonds on the split, crisscross shank.

"It's tiny compared to my love for you."

She leaps from the chair into my arms.

I catch her and cover her face with kisses before finding her lips.

The blazing kiss is fire.

Passion.

Love.

Chapter 32

Jules

Three weeks later

Three months ago, when I first stepped inside Dark Compulsion, I was Wild Strawberry. Tonight, I'm Ofira—a bona fide member. I balked at the steep fee, but my fiancé wouldn't hear of it. Granted, members get a generous discount for their better half, but it's still an eye-popping number.

As I step inside the club, I'm instantaneously transported to the day that changed my life forever. The day serendipity played in my favor. Sydney insists I should name my first born after her. I can't help but laugh. I doubt I'll grant her wish, but she's unquestionably my fairy godmother. The girl who was down on her luck infiltrated a naughty ball and scored a prince charming. Speaking of my best friend, she isn't a member. The astronomic fee is a bit too rich for her blood. Not that it matters, because Sydney had other plans. She's been dating one of her client's sons for a couple months now, and things are going so well. I couldn't be happier for her.

I make a slow tour of the club, taking in the action. This is my second time back since the *Ruined* theme party. Between the upheaval in my life and gearing up towards the crowd-funding campaign, Levi and I barely had time to sleep, let alone partake in naughty parties. The third time around, I wouldn't say I'm comfortable, but I'm no longer a fish out of water. Case in point. The pretty brunette strutting past me in nothing more than a man's white shirt, opened to reveal her naked voluptuous body, doesn't even make me blink... much.

Wow.

Like the first time, there are plenty of drop-dead sexy women and incredibly hot men dressed to kill. On that first magical night my man could've been paired with anyone here, but I was the lucky one.

I accept a glass of champagne from a passing waiter and I spot Zeus. He's wearing an expensive, no doubt bespoke, dark as night suit. He looks impeccable. His silver cufflinks glimmer under the lights as he lifts a tumbler to his lips. Colorful tattoos peek out from under the sleeves of his black shirt. The owner of the club is one good-looking, debonair man. Not that he has anything on my fiancé, but if he were to smile, panties would drop... more than they already do. He's in the middle of an animated conversation with two couples. His gaze lands on me. He gives me an appreciative onceover and nods. I respond by lifting my glass of champagne. Someone calls for his attention. His cognac-colored eyes shift, his focus zoomed in on a tall silver fox in a burgundy suit.

I check my Cartier *Ballon Bleu* for the time. The luxury watch is a splurge. Our first month as an official business was so epic, I wanted a memento. Every time the watch catches my eye, I'm reminded how I went from near despair to top of the mountain in a matter of weeks.

Time to go meet my fiancé.

We're celebrating our return to Dark Compulsion with a bang. Even though we talked about it at length, and I agreed, I'm a bit nervous. I polish off my drink in one gulp before snatching another glass from another waiter's tray. With champagne in hand, I stride through a sea of bodies until I exit the main party room. I ride the elevator with a couple who can't keep their hands off each other. The guy has his hands under her skirt, and from her helpless moans I'm guessing his fingers are teasing her clit.

More power to you, girlfriend.

When we reach my floor, I'm a little hot and bothered.

"Enjoy the show," the woman calls from behind me.

I turn around as the elevator doors are about to close.

She flashes a complicit grin while riding her companion's hand.

My excitement quadruples.

My feet carry me down the corridor to our assigned room.

I pull out my club card and swipe it. Cautiously, I push open the door.

My heels clacking against the wood floor announce my presence.

Levi looks up from where he's sitting, tumbler in hand.

He came straight to the club from LAX. He was in Dallas with Linc. It was a forty-eight-hour trip they couldn't get out of. Even though they have a top-notch team that takes care of the last round of checks, this concert has an extra layer of complexity because the artist was dead set on a revolving stage. Since he was arriving late, he booked a room at the Quintus Hotel so he could shower and change.

He sets his drink on a side table and eats up the floor with his long strides until we're toe to toe.

His heated gaze travels the length of my body.

"I love the dress and the strappy heels," he says, lust shining bright in his eyes.

I opted for an elegant designer wrap dress in a vibrant shade of crushed strawberry that hits me above the knee—a nod to my temporary club name. I paired it with strappy white heels. Three months ago, I couldn't even afford to look at such an outrageously chic and pricey outfit. Today, I'm wearing it with pride. I kept the jewelry to a minimum, but played up the makeup. I didn't do much with my hair. I allowed my long locks to cascade over my shoulders. Levi prefers it that way.

I take him in from head to toe. "I love the suit."

Levi in a suit is undeniably drool-worthy. Levi in a suit jacket without a tie, a few buttons of his shirt undone *and* wearing jeans? Well, that's an invitation for misbehaving.

"Did you miss me, sweetness?"

"Did you miss me?"

"Are you going to parrot everything I say?"

"It all depends."

He grabs me by the nape, pulling me closer. "I couldn't get here fast enough."

His words are as warm as sunshine.

"I missed you, baby." I smile.

He brushes a strand of hair behind my ear, his aqua eyes boring into mine. "What did you miss the most?"

Instead of answering, I offer my lips.

He teases, letting his lips ghost over mine.

I hiss a hurried breath, shuddering in anticipation.

A tremble builds inside me, causing my body to vibrate.

I get on my tiptoes, demanding more. He pulls away.

"Are you going to kiss me?" My annoyance is loud and clear.

He gives me a cocky grin. "Is that a demand, little one?"

"It's been two long days."

"That wasn't an answer."

"Please, kiss me. I missed your lips so much."

"I much prefer hearing you beg."

He tangles my hair in his hand, tugging me close.

His eyes brush along my face, stopping at my mouth.

I'm about to plead again when his lips meet mine, urgent and desperate.

I gasp against his kiss, my body sighing in relief.

He fucking devours my mouth, claiming me as his.

God, yes.

Sparks shoot straight to my needy clit.

When he pulls away, I grunt in disagreement.

"Patience. The night is still young," he says. "Come on. Let's sit down. The show is about to begin." He grabs my hand and leads me to the two chairs facing a wall.

I sink into the seat and drop my clutch on the table.

I cross my legs in an attempt to tame my throbbing clit. I'm aching to have him deep inside me, but I agreed to this, so he's right, I have to be patient.

Levi walks to the wall and draws the curtains back on a one-way mirror.

"Oh wow." The words fall out of my mouth.

I blink.

I knew what tonight was all about. Still, talking about it and doing it are worlds apart.

The couple making out on the other side of the mirror knows someone is watching. That's the whole point. She's naked, and he's shirtless, but he's still wearing his jeans.

They're exhibitionists.

Tonight, we're voyeurs.

Levi didn't introduce me to porn—Sydney did—but he introduced me to raunchier videos. For weeks now, he's been seducing me to the idea of watching a live couple in the throes of passion. So here we are in Peek-a-boo room #14. If the sexy action from the elevator is anything to go by, I'm up for watching others get down and dirty.

Levi taps a few times on the glass, letting the couple know we're ready to start.

He turns his attention to me. "Did you follow my order?"

"I did," I say.

"Let's see."

Biting my lower lip, I uncross my legs in an exaggerated motion to give him a peek.

"Nice." He nods. He insisted on me going commando. "Tonight should be dirty as fuck," he says, sitting in the chair next to me.

The couple break their embrace, almost as if they know we shifted our attention to them. The woman looks in our direction, smiles, and wiggles her fingers to say hello. Her brown eyes sparkle with mischief.

The guy waves too.

"That's her husband," Levi says. "His club name is Volney. Hers is Laramie. They met at the club at a theme party."

"Like we did," I say with a smile.

He winks.

"They love having an audience," Levi says. "They're here nearly every weekend—from Friday to Sunday night—which explains why they're among the top-rated exhibitionists at the club."

"There's a rating system?"

He nods. "Only for the Peek-a-boo rooms. You want to know what you're getting in advance."

"I see."

"Volney is forty," Levi says. "She's twenty-two."

"That's quite the age difference."

"They met at a daddy-baby girl theme party. He came as a wingman with a friend and they fell in love at first sight."

"What a story."

"Two years later and they're still going strong," he says. "That guy can go all night long. Their sex drive is legendary, so is the size of his dick."

My eyebrows hit my forehead.

"You'll see."

I shift my attention away from my fiancé.

Crawling on all fours, the busty and curvy brunette approaches the mirror. Laramie's breasts are massive, swinging left to right when she moves. She sits on her knees and licks her lips in the most provocative way.

My head jerks back when she grabs one watermelon-size breast in both hands before bringing it to her lips. She slides her hard, pink nipple into her mouth and sucks on her own tit, her eyes still staring straight at us.

Mother of God.

"She's a filthy slut." Levi grabs my hand and lacing our fingers together.

The busty brunette's eyes roll to the back of her head when she closes her teeth around her nipple and bites down. She ratchets things to another level of bawdiness by pressing her breasts together, wiggling her tongue between her giant tits. As a curtain call, she slides her erect nipples into her mouth, sucking on them greedily. It's as if she's making love to her tits. It's ridiculously sensual. And it's clear from the way her husband is holding back, that this show is just for us.

I squirm in my seat.

"You're turned on," Levi says.

I respond by sliding a finger into my mouth and biting against it, fighting to hold a tremble at bay.

He grins.

Meanwhile, the show goes on.

The silver man appears behind his wife, fists her hair and all but drags her back, leaving her pussy on display. He gestures to the floor, and she gets on her knees. He gestures again, and she pulls his jeans down his legs, revealing his cock.

My jaw drops.

"I told you," Levi says.

My head whips in his direction, my eyes bulging out of my skull. "You said big. That's porn-star big."

He nods.

The man clenches his massive cock in one hand, stroking it in long languorous strokes. He says something to his wife. From the way she nods, I bet it's, *"You want my cock?"*

She licks her lips and opens wide.

He seizes her head in his hands and drives himself between her parted lips.

Good God.

My face bursts into flames, but I don't look away. I can't.

I watch the slide of the man's huge cock between his wife's pink lips, his skin glossy with her saliva. The guy's porn-star dick is thick.

How does she manage to take him all in without choking?

Lewd doesn't even begin to describe it.

Anything I've seen online so far pales in comparison to being a voyeur.

Levi's eyes are on me, but I don't dare to glance in his direction.

He brings my hand to his lips and trails soft kisses on my skin.

I press my knees together, squeezing.

It does little to subside my mounting desire. On the contrary.

From this angle, the woman's ass is facing us, so there's

nothing obstructing our view of the man's handsome face. The passion reflected in his expression tugs at my breath. Love floods from every inch of him. It's so powerful, I feel it at my core. It's the same expression I see reflecting in Levi's eyes when I'm on my knees sucking him off.

My fiancé reaches out, his fingers moving my hair off my neck so he can set his lips there.

A wave of goosebumps erupts along my body, and I whimper in need. I offer him better access by tilting my head to the side, my eyes never leaving the couple.

Levi kisses, licks, and bites my neck.

I moan.

The man strips out of his jeans, kicking them to the side. He's naked. He has a good body, nothing to sneeze at, but it's a far cry from Levi's sculpted muscles. He helps his wife up and together they move to the low bed set behind them. He climbs on first and lies flat on his back.

She straddles his head, placing her feet flat on the bed, hovering above his face. The man sticks out his tongue, beckoning her. She parts her pussy lips with both hands and lowers her body until she's sitting on his face.

"This is the best part."

I glance at Levi.

Lust burns bright in his blue eyes, no doubt a mirror of my own horniness.

He tilts his head to the couple. "You don't want to miss the way he ravishes her pussy."

I move my gaze, returning it to the dirty couple.

The BBW curvy woman rocks her wide hips back and forth, her enormous breasts swaying to the same cadence.

It's slow and steady at first, but she picks up the pace.

My eyes widen in shock when she grabs her husband's hair, lifting his head to her pussy, riding his face in a rough and unrepentant way. Her long hair flies all over the place. Her pretty face is sheened with sweat. She's abandoned to the moment. As much as I'm enjoying the show, I'm a bit jealous.

Her husband grabs hold of her soft stomach, holding her tight. His tongue probes, toys and licks her clit. He's fucking devouring her pussy.

For a few long beats she rides his face fast and furious until she changes position. Instead of worshipping her clit, the man is now licking her ass with gusto.

"You love it when I do that to you," Levi says, low in my ear.

I nod, a wicked smile tugging at my lips.

To my surprise, he grabs a remote control from the table—I hadn't noticed until now—points it at a box on the wall, and the next thing I know, moans and grunts fill our room.

My wide eyes shift to my fiancé's. "We can hear them?"

"They can't hear us." He answers my unspoken question. "I didn't want you to feel like you were drinking from a fire hose, so I held back. Now that I've added the sound, it's about to get a lot dirtier."

The woman's hips move faster, matching her frantic fingers skating over her clit.

The sound of slickness is dizzying.

Wow. Wow. And wow.

This is filthy with a capital F.

Jesus.

She chants, *oh my God*, over and over again.

Her husband grunts in response.

Heat pours through my veins.

This is so sinful.

I uncross my legs, praying the cool air dowses my pulsating pussy.

It's wishful thinking.

My whole body is ablaze.

Levi's fingers walk across my thigh, slipping beneath the bottom of my wrap dress.

I gasp.

"No bra?" I shake my head. "You're begging for it."

"I am." I arch my back, making it easier for him to play with my breast.

He pinches my nipple hard, twisting it until it aches.

I close my eyes as pleasure ripples through me.

Goddammit.

His hand travels to my belt. He makes quick work of undoing it before parting the fabric, exposing my naked body.

His big hand strokes my skin. "Fuck, I missed this body," he says.

"Fuck, I missed your touch."

His hand travels below my bellybutton. I hold my breath. When his fingers part my pussy, I nearly combust.

Holy fucking shit.

Levi jerks his chin to the couple. "You want some of that?" his voice is dark and smokey.

I can only nod.

I'm panting so hard, I'm close to hyperventilating.

"You know the rules," Levi says. "If you don't tell me what you want, I can't give it to you."

"Yes," I say in a trembling breath. I'm half out of my mind with need.

I know they can't see—or hear us—but still, this is unbelievably risqué.

"Fuck, fuck, fuck," the woman says, her head lolled back, her husband tongue-fucking her ass with determination.

"You want my tongue that deep up your ass?"

"Yes," I say. The way he stares at me inebriates my sex-drunk mind. "Up my ass. Up my pussy. It doesn't matter, as long as you make me come."

"Listen to you beg, little one." His tone tells me he's pleased. So does his wolfish grin.

He gets up and comes to stand in front of me, blocking the show of the bodies connected on the bed.

He peels out of his suit jacket, undoes a few more buttons of his shirt, exposing his tattoo, and rolls the sleeves to the elbow.

He has something in mind. The question is, will I survive?

The love of my life, with mesmerizing blue eyes and a filthy mouth, which turns my insides into molten lava, lowers to the floor.

I'm filled with a mixture of anxiety and excitement.

"Spread your legs for me."

Oh. My. God.

I don't budge, unable to get my brain to function.

I blink, held immobile by the raunchiness of his command.

I was prepared to play the role of voyeur and I expected that afterwards things would get hot and heavy between us, but I'm unprepared for this.

He curls a hand under my chin and tugs my head back to look up at him. "I said, spread your legs."

I exhale a stuttering breath and obey.

"Scoot to the edge of your seat so it's more comfortable."

I do as I'm told.

"Good girl." His head dips down, sealing his lips over mine. The kiss is too brief, but I don't complain. He parts my dress until it falls open.

My gaze moves to the couple lost in their kinky passion.

With his eyes locked onto mine, Levi pulls a breast into his mouth.

I bite down on my lower lip and strangle back a cry of pleasure when his teeth close around my nipple right on the edge of pain.

Fuck.

My pussy is shamefully wet.

The taboo element of the experience is unbelievably arousing.

The mouth working my breast is sinful, but my body demands satisfaction lower. My hands ache to force him down there. I might have to pay for my effrontery, but so be it. I tangle my fingers in his silky brown hair.

"What do you want?" It's as if he can read me like an open book.

"More."

"More of what?"

"More of your mouth."

"You mean like this?" He trails soft kisses between my breasts.

"Lower," I say.

"Like this?" He travels down to my bellybutton.

"Lower." My voice trembles.

"I know what you're doing." He grins.

My grin matches his.

I could be more precise, but it wouldn't be as much fun.

"You want me to worship your sweet pussy like that guy is worshiping his wife's cunt?"

"Yes."

He licks just below my bellybutton, causing me to flinch. He licks again, this time lower and so close to my desperate pussy.

Yes.

His fingertips touch my knees, gently pulling them back.

"You're trembling," he says.

I nod.

"I'm going to give you a good reason to tremble." Making good on his promise, he dips his head between my legs.

He slides his tongue inside my pussy, and I gasp.

I moan when his tongue laps at me, then slides up, tongue-fucking me.

My hands ball into fists and my manicured nails dig into my palms. My chest is heaving hard.

"Shit." The woman's breathless voice echoes in the room.

My gaze bounces to her.

"Fuck, Big Daddy, I'm getting close." She's riding his mouth so fast, her tits bang against her chest each time her hips gyrate.

"Come for me, you filthy slut," the man says. "Let me fucking drink you."

His command makes me vibrate in my seat.

Jesus.

This is so forbidden, I'm certain I'm a breath away from going down in a blaze of sin so hot it would melt steel.

The woman's rhythm slows to a halt. She lets out an enormous gasp, followed by a slew of profanities. She lifts her hips and to my amazement, she gushes her abundant juices in her husband's welcoming mouth. She chants *Oh, yes, Big Daddy* so many times, I lose count.

It's almost as if her cries trigger Levi.

He picks up the pace, his tongue swirling, lapping, licking, flicking.

I buck in the seat, arching my back for more.

He doesn't disappoint.

His tongue continues its wicked stroke as he slides two fingers deep inside me, pumping in and out.

Yes, yes, yes.

I'm right on the edge.

He peers up at me with his big blue eyes.

My hooded gaze peers back, the show long forgotten.

Sweet tension builds at my core.

My leg muscles tense. "Levi, I—I'm—"

He lifts his head. "Come all over my fucking tongue, sweetness."

A few more licks, and I'm floating.

"Oh, God. Oh—"

I let go, swept away in a blissful climactic wave.

My head lolls back.

I come.

And I come.

And I come.

My breath is labored, and it takes a while before I find my bearings.

On a long exhale, I peer down at my fiancé.

Levi's lips pull back into a pleased smile.

My core clenches.

The dangerous expression on his face is enough to make me come again.

"You're fucking perfect, Jules."

"I love you," I say on a broken breath, no louder than a whisper.

"No more than I love you."

Epilogue 1
Jules

Two weeks later

My eyes are lost in the horizon as I admire the Pacific Ocean from the upper deck of the mansion doubling as a chapel and wedding venue. A warm draft tickles blonde strands of hair around my face. I love this time of day, when the sky turns into a spectacular painting, a perfect blend of dark blues, golds, fiery reds and brilliant oranges. For months, I was so blinded by my worries, I'd forgotten what a sunset looked like. Not anymore.

I lift my eyes to the tranquil sky.

"Mom. Daddy. I miss you... especially today," I say. "I wish you could meet Levi. You'd love him as much as I do."

A familiar longing pulls at my heart.

I touch a hand to my stomach, hoping to suppress the momentary wave of sadness.

It's an emotional day for me. From my misty eyes, you wouldn't suspect this is the happiest day of my life. I'm so elated, words can't capture my immense joy. At the same time, my heart aches, and every so often, I dissolve into tears—like now. I snuck out of the festivities not only because I needed a respite, but because I needed a moment alone with my parents.

"Monterey, California is spectacular, you guys," I say, wiping a tear from my cheek. "I wish you could see what I see." I suck in a sharp breath. "I wish you could see me in my pretty dress..."

It's official. I'm Mrs. Jules Salinger Aldridge.

Three hours ago, Levi and I exchanged our vows in front of a cheering crowd.

Since Mom died, I knew I would never have all those pre-wedding mother-daughter moments most women share with their mother. After Daddy died, I knew I wouldn't be trailing by his side, hanging from his arm on my way to my husband-to-be. Mentally, I was prepared. Emotionally, I wasn't. Thank God, Levi's father was my pillar today—my wedding day.

Voices echo from the garden below.

It's a full house.

So many friends are present on our big day.

I'm blessed.

Without Larkin, we would've had to cram a large group of people in our backyard. It wouldn't have the same prestige. You wouldn't believe the number of venues that literally laughed in my face when I told them I had a five-week lead-time before my wedding day.

From the first day we laid eyes on each other, our relationship has been a bit over the top.

It's the same for our wedding.

We didn't want to wait a year—or even six months—and we didn't want a Vegas wedding. Larkin came to the rescue. His Monterey house was in between rentals, so it was perfect.

"Here you are." A familiar voice jolts me out of my thoughts.

I turn to face my devastatingly gorgeous husband as he struts towards me, both hands tucked into the pockets of his pants.

This man is my husband.

Someone needs to pinch me now.

"What are you doing—" his words cut off and his step falters. I can only assume I look like a hot mess. "Sweetness..." He approaches, a shadow of concern in his gaze.

"Hey." My voice is feeble. I swipe my fingers under my eyes to wipe away my tears. It's futile.

He reaches out and cups my face. I take in the scent of his expensive cologne. "You're crying."

I nod.

"You were laughing your head off not long ago. What brought this on?"

I place a hand on his chest, smoothing the fabric of his jacket. He rejected the idea of a tuxedo, favoring a bespoke black suit that accentuates his muscular frame, from his broad shoulders, to his solid chest, and down to a lean, trim waist. He looks amazing.

"Talk to me, wife."

Wife. The most beautiful word ever after love.

The brave face I've had firmly in place, crumbles. "I was keeping it together. I never imagined it would hit me all at once like a tidal wave. I miss them so much, my heart aches."

A few beats pass before he speaks.

"Your parents, my mom, Annmarie, and my little girl are up above partying with God and the angels." His is voice is warm. "They may not be here"—he points to the floor—"but they're here." He taps against his heart. "And here." He taps against mine.

My gaze lowers.

"They *are* sharing our joy, sweetness."

I glance up. "I keep telling myself that, but it's still so hard."

He runs his thumb over my lower lip. "I understand."

He pulls me close to his body and wraps me in his strong arms, his warmth seeping through me.

My safe place.

I close my eyes.

This man holds my heart in the palm of his hand.

I'm not sure how long we stay like this, him rocking side to side.

He pulls away from me until his gaze bores into mine. "You're going to be okay?"

I nod. "The sadness comes and goes, but yes, I'll be okay."

"I didn't only come up here to find my beautiful wife. I've been told it's time for the cake cutting, and then the tossing of the bouquet and garter."

I laugh.

"By you've been told, you mean, Sydney?"

"No, I mean, Riley." He chuckles. "She's hoping to send her boyfriend a message."

Riley Carrington, a boisterous and bubbly redhead with a big personality is also here. Sydney nearly died. She's a huge fan of the popular Food Network chef and food blogger. I met Riley Carrington at a few of Shane's barbecues and parties. She's also a client. She couldn't wait to get her own Cycle Thonix bike. She even got a couple for her brother's ranch in Summerville, Texas—one for Jake and one for Hunter, Jake's business partner and best friend.

"She's too much." I laugh.

"Yes. She. Is," he says. "But you've got to love her."

"I guess there's no pressure weighing on your shoulders since none of your boys are going to be fighting over the garter. On the contrary, they'll be fighting to distance themselves as fast as humanly possible."

"I'm certain they'll conveniently be absent, or lost in the bathroom or garden. And that includes my brother, unless he uses Micah as his scapegoat."

"I'm sure you're right."

"As for Larkin, the garter is smart enough to stay the hell away from him."

I laugh.

Random Misconception rocked the crowd until our feet hurt with a playlist of danceable tunes and ballads—all with a rock edge. Holt, the fourth member, flew in from London with his adorable little girl.

My wedding day is beyond anything I could've dreamed of. Marrying Levi is a blessing, but being surrounded by all of these new friends warms my heart.

"Everyone is waiting, Mrs. Aldridge." My husband laces his fingers with mine and brings my hand to his lips before dropping a soft kiss.

An unbidden smile steals across my lips, "God, I love it when you call me Mrs. Aldridge."

"That's a good thing because it's your name for the rest of your life."

We exchange a wide smile.

"Come on, let's go," he says, guiding me to the stairs. "The faster we feed these people cake, the faster I can have you all to myself. I can't wait to consummate this marriage, Mrs. Aldridge."

"Mr. Aldridge." I feign outrage. "Is that any way to talk to your wife?"

He leans into me, his lips flirting with my earlobe. "You're right." The words are a husky whisper in my ear. "Why sugar-coat it?" He grabs my hand and places it on his crotch and grinds into the palm of my hand. "I've been hard since I saw you walking down the aisle in your gorgeous princess dress.

Since you agreed to be my wife, I've been counting down the minutes until I can rip your virginal white panties off your sinful body with my teeth, so I can bury my hard cock inside your sweet little ass, Mrs. Aldridge."

Holy hell.

"And, FYI, I intend on keeping you naked and barricaded in this house for five days once we get rid of all of these people. Don't count on a second of rest." He stares at me with suggestive bedroom eyes, half-lidded and sensual as fuck. "Better?"

There goes a good pair of panties.

The wolfish grin parting his lips is as stomach-fluttering and potent as the one he gives me when I know I'm in for a long night of multiple orgasms.

Epilogue 2
Levi

As far as I'm concerned, love isn't measured in months or even years. It's measured in heartbeats. I love my girl with every fiber of my being, and I know with absolute certainty she loves me. Why wait to start the rest of our life together?

I would've been happy with a courthouse wedding, but Jules deserves better. Thank God I have the right connections, and so many people cared enough to make our big day one we'll never forget.

Larkin came through for us when he offered his spectacular mansion, overlooking the Pacific Ocean.

Dominika insisted we weren't to hire a wedding videographer. Since she's a guest, and not allowed to work, a couple members of her team are capturing every moment on video.

Shane put his other talent to use when he insisted on doubling as our photographer.

The best rock band in the world, albeit retired, gave an unforgettable live performance.

Sydney worked her magic with myriad bouquets decorating the mansion.

We lucked out when a top local caterer was able to fit us in after a cancellation. Something about the bride-to-be running away with her fiancé's father. Very scandalous.

Everything else just fell into place.

The champagne has been flowing all night and everyone is tipsy on happiness... and on too much booze.

I couldn't ask for more.

For the closing act, we decided to shake things up by breaking with tradition, hence the commotion.

After removing my gorgeous wife's garter with my teeth to the hoots and hollers of my boys, Jules and I are standing in the middle of the expansive living room, facing each other. The announcement of the garter-slash-bouquet toss tandem event is causing a buzz among our guests.

"This should be fun," Jules's hazel-green eyes twinkle as she meets my gaze.

Goddamn, she's fucking stunning.

And she's mine.

I sweep a strand of hair behind her ear. "These women aren't joking around," I say, swinging my gaze over her head. "I sense we might end up starting a war."

Jules giggles.

The women are standing behind her, and *three* brave men are standing behind me. As predicted, my boys are standing a state away. Larkin escaped in the gardens a few minutes ago. I figured as much. To my surprise, Riley is dragging him back inside by the hand right now. Grudgingly, he follows behind her. That woman has no idea who she's dealing with.

"Let's get ready to rumble." The MC's voice booms through the speakers.

Laughter roars through the crowd.

"All right, Mr. and Mrs. Aldridge, you're about to make dreams come true for one lucky lady and one poor sucker." The MC's mouth twitches into a sly smile. "Is the happy couple ready?"

Jules nods.

"Ready," I say.

"On the count of three," the MC says into the microphone.

Our guests shout their approval.

The countdown begins.

On the count of three, Jules tosses the bouquet over her head with all her might at the same time as I throw the garter over mine.

I turn around.

Jules has been holding back on me because that throw is what sports championships are made of.

The bouquet sails through the air.

That's enough to get the crowd of women into a mad frenzy. They tackle each other. Hands claw the air, fingers curling, begging as they attempt to grab the coveted prize. A redhead intent on snagging it first, leaps into the air like a baller, just to bump into an eager brunette, who bumps into Sydney, who bumps into a blonde with short hair, leaving the field wide open. Dominika steps aside to avoid the train wreck, just to catch the bouquet when it collides with her chest.

Talk about strange twist of fate.

She stares down at the bouquet in her hands, dumbfounded.

Big questioning blue eyes search the crowd for an answer. Then, they meet mine. Dom's gaze bounces from the flowers up to my stunned eyes. She does that a few times.

She's bewildered.

It's like she doesn't know what to do with the flowers she's holding.

Then, her gaze slides past me.

Shock is replaced with disappointment. No, dejection.

Curious, I turn around.

Rod is standing near the piano, staring at her, his expression unreadable. Dominika isn't looking at her best friend. Her eyes are pinned on the tall, rail thin blonde wearing a revealing silver dress and ridiculously high heels. She arrived with my fuck up of a cousin, Dean. She's his flavor of the day.

Speaking of the idiot, where is he?

I peruse the living room, looking for him. His drunk ass must be outside chain-smoking. By the way his date is hanging off Rod's shoulder, I'm willing to bet she isn't interested in my cousin's cock for tonight. The blonde must clue in on the fact she's stepping on toes because her chest protrudes, proud like a peahen. The way her mouth quirks in a devious smirk says it all. The tension in the room is so tight, it's like all the air has been sucked out of it. If Dom's blue eyes were lasers, the blonde would be six feet under.

With a twirl, Dom turns on her heel and rushes to the garden, the bouquet still clenched to her chest.

I shake my head at Rod.

He gives me a, *What the fuck?* look.

"Rod is blind," Jules says in a soft voice from beside me.

"He is," I say. The idiot is fucking his way through LA, looking for something that's right under his nose. *Dumb ass.* I grab Jules in my arms. "Thank God I was smart enough to marry you. I'm never letting you get away, Mrs. Aldridge."

"I wouldn't want it any other way, Mr. Aldridge."

The Next Book Boyfriend
Dominika's POV

I stomp out of the living room in a hell-bent fury, leaving the embarrassing scene behind.

Not one to draw attention to myself—let alone cause a scene—I had to get out of there before I dissolved into tears or bitch-slapped that stupid, desperate blonde vying for Rod's cock. For God's sake, she arrived with Levi's cousin Dean and from the way they were making out earlier, it's clear they have a thing going on. Now she's moved on to another man. How skanky can you be?

I'm so outraged, I'm surprised fumes aren't shooting out of my nostrils.

Same shit. Different event.

I should know better.

Silly Dom. A tiger never changes his stripes.

I was having a pretty good time until the blonde decided to latch onto my best friend like a chimp latches on to its mother.

Why do I even care who Rod fucks?

Dammit.

I hate these conflicting waves of emotions that consume me every time I'm around my best friend these days.

Rushing on my heels, I make my way to Larkin's lush gardens in the hopes of losing myself for a few long minutes until I regain my composure.

"Dominika, wait!" a voice says behind me.

I stop in my tracks and turn around.

Sydney, Jules's best friend, comes running after me.

She stops right in front of me and smiles wide.

I respond by lifting the corner of my lips, but the smile never touches my bruised heart.

"You promised you'd hook me up with the secondhand shop where you bought this amazing dress." She waves a finger up and down the length of my body.

I suspect that's not why she came running after me, but I play along. "I will."

"Good. Renting the runway is great, but if you can own it without it requiring a trust fund, that's even better." She laughs.

"This boutique is a new to me shop, but like I said, they have a great selection for girls like us."

In a city where Amazonians seem to reign supreme, it's comforting to be standing in front of a woman who's as petite as I am.

She gives me another onceover. "I'm super excited."

For Jules and Levi's big day, I deviated from my usual low-key fashion, which tends to be a monochromatic palette of black and white shades. I selected a gorgeous gunmetal dress that elongates my short body. The sequins are a bit more dazzle than what I gravitate towards, but it's tasteful and it doesn't reveal too much. I was so pleased with my fashion selection until Dean showed up with his date who so happens to be wearing an in-your-face silver dress that leaves nothing to the imagination.

What a pleasant coincidence. Not.

"You're getting some air?" Sydney says.

I'm simmering down so I don't go off like a damn pressure cooker. "You could say that."

"Great catch, by the way." Her blue eyes shine bright with malice. "You should've stayed a little longer for everyone to cheer you on."

That's when it hits me. I'm still clinging onto the flowers for dear life.

My eyes meet hers. "It wasn't planned," I say. "I was trying to get out of the way to let the hopeless romantic souls—which includes you—fight for the victory."

"Guilty as charged." She giggles. "Not that it matters anymore since you're the winner."

"Lady Luck sure has an ironic sense of humor," I say.

"Here"—I extend the flowers to Sydney—"you should have them. You were in the running, I wasn't." I'm not upset at the bouquet or at Jules. My beef is with Rod Wolfe, more specifically his inability to be anything other than a manwhore. Still, why keep something that is of no use to me?

Spooked blue eyes grow wide. "Oh no, no, no," she says. "I'm pretty sure if I take them, I'll be cursed... so will you. I intend on getting married one day. No way am I going to jinx myself. You caught the bouquet, you keep the bouquet."

I let out a wry laugh. "This is a silly, outdated old wives' tale. It takes a hell of a lot more than catching a bouquet to walk down the aisle."

She frowns. "You're not much older than I am. Why do you sound like you've given up?"

"It's nothing," I say.

"So it has nothing to do with the tramp hanging from Rod's arm?"

I sigh. "Was it that obvious?"

"People in Iceland could feel the tension between the two of you," she says.

I wince. "It wasn't my intention to usurp Jules and Levi's moment."

"Those two are high on love, so there isn't much that's going to throw them off. That said, your resting bitch face is pretty menacing. Bravo, girlfriend. No doubt, it's been perfected over years of intense practice."

I laugh at her comment.

"On a serious note, Dom," she says. "I know we don't know each other very well, but I'm a great listener. And right now, you look like you could use a friend."

I hang my head low, my gaze fixed on the spectacular white wedding bouquet in my hands.

I take in a deep breath before locking eyes with her. "I appreciate it, Sydney, but I'm not sure talking about it will change anything between Rod and me."

"Let me guess. You're pining after your best friend and you don't quite know what to do with yourself."

Great. The whole world knows.

She cocks an eyebrow. "Did I hit the bullseye?"

I respond with a small nod, not trusting anything that might slip from my lips.

"Does he know?"

"Rod will always be a playboy. With just one glance, women drop their panties when he walks into a room." *Why would he settle?*

"It's a given men like Rod are players. This is LA, after all—the land where marriages that last more than a year are celebrated with as much zeal as a Super Bowl win. Still, that doesn't answer my question."

"Rod is out of my league."

"That's how Jules felt about Levi," she says. "It took a long time before Jules was willing to believe she was good enough for a guy like that."

"It's different between Rod and me. We go way back—"

"Even better," she says. "You can cut through the bullshit and jump right into what matters."

I let out a sarcastic laugh. "The day Rod Wolfe settles down is the day hell will freeze over."

"You're speaking on his behalf."

"I know Rod, Sydney."

"What's the worst that can happen if you were to open up to him about how you feel?"

I might lose my best friend.

If that were to happen, it would unravel my world.

I'd be nothing more than a drifter without a compass.

I can't allow that to happen.

I offer a one-shoulder shrug. "It's a non-issue, anyway."

She frowns at my cryptic response. "What do you mean?"

"I'm starting an intense training course next week. I'll be off to New York, then Europe." A little distance will help me get my head screwed back on straight.

"You can't brush your feelings under the rug," she says.

I've perfected the art. "Six weeks where Rod and I won't be in each other's way should clear the air between us. By the time I come back from my training, we can go back to just being Rod and Dom." Minus the weird vibe playing between us and those stupid butterflies constantly fluttering in my tummy.

Sydney frowns. "That's it?"

"That's it."

She's dumbfounded.

When she recovers, she says, "Okay. Rod is a no go. Got it." The way her eyebrows knit in confusion suggests the contrary.

"Let's go back inside. I need another glass of champagne." *...or three.*

My lifelong sentence is to be locked in the friend zone dungeon until the end of time, without a hope of ever escaping. *Sigh.*

Unrequited love is an easier pill to swallow than watching the demise of a decade-long friendship.

~

Bonus Scene

For a bonus scene about Levi and Jules (you get a peek into Levi and Jules five years later), subscribe to my newsletter.
www.MyRomanceAddiction.com

Who's The Next Book Boyfriend in This Scorching Hot Series?

Bachelor forever Roderick (Rod) Wolfe is the next hotshot on the list.

You must be curious to find out the turn of events between Rod and his best friend Dominika. After all, that was a pretty emotional discussion between Dom and Sydney in the gardens.

Is it that easy for Dom to sweep her feelings under the rug?

I think you're already clued in on the trope for the next romance in this series, but you know me, there's so much more to discover...

Out of all my alphas, I have to say Rod is my first damaged hero. Mark my words, he'll quickly become your new favorite alpha book boyfriend.

Rod and Dom's story is a breathtaking friends to lovers romance so deep, so gripping, so engulfing, you'll need days to recover.

Binge-read now: Always Mine

Reviews are a beautiful thing.

It only takes a few minutes to leave a review, which makes a huge difference for an indie author like myself.

**Here's the link to leave a review for:
Always You**

Scarlett's Book Banter

Dear Sexy Reader,

Gosh, I love when we meet here.

This is where I talk to you, my reader, about what was going on in my head—or/and life—while writing this romance.

There are so many aspects of Levi and Jules's love story that took me by surprise.

One of the biggest one is the involvement of the Dennison brothers.

When I first plotted the novel, I intended on having Larkin as a silent investor who provided the financial backup Jules needed to turn her father's company around. It's only when I started thinking of a potential spokesmodel for her company that I thought of Collin and Shane. Instead of giving them a secondary role, I decided to make them integral characters of the story.

Not only was it great fun, but it allowed me to know these two a lot more.

We get a glimpse of their personality in Hunter Evan's story (aka **Infatuation Duet**), but that wasn't enough to flesh out a full novel. Sure, I could've relied on a serious brainstorming session, but having them part of Levi's story was a lot more thrilling.

I hope you loved reading Levi and Jules story as much as I loved writing it.

About the Dennison Brothers

Collin and Shane Dennison were first introduced in **Infatuated (Infatuation Duet Book 1)**, which is a duet part of the *Summerville series*. I never intended for those two characters to be more than secondary characters. That said, so many readers fell in love with the Scottish Irish twins—that's a mouthful—I had to find a story for them.

That's one of the reasons I wrote Levi's story. As I was writing the books in this series, it hit me, the Dennison brothers were included in nearly every book, yet we really don't know who they are. I remedied the situation by giving them a more robust presence. This will be the foundation when it comes time to writing their romance.

It Was Always You Series

★★★★★ "...I need more of these playboys in my life!" —P. Turner's Book Blog

"I am not sure how Scarlett does it, but these books just keep getting better and hotter!

Straight away I am absorbed into the world of these certified playboys. Moody, mysterious and very Alpha I just could not get enough of their characters.

The women in these books are no shrinking violets and give just as good as they get. I love the way all the characters are referenced in each other's books so they interlink. My personal preference is to read them in order, but all of the books in this series can be read as standalones.

This was my first series by Scarlett, but I cannot wait to see if there will be more in the series and I need more of these playboys in my life!" — P. Turner's Book Blog

I'm so humbled by that review.

There are six scorching hot romances in the **It Was Always You** Series.

They're all meant to be read as standalones, but it makes a lot more sense to start with Book 1 and keep reading. Not to mention, it's a lot more fun. Many of the characters make cameo appearances in other books, so you get a snippet into the future. Don't worry, there are no spoilers. I'm pretty much of a stickler about that.

The heat level in each book increases in crescendo waves, and the sexy times are as unique as the main characters themselves.

Once you step into my world of dangerously sexy LA hotshots, there's no turning back. Your only salvation is to keep reading to your heart's content.

Fair warning, I'm not responsible for ruined panties... and there will be many. Trust me.

Who's the next book boyfriend on the list?

Bachelor forever Roderick (Rod) Wolfe is the next hotshot on the list.

Always Mine is a breathtaking friends to lovers romance so deep, so gripping, so engulfing, you'll need days to recover. Rod Wolfe is a possessive, jealous billionaire who takes no prisoners when it comes to protecting the woman who was destined to be his.

"First time reading this author and I am HOOKED! Great story!" – Sarah Barr

"I love this story. As usual, Ms. Scarlett, you didn't disappoint me. Your stories grab the reader with a hook in the beginning and never let go. Bravo!" – J. D. T.

"I absolutely loved the book." – Mamie G.

Tropes you love...

Unrequited love

Best friends to lovers

Former rockstar turned CEO

Her pass comes to haunt her

Overprotected hero. He'll protect her at any cost

Jealous hero

Workplace romance

He falls first

Red-hot passion

Binge-read now: Always Mine

That's it for me.

Back to writing.

Much love,

Scarlett Avery

P.S. Reviews give me wings. I LOVE to fly.

P.P.S. I keep writing because of your hunger for my stories. Thank you for your fervor, love, and loyalty. I'm humbled and incredibly grateful. Without you, there's little reason to keep coming up with new stories.

P.P.P.S. For access to the Bonus Scene, go to:

www.MyRomanceAddiction.com

If you've already signed up to my list from previous books, you can visit the same page to download the Bonus Scene and/or Storyboard for this romance.

~

Welcome to the City of Angels where sparks fly and ignite into burning love. The beaming California sun pales in comparison to the wattage of passion in this series and the spinoff series. Framed by the Pacific Ocean, palm trees, an abundance of colorful flowers, and breathtaking views, Los Angeles is the city these commanding billionaires call home. These movers and shakers might be bone fide forever bachelors, but they'll risk their hearts for the women who bring them down to their knees.

It Was Always You Series

These sexy as sin tattooed billionaires are notorious forever bachelors... that's until they cross paths with the women who bring them to their knees. And when they fall, they fall hard.

Always You (Levi and Jules)

Always Mine (Roderick and Dominika)

Always Destined (Lochlan and Kyla)

Always Forever (Holt and Everly)

Always Us (Jace and Eliana)

Always Love (Jagger and Stasia)

Holt's baby brother, Beckett, kicks off an illegally hot series.

The Moguls Series

These commanding CEOs and COOs go after the women who steal their hearts with guns blazing.

Bossy Mogul (Beckett and Arianne)

Off Limits Mogul (Rhys and Keira)

Ruthless Mogul (Phoenix and Michaela)

Damaged Mogul (Gage and Lily)

You'll find **all my books** and **reading order** on my site:
www.ScarlettAvery.com

About Scarlett Avery

Two-time *USA TODAY* and Amazon TOP 21 bestselling
author Scarlett Avery unapologetically brings book boyfriends
to their knees. Only smart, sassy, and vulnerable heroines are
brave enough to unravel these heroes.

Scarlett's love stories are intense and passionate, emotional and
steamy, layered with some delicious angsty scenes that always
leave you begging for more.

She writes romance because with every story, she goes through
the beautiful adventure of falling in love.

On a personal note...

Scarlett lives in the North Pole (aka Canada).

The Thomas Crown Affair (1999) is her favorite love story.

Love Actually is her all-time favorite Christmas movie.

She's a polyglot who'll gladly listen to the same audiobook in
multiple languages when it's available.

She could live off elaborate cheese boards accompanied by

French or Portuguese bread and a fantastic glass of white wine. Same goes for a mezze platter with Greek pita bread.

She has a serious love affair with Italian gelato and ice cream. During summer months, you're sure to catch her sipping on an Aperol spritz because, OMG those are so amazing.

Made in the USA
Las Vegas, NV
02 January 2026

38432828R00184